THE DIRTY
TRUTH

KN

OCT 0 8

THE DIRTY TRUTH

BRENDA HAMPTON

www.urbanbooks.net

Urban Books
1199 Straight Path
West Babylon, NY 11704

ISBN- 13: 978-1-60162-076-7
ISBN- 10: 1-60162-076-4

First Printing November 2008
Printed in the United States of America

10 9 8 7 6 5 4 3 2 1

Distributed by Kensington Publishing Corp.
Submit Wholesale Orders to:
Kensington Publishing Corp.
C/O Penguin Group (USA) Inc.
Attention: Order Processing
405 Murray Hill Parkway
East Rutherford, NJ 07073-2316
Phone: 1-800-526-0275
Fax: 1-800-227-9604

ACKNOWLEDGMENTS

My Heavenly Father, thank you for opening my eyes so I could see the path that you laid down before me. I've been taking this journey for a while and it has been so much more than what I could have ever imaged. Because of YOU, no mountain is too high for me to climb, and my challenges are considered blessings.

To Carl Weber and his wonderful wife, Martha, thank you for assisting me in keeping my literary dreams alive. There are no words to describe how grateful I am for your continuous support and I look forward to a long lasting relationship with the entire Urban Books Family that have been a true joy to work with.

To the Hampton, Littlejohn, Walton and Ball Families, a special thanks to all of you for hanging tight with me. Many of you believed in me, even when I didn't believe in myself. Without your continuous love and appreciation for me, I would be lost. I love you all and I wish everyone of you the best.

To my readers, author friends, book clubs and bookstores who give me more than what I could ever give in return . . . THANK YOU SO MUCH. Your dedication, support and love for my work means the world to me, and ten books later, I promise to keep on bringing all of you the excitement that a Brenda Hampton novel can bring. With that being said . . .

LET THE DRAMA BEGIN!

THE DIRTY TRUTH

CHAPTER 1

It wasn't until I sat at Cassandra's funeral, completely torn apart from what had happened that I realized something wasn't right. I'd known her for the past six years and thought I knew every friend she had, every family member, and, of course, every past male companion as well. But when I saw this muscular police officer dressed in a uniform sobbing more than I was—and receiving more attention from Cassandra's family than I did—I couldn't help but feel there was more to this story.

When the police questioned me about Cassandra's murder, they insinuated that she had another man, but I didn't believe them. I figured they were just trying to rattle me. But as I watched Cassandra's close girlfriend, Annette, and her cousin, Felicity, comforting this brotha, I was starting to think maybe there was indeed another man. I overheard Felicity introduce him to another cousin as a very close friend of Cassandra. I'd never met him before, and Felicity sure didn't introduce him to me.

I figured this cold treatment I was getting from some family members, especially Cassandra's parents, was because the police had questioned me as a possible suspect. It was obvious that her parents blamed me for her death. I couldn't make them understand that it was just normal procedure for the police to question me, since I was the one who found her body.

As the funeral wrapped up, everyone headed for the cemetery. Cassandra's aunt Ruby grabbed my hand and walked with me to my car. "Don't worry," she said. "Everything is going to be fine. The police are going to find out who is responsible for this." At least she didn't think I was guilty.

While parked in line at the cemetery, I wiped my tears and sat calmly in my black Acura during the burial service. I slid on my dark shades and waited for everyone to leave, so I could go to her gravesite alone and give my last good-byes to the only woman I'd ever loved. I thought about how we'd been the best of friends. Just two weeks away from getting married, I walked into her condominium to find her throat slashed, her body badly beaten like some damn animal.

Before then, we had it all. There was nothing wrong with our relationship, and in addition to getting married, we planned on having plenty of children. Cassandra knew how much I wanted kids and promised me we'd do everything possible to make a baby on our honeymoon. She was such a sweet person, and that's why I couldn't understand why someone would want to hurt her. There were so many unanswered questions, and I was determined to find out what in the hell went wrong.

After further investigation, the police said they suspected that someone close to Cassandra was responsible. There was no forced entry, nothing was missing from her condo, and they found a note I completely overlooked on her dining room table, which read: YOU HAD IT COMING, BITCH!

Those were the words that wouldn't allow me to let this go. What in the hell did she have coming? Who was so angry with her that he wanted to see her dead? I was dying inside, and to put my mind at ease, so that my lady could rest in peace, I had no intentions of letting this go.

I grieved in my car at the cemetery and watched everyone from a distance as they gave their good-byes. I dropped my head and closed my eyes, and in my mind, I heard Cassandra's beautiful voice singing sweet melodies to me. Whenever I felt down, she'd always sing to me, and her voice would send chills throughout my body.

My thoughts of her made me break a half smile, and when I opened my eyes, I saw everyone heading back to their cars. Annette and Felicity came up to my car, and I lowered my window. Felicity bent down and spoke calmly to me.

"Brandon, are you going to Aunt Ruby's house?"

"No, I prefer to be alone right now."

"You really shouldn't be. Cassandra would want us to lean on each other for support to grieve together."

"I know she would, but she also knew how much I liked to be alone."

"Well, get some rest and call me or Annette if you need anything."

"I will, and thanks."

Annette and Felicity waved good-bye, and I waited around until nearly everyone had left. When I looked at Cassandra's gravesite, I noticed the police officer who had been crying at the funeral. He was watching the gravediggers lower her casket with a pained look on his face. I wanted to know who he was, so I got out of my car and paced myself to where he stood.

By the time I reached him, the gusty wind had blown open my long black trench coat, and my black leather shoes were covered with mud from the soggy grass. He turned and looked at me.

"Brandon Fletcher," I said, holding out my hand for him to shake.

He looked at my hand, and then held out his. "I know who you are. I'm Jabbar. A friend of Cassandra's."

"Well, how is it that you know me and I've never seen or heard of you before? For the record, Cassandra and I were engaged—"

"I . . . I doubt that," he said, "but now isn't the time or place to discuss this. I know you have questions, but I'm not prepared to answer them yet." He spoke sternly, and reached into his pocket to give me a card. "Call me in a few days so we can talk."

I took the card hesitantly and nodded as Jabbar walked off toward his vehicle. Still, I felt very confused. I looked down at Cassandra's casket, which was already in the ground. I wanted answers, but it wasn't like she could give me the answers I needed.

I stayed with her for at least thirty minutes, thinking about the good times we shared. I visualized her pretty smile and chuckled about the way she'd rub her nose against mine and sing to me whenever I was upset. Our dinner the other night was so special, and if I had known it would be our last time together, I would never have teased her about burning the roast. She seemed a bit offended, but I made up for it by sending her roses the next day. Hopefully she'd forgiven me, and as I whispered the words "I'm sorry," it was as if I heard her voice telling me that everything would be okay. I truly hoped so. After I wiped away the tears that had fallen down my face, I gathered myself and headed for home.

When I opened the door to my high-rise loft on Washington Avenue, Cassandra's amazing, sweet scent hit me. I walked over to the fireplace and picked up a picture of us from the mantle. I held it in my hands and then placed my lips on hers, as if I could really feel them; then I placed the picture right back where it belonged and would forever stay.

I went into the bathroom and stepped into the shower without taking off my black suit. The water poured down on me as I angrily removed my tie. I dropped it on the floor and then ripped my crisp white shirt apart. The buttons popped loose, and as I stared down at them, I tightened my fists, slamming them into the shower wall. When my rage was spent, I took several deep breaths to calm my nerves. I wiped the cold water that dripped from my face and then removed my clothes. My naked body fell against the wall, and I eased my way to the floor.

When I finally opened my eyes, I realized I'd turned off the water, but drips of cold water still trickled down on me. I tightened the faucet. With thoughts about Cassandra still stirring in my mind, I had no clue what time it was.

I dried myself and looked at the alarm clock in my bedroom. It showed 2:15 AM. Feeling overwhelmed, I plopped down on my bed and smothered my chocolate body in my royal blue satin sheets. I shut my eyes again and prayed for my misery to be over with soon.

While lying in the dark, I reached over and felt for Cassandra's warm and smooth, awesomely framed body. I visualized playing with her short, neatly layered hair and thought about making love to her once again. As I reminisced about her thick lips touching mine, the phone rang and startled me.

"Hello," I said softly.

"Brandon?"

"Yes."

"It's Ruby. Why didn't you come by with everyone else? And why haven't you been answering your phone? I've been trying to reach you all night."

"I fell asleep in the shower and didn't hear the phone.

Plus I wanted to be alone, Ruby. Please don't take it personal. I'm sure you understand."

"I do. But remember, no matter what, you're still like family to us. If you need anything, we're here for you, okay?"

"I know."

There was silence; then Aunt Ruby said good-bye before hanging up.

I hadn't eaten all day, so I went to the kitchen to find something. I made a bologna sandwich, and then went into my studio to meditate.

My mind was focused on Jabbar; his connection to Cassandra was a complete mystery to me. I still didn't want to believe she could have been having an affair. Her schedule was very busy, and I thought there was no way she could have had time to see another man. Besides, we were so damn happy together. We'd had very few arguments, and if we did, we'd always worked through our disagreements. We spent an enormous amount of time together, and even though her job as a travel agent kept her busy, she always made time for us. Being an artist, I pretty much had my own schedule. And, no matter what, she'd always let me know where she was.

As a travel agent, she made way more money than I did, but she never complained about my struggles to become a full-time artist. She'd been there for me every step of the way. There were times that I didn't have enough money to pay the rent, so she stepped up to help a brotha out. Bottom line, she'd done everything in the world for me, and I had done the same for her. Now, though, how would I ever move on without her? I didn't know. I was already missing her backrubs, her surprise candlelit dinners, her daily love letters, and her simply just calling to say how much she loved me.

Unable to shake those feelings from my mind, I squatted on the floor and gazed at the painted picture in front of me.

I'd never gotten around to finishing the portrait of Cassandra in a long red evening gown, so I reached for my red paint and brush. I dabbed the brush on the canvas, and took my time as I tried hard to make the picture appear realistic.

By morning, the sunlight beamed through the window and I was still at it, trying to bring the picture back to life. I put down my brushes and walked over to the window to look outside. It was a beautiful day. The St. Louis Gateway Arch was in my view, and the blue sky was clear and bright. Not wanting to torture myself for another day, I called my best friend, Will, to see if he would meet me for breakfast at Lucille's, a nearby food joint. He agreed to meet me in an hour.

Traffic was crammed, and by the time I reached Lucille's, Will was already there. He stood outside and paced back and forth, smoking a cigarette. If I didn't know better, I would've thought he was a crackhead because of how thin he was and the way his eyes bugged. He shot them in my direction, and when I made contact, he quickly dropped his cigarette on the ground and smashed it with his shoe. I often complained about his smoking habits and his bad breath, so he always tried to avoid smoking around me.

When I got out of my car, Will gave me a handshake and patted my back.

"Brandon Lee Fletcher, what's up, man? How ya feeling?"

"Not too good, Will," I said as we walked into Lucille's. We sat at a booth in the far corner of the restaurant. Will reached in his pocket for another cigarette, and then looked at me with his reddish glazed eyes. I could tell he'd had more than a cigarette before meeting with me.

"Oh, I forgot," he said, placing the cigarette back into his pocket. "I'm gon' die of lung cancer, right?"

"Hey, man, smoking is your preference. I be trying to look out for you, that's all."

"I appreciate you looking out for me, but let me know what your best friend can do for you."

I looked at Will and my eyes started to fill with water. "I want my baby back, man. It's been so tough living without her and I—"

"Well, nothing in this world gon' bring her back. You need to regroup and focus on your future. Cassandra was cool, but you know that we didn't really click. She always looked down on me, and I didn't like that shit. But this ain't about how I felt about her. I know losing her hurts you like hell. . . . But at this point, all you can do is move on."

"I know she's not coming back, but I've got to find out why this shit happened. Have you heard anything in the hood, or have you had a chance to talk with your boy Antwone yet? By now, I'm sure he's probably heard something."

"I mentioned it to him and he told me he'd get back with me. I explained to him what happened and he said it sounds like Cassandra was killed by somebody she knew. The question is, who?"

"I couldn't agree with him more."

The waitress came over and took our orders. When she came back with our orange juice, Will flirted with her.

"What's your name, baby girl?" he asked while rubbing her hand.

"Stacie." She blushed.

"Um, well, uh, Stacie, do you think I can get your phone number? I promise you that I won't call you until tonight."

She blushed again and wrote down her number on a napkin. She gave it to Will and he put the napkin in his pocket.

"Did you see how easy that was?" he asked.

"Yes, I did."

"Well, straighten up and please get back into action. I know how much you loved Cassandra, but you have a whole life ahead of you. You'll be thirty-one next month, and you walking around like it's the end of the world. I'm starting to see kinks in your hair, and your facial hair, well, it could use a trim. I'm used to a nigga's hair lined up and beard trimmed. What's up with that?"

"Will, this is probably the first time you've seen my fade out of whack. And as for the beard, I haven't felt like shaving. Man, don't you understand how difficult this is for me? Cassandra is all that I had. She was everything to me, and since my family moved to Alabama, you know all I had was her."

"Yeah, yeah, yeah . . . I understand that, but life goes on. All I'm saying is you can't bring her back, bro. Cassandra would want you to move on, so why don't you?"

Will and I sat at Lucille's for the next hour or so and discussed what we thought had happened. We agreed that someone close to her had someone else do their dirty work.

"Who, though?" Will asked. "You know her family way better than I do, and didn't you say she had some crazy-ass cousins?"

"Man, we all got crazy-ass cousins, including you. I'm really puzzled about her murder, and my mind is drawing a serious blank."

"What about her whack-ass mama and her Aunt Ruby? Didn't you mention something about them practicing voodoo?"

"Yeah, they're into that kind of stuff, but that has nothing to do with killing people. And even though Cassandra's relationship was kind of shaky with her mother, she got along very well with Aunt Ruby."

"If you ask me, I think you might have yourself a suspect. Having a shaky relationship with your own mother can lead to so many other things. When the police questioned you, did they mention anyone else?"

I shook my head and didn't mention anything to Will

about Jabbar. I didn't want him to know that Cassandra had possibly been seeing someone else. The thoughts of it were tearing me up, and I hoped that their relationship wasn't as serious as I thought it might be. Will had previously mentioned that he'd thought she was seeing someone else "on her level" because, according to him, she was too ambitious for a brotha like me who was still trying to find his way. He often complained about how she disassociated herself with my friends and appeared to be so uppity. I explained to him that she was a mature woman and didn't see the need to hang out with us all of the time. Cassandra always spoke well of Will, and laughed when I told her about his accusations.

With my hands deep in the pockets of my boot-cut faded jeans, I waited outside for Will to wrap up his conversation with Stacie. Hair trimmed or not, two ladies passed by and complimented my light brown slanted eyes, and bowed legs. They said that I reminded them of Tyson Beckford. I thanked them for the compliment, and they joked about my thick lips, which were identical to his too. I smiled, and as they walked off, I watched Will strut down the sidewalk like a pimp, as if he were a mack daddy. To me, he wasn't that good looking, and many women were turned off by how short and frail he was. His nappy hair didn't help much either, but his charm, friendly smile and compliments to women worked magic.

Will stepped up to me, and I teased him about moving on up in the world, pertaining to women. Stacie didn't look bad at all: thick figure, bright smile, long braids and caramel skin. I commented that his wide smile must have *moved* her, and Will laughed as he got into my car.

"You're damn right I'm moving on up. I'm moving on out too. Mom's getting sick and tired of me hanging around the house, so I gotta find an established woman to chill with."

"Man, when are you going to get your own shit? Wouldn't

you say it was about time you had something to call your own?"

"Hell, naw. I ain't got time to be paying no rent when somebody else can pay it. I'm supposed to lay back and enjoy the life of luxury around me. Besides, if you're tired of me living off my mother, then let me stay with you. Your loft is big enough for the two of us, and since Cassandra—"

"Don't even think about it. For once in your life, you need to stand up and be a man. That way, can't nobody kick you out and tell you what you can or can't do."

"I know, and trust me, I'm working on it. In the meantime, I know you got your own place and everything, but Cassandra did kind of make a way for you, didn't she?"

"Yes. She helped me out financially, but I did plenty of things for her in return."

"Many things like what? Fuck her all the time? That's the only thing I recall you saying that you did."

"Will, please. Yeah, man, I did sex her all the time, but I also cooked, cleaned, pampered her . . . you name it, I did it! I gave her all of me and then some."

"I know you did, and you know I'm just messin' with you, right?"

"Yeah, but I'm serious when I say that you need to get your own shit. I can't let you stay with me, man. I like my privacy. If there's anything else I can do, holler at your boy, but living with me is a no-no."

"Fo' sho'," Will said. He opened the door and looked over at me. "Listen, man. Take care. And I promise you that we'll find out what happened to your woman. Ya hear me?"

I nodded and gave Will a high-five before he stepped out of the car. As I drove off, I looked in my rearview mirror and saw him lighting up another cigarette. I smiled and shook my head.

Instead of going home, I drove to Cassandra's condo. I

knew her parents and Aunt Ruby had pretty much cleared out the place, but I sat outside remembering all the wonderful memories we shared. Making love to her was at the top of my list, and I snickered from the thoughts of us sharing laughs and going for late night walks in the park. A few more tears fell, and I vowed to never stop by her place again.

CHAPTER 2

My alarm clock was set to wake me around 7:00 the following morning. But when I heard the doorbell buzzing and looked at the clock, it was already 11:00 AM. I grabbed my robe and hurried to the door to see who it was. When I looked out the peephole, I saw Felicity.

"Hey, Brandon," she said, entering the room.

"What's up, Felicity? What brings you by?"

"Don't tell me you forgot."

"Forgot what?"

"So, you did forget."

"Again, what did I forget?"

"I know you've had a lot on your mind, and trust me, we all do. I'm missing my cousin like crazy, but she did say it was okay for you to paint my picture. You remember my picture, don't you?"

"Sorry. I remember now, but I did forget. My mind—"

"Of course, I understand." She placed her hand on the doorknob. "Look, if you want me to come back some other time, I will."

"Naw, that's okay. Besides, you said that you wanted to give this picture to your man for your anniversary, right?"

"Yes, and it's tomorrow. I would've called sooner, but I knew you were probably not feeling up to it after the funeral and everything."

"I'm not, but I made you a promise," I said, walking back to my studio. Felicity followed. "You can change into whatever you want to over there." I pointed to a room divider in the far corner.

"No need," she said, opening her coat. "I told you I wanted something simple."

Felicity dropped her coat and stood naked. When she walked over and stood on the small stage in front of the 40x60 canvas that was propped up on an easel, I gazed at her juicy thick breasts, her trimmed coochie, and her apple bottom ass. She placed her hand on her hip and smiled. I was in another world, and hated to admit that I admired her well-shaped body.

I remembered Cassandra saying that Felicity was a freak, but it surprised me that she'd shown up with nothing on under her coat. I was horny as hell, and I'm sure she noticed my wandering eyes drop between her thighs.

"How would you like for me to pose?" she asked.

I licked my bottom lip and walked over by her. "First, I prefer that you leave a little something for your man's imagination. It'll make the picture much sexier, but that's just my opinion."

"You're the expert here, so I'll pose however you'd like me to."

I placed my hand on top of my forehead. "Give me a minute to get my thoughts together. I need to go put on some clothes, shave and brush my teeth. I'll be back in a bit."

I excused myself because Felicity had a brotha on the rise. She was a bi-racial woman, and she looked beautiful. I was looking forward to the pleasure of painting her face and her bodacious body. But I thought about how awkward this felt. My dick hadn't gotten this hard for another woman in a very long time. I surely wouldn't mind having sex with Felicity, and maybe I did need to move on like Will said. I hoped she didn't notice the growth down below, but maybe the expression on my face was enough.

When I re-entered my studio, Felicity was still naked, but I turned my head to momentarily avoid her. I searched through my props so I could add a sense of creativeness to her picture. I came across a black velvet chaise and slid it over to the stage for her to lie on. She sat and I placed her arm on the armrest then positioned her legs where they crossed and hid her pussy. I teased her naturally curly thick hair, and asked her to hold good posture so her breasts could face me. To match her steel gray eyes, I found a piece of silky silver material and placed it on the lower part of her body to cover her.

As I started to draw her, she complained about how uncomfortable she was. Within the first thirty minutes, we took three breaks.

"I'm sorry, Brandon. My back is killing me," she said, sitting up again.

"I know it's uncomfortable, Felicity, but if you want this done today, you'd better be up for the long haul."

"Can't you work faster?"

"No, I can't. If you want perfection, and I'm sure you do, then you'll have to be patient."

"Okay," she said, getting back into position. "But now I'm starting to get hungry."

I smiled at Felicity and shook my head. She laughed and watched as I got back to business.

For the next hour, Felicity didn't complain one bit. She kept talking to me, though, and I had to remind her how important it was for her to keep still. Once she started fidgeting again, she rolled off the chaise and lay flat on her back. She stretched out her arms and screamed out loud.

"Okay," I said, putting down my sketch pencil. "Let's get something to eat."

She rolled over and got up. "I thought you'd never make that suggestion."

Felicity put her coat on and followed me into the kitchen. When I realized I didn't have much for us to eat, I called Pizza Hut and ordered a veggie pizza. Waiting patiently for the pizza to come, we sat side by side on two barstools in front of the stainless steel kitchen island.

Felicity looked around. "Brandon, your place is put together very well. I love the contemporary furniture, and I see why Cassandra liked to spend so much time here."

"It's cool. I got a lot of my furniture at estate sales, and I am one brotha who can't afford to splurge on expensive furniture."

"Used furniture or not, you have good taste." Felicity stood up and stretched again. "My body is so tight. I didn't think I would be this uncomfortable."

"It's more work than you think. Trust me; I'm not the only one who has to do all of the work."

"Yeah, I see. The naked picture you painted of Cassandra was so beautiful that I definitely had to have one for Kurt. You're a talented man, Brandon, and I hope what happened to Cassandra doesn't interfere with you continuing your work."

"No, it won't. Actually, my work is what keeps me at peace. I'll never give up on it."

"Well, good," she said, sitting back down. She looked over at me. "I . . . I really didn't want to bring this up, but are you going to be okay? You seem like you could use a friend to keep your mind off your troubles. And remember, I knew you before Cassandra did."

"I haven't forgotten, Felicity." Our co-worker, Gary, had introduced me to Felicity. I took her out on one date, but for some reason, it just didn't work out. That's when she introduced me to Cassandra. I teased Felicity, "I haven't forgotten that date we went on, either. I guess you wasn't feeling me, huh?"

"I was feeling you, but I was feeling Kurt too. Cassandra didn't have a man at the time, so I hooked the two of you up. Y'all connected, and that was that. Now, answer my question. How have you really been feeling?"

"Downright awful. I guess the sooner I find out what happened to her, the better off I'll be. There are just so many unanswered questions, but I'm confused and don't know where to start."

"I want to know who's responsible too, and I can't wait until whoever is responsible is brought to justice."

I looked over at Felicity. "I know this has nothing to do with Cassandra's murder, but do you know anything about this police officer, Jabbar? I got the impression that you and Annette know him quite well."

Felicity gave me a funny look, and then removed herself from the stool. "Brandon, I don't feel comfortable talking to you about Jabbar. He was very close to Cassandra, but that's all I can say."

I took a deep breath and almost hated that I'd brought up his name. If her cousin was seeing another man, would Felicity feel comfortable telling me so? I wasn't sure, but pressing the issue was worth a try. I dropped my head and stared at the ground, not wanting Felicity to see my hurt. "I . . . I know you don't want to get involved, but I'd really like to find out more about their relationship. There's not much I can do at this point, but I'd still like to know."

Felicity walked over and rubbed my back. She took my hand and squeezed it together with hers. "Brandon, Cassandra loved you a lot. Don't you ever doubt her love for you.

And when the time comes for you to know more about Jabbar, you'll know it. I don't feel comfortable poking my nose where it doesn't belong, and I hope you understand that."

I nodded and Felicity lifted my chin then stared deeply into my eyes. She rubbed her fingers along my thinly trimmed beard and traced my goatee. "Cassandra was so lucky to have you, as you her. When Kurt and me were having our issues, there were times that I was mad at myself for introducing you to Cassandra. She seemed happy with y'all's relationship, and a part of me was kind of jealous. Sometimes, I was uncomfortable being around the two of you, and I was afraid that Cassandra would notice my attraction to you. It was so obvious, and I figured you must have known."

"No, I didn't. I was deeply in love with your cousin, and if any woman had shown interest in me, I wouldn't have noticed."

Felicity looked embarrassed and removed her hand from my face. I appreciated her being honest with me, but I had to be honest with myself too. I was disappointed when Felicity didn't want to go on another date with me, but meeting Cassandra was the best thing that had ever happened to me. Now, though, Felicity's sexiness couldn't be ignored.

When the doorbell buzzed, I headed for the door to pay for our pizza. We quickly ate, and then went back to my studio to finish her painting. Felicity had trouble repositioning herself, so I helped her get back into the same position she had been in before.

"You're really good at this, you know?" She grinned.

"Yeah, I do," I said, moving her hair away from her face. She gave me a long and hard stare.

"How much longer is this going to take?"

"Not too much longer. I'm just about finished sketching you. Once I finish, you can relax. I can paint it later and have it ready for you by tomorrow morning."

"Thank you."

I went back to my chair, but as I started to sketch Felicity, my dick was on the rise again. I hoped that she didn't notice how uncomfortable I was. I'd painted plenty of naked women before, but there was something about Felicity that made my palms sweat. But I knew that now wasn't the time or the place for me to act on my feelings.

I started thinking about how Cassandra and I used to make love, so I took a break and placed my drawing pencil down on the easel. The guilt for admiring Felicity was kicking in, and all I could do was close my eyes to erase my thoughts.

"Are you getting tired already?" Felicity asked.

"A little bit, but don't move. My hand just caught a slight cramp."

Felicity didn't move. I fought my attraction to her and tried to finish her picture as quickly as I could.

Almost an hour later, I was finished. Felicity rushed over to see it. A few tears rolled down her face.

"That couldn't be me," she sniffed.

"Well, it is," I said, feeling proud of my work.

"Kurt is going to love it! I can already tell what the finished product is going to look like."

"Yeah, well, get your butt out of here and let me finish. I don't have anything else to do today, so there shouldn't be a problem with me finishing by tomorrow morning."

"G'on with your bad self. Before I go to work tomorrow morning, I'll stop by and pick it up. How much do I owe you?"

"Normally, I charge three thousand dollars for something like this, but I'll let you have it for . . . let's say half?"

"Then half it is," she said, reaching her hand out to shake mine.

Felicity put her coat on, and before she left, she gave me a squeezing hug and told me she'd see me in the morning.

* * *

I spent the entire evening painting Felicity's picture. There were some setbacks, as the thoughts of Cassandra and Jabbar weighed heavily on my mind. I wondered if he'd made her smile like I did. If she sang to him and rubbed her nose against his when he was upset. Did they have crazy and wild sex like we often had? What attracted her to him?

I took a break and decided to return some of the phone calls I'd been avoiding. There were several messages on my answering machine. Ruby seemed extremely worried about me and begged me to call her back. Will bugged me about a place to stay, and Cassandra's mother called and apologized for putting the blame on me for Cassandra's murder. Her father wasn't speaking to me at all, because for whatever reason, he still felt I had something to do with her murder. It hurt me like hell that they'd even think something so ridiculous, and I wasn't about to forgive either one of them so easily.

When I called Ruby back, she didn't answer, so I left a message for her to return my call. As for Will, he said he was busy talking to Stacie on the other line, and he promised to hit me back later. I got back to Felicity's picture and worked hard at finishing it.

By midnight, I turned off the main lights and dimmed the track lights so I could put the finishing touches on the painting. Her beauty stiffened me even more, and I found myself thinking about being inside of her. What if things had worked out between us? What if Kurt was never in the picture? I was disgusted with my thoughts, and I knew they stemmed from my suspicions about Cassandra and Jabbar. I was in need of something to make me feel better, because as much as I wanted to force their relationship to the back of my mind, it was obvious that he was her man, just as I was.

As I gazed at Felicity's picture, I was quite impressed with the final product. Exhausted, I lay on the floor next to a painting of Cassandra in a red dress. All of a sudden, feeling frustrated about her relationship with another man, I dipped my brush into some paint and painted over her picture until her image was completely destroyed. I held my chest and squeezed my eyes together.

I knew that speaking to Jabbar would clear up some of the questions I had about Cassandra, but I refused to call him. Maybe a part of me didn't want to know the truth. Or maybe it didn't even matter now that she had cheated. What really mattered was that she was dead. Maybe it was time that I chill and let the police find out who was responsible. They had questioned me, but I wondered if they had questioned anyone else. I sure as hell hoped that the truth would soon come to light.

By morning, I was cuddled up on the floor with a blanket and felt soft hands touching my face. I slowly opened my eyes and saw Felicity standing over me. Her makeup looked as if it was perfectly painted on her face, and a strand of her curly hair dangled in front of her right eye.

"Brandon, are you okay?"

I rose up on my elbows and squinted. "Yeah, uh, I'm fine. What time is it?"

She looked at her watch. "It's a quarter to seven. I told you I was coming by early, remember?"

"Yes," I said, getting off the floor. I looked over at her picture and tightened the belt on my loose-fitting silk pajama pants. "Did you see your picture yet?"

"Of course I did. And please don't give me any discounts. You did a phenomenal job, and you deserve to be paid in full."

"If you insist," I said, stumbling my way into the kitchen to turn on the coffee pot. Felicity followed.

"Yes, I insist. . . . Aren't you going to ask me how I got in here?"

"Yeah, how did you? I can't remember if I locked the door or not."

"Brandon, you really need to get a hold of yourself. The door was wide open and I was scared to come in here. Considering what happened to Cassandra, I wasn't sure what to expect."

"I've been so out of it, Felicity. I don't know if I'm coming or going."

"I understand, but you've got to get yourself together. I've never seen you like this." She moved in closer and rubbed the side of my face. "If you need me, I'm here, okay?"

"Thanks." I got ready to pour my coffee. "Would you like some?"

"Yes, I would." She took the cup away from me. "Go sit down. I'll get mine and yours."

I smiled and took a seat at the table. Felicity placed my coffee in front of me and sat beside me. She teased her curly hair with her fingertips. "Would you do me a huge favor?" she asked.

"Sure."

"That picture isn't going to fit into my car. Would you mind bringing it to my place around six o'clock this evening? Kurt and I are having a late dinner at eight o'clock, so I'd like to have it there before he arrives."

"That's not a problem. Just make sure you're there."

"I will."

Felicity and I finished our coffee, and still feeling beat, I moseyed to my bedroom to lie down. She stood next to my bed and pulled the sheets over me.

"Please get some rest, Brandon. I know you're angry, but don't take this out on Cassandra."

"I'm not."

"If you're not, then why did you destroy her picture?"

"I don't know." I took a deep breath and sat up on my elbows. "Hurt, I guess."

Felicity sat on the bed next to me. "Hurt about what? That Cassandra is dead, or that you don't know what actually transpired between her and Jabbar?"

"Both. I feel so—"

I took a hard swallow, and before I knew it, I reached over and pulled Felicity's face to mine. I licked her lips, and when she tried to pull away, I stuck my tongue deeply into her mouth. Surprisingly, her resistance stopped. She placed her hand on the back of my head and rubbed it. Our kissing became more intense. I felt a serious need for her, and I could tell that she had a need for me too.

"What was that for?" she asked as she backed up and wiped her lips.

I looked at her with my sore, baggy eyes, and then shrugged my shoulders. "You said if I needed you—"

"But . . . but not like this, Brandon. I know I told you how I felt about us before, but I do have a man."

"I'm aware that you have a man, but I . . . I'm just reminding you about what you said. It seems like you're trying to play some kind of game with me, Felicity."

"That's not what I'm trying to do. I've always felt a connection with you, but Kurt—"

"Kurt has been unfaithful to you for a very long time, and you know about his other women. Don't go pretending as if you care that much about a man who constantly cheats on you."

Felicity rolled her eyes. She must have known that Cassandra had discussed their relationship with me. I sat up and stared at her with a desperate look. She could tell what I wanted, and for the moment, she knew exactly what I needed. Without saying a word, she stepped out of her shoes, and her suit jacket hit the floor. She unbuttoned her blouse and wasted no time straddling my lap. I was just as anxious as she was, and assisted her with removing her blouse and bra. I held her perky, peach-scented breasts, and when I started to suck them, Felicity moaned and dropped her head back.

Before I could remove her skirt, she pressed her hands against my chest and lightly pushed me back. She placed her lips on the side of my neck, and I lay silently while gazing at the vaulted ceiling. Felicity lowered herself and allowed her lips to touch every part of my body to arouse me. By the time she reached my goods, I held bunches of her hair in my hand, while satisfying pleasure was given to me down below.

I was so hungry for Felicity that I cut her blow job short and made my way on top. Her long legs rested high on my shoulders, and I pecked down them. Felicity rushed me, pulling her panties to the side and forcing my dick inside of her wetness. I closed my eyes and slowly worked against her slippery walls.

I started to feel guilty about what I was doing and stopped my motion. Felicity placed her hands on my muscular ass and dug her nails into it.

"Don't stop, please," she begged.

I leaned down and gave Felicity a peck on her lips. Memories of making love to Cassandra swam around in my head, but Felicity's juicy and warm insides helped me stay somewhat focused.

By the time we finished, my stomach turned in circles. I could hear Felicity in the shower as I lay back, resting on the bed. What in the hell was I thinking? Cassandra's gravesite didn't even have grass growing over it yet, and there I was, already fucking another woman. Was I crazy? I wanted Felicity to be Cassandra so badly that while we were having sex, I was thinking and believing that she was. Maybe I was wrong, but I couldn't help myself. A part of me felt so damn weak inside.

Felicity stepped into the room and my guilty thoughts were interrupted. Without any clothes on, she pulled the sheets back and climbed into bed with me. We both lay sideways and looked at each other.

"Brandon, I know you're probably having some regrets, but if I didn't want this to happen, it wouldn't have."

I spoke in a soft whisper. "Why did you allow me to take advantage of you like that?"

"You didn't take advantage of me. Like you said, Kurt and I have had our share of problems, and a few indiscretions on my part shouldn't hurt him."

"It's that simple, huh? You make it sound so simple."

"Yeah, it's that simple, especially since I often wondered what sex would be like with you."

"But . . . but today is your anniversary, isn't it? Why did you decide to put yourself out there like this on your anniversary?"

"Because I wanted to. I'm going to celebrate my anniversary with Kurt, and so be it."

"No regrets at all—just like that?"

"Brandon, there are some people who do things that simply make them happy. My intention wasn't to come over here and have sex with you on my anniversary. It just happened, and there's nothing I can do to change it. I enjoyed myself and I have no regrets. You might not understand that because of your dedication to Cassandra, but trust me; what transpired between us was bound to happen someday."

"So, are you saying that you had plans for us?"

"No, I'm not saying that, but since you already know, my relationship with Kurt has not been on solid ground. I love him a lot, and I tend to go above and beyond sometimes to show him just that. He has his faults, but I haven't been the perfect little angel either. I haven't stepped out on him for some time now, but it felt good being with you."

"I . . . I guess Cassandra must have felt the need to be with someone else too. Our relationship wasn't shaky, though. I never, ever cheated on her, so I don't quite understand your way of thinking when you say that you have love for Kurt, yet you can cheat on him."

Felicity shrugged her shoulders. "You just never know, Brandon. Some things you just never know."

Felicity and I talked for a while longer. I was still tired from being up all night, painting her picture, so she put on her clothes and got ready to leave. I told her I'd drop the picture off before 6:00 PM. Once she was gone, I lay back on the bed, wondering if this thing between me and Felicity was just a one-time encounter. Maybe she would leave Kurt just to be with me. But was that what I really wanted? Was I ready to move on and get over Cassandra? I really wasn't sure.

CHAPTER 3

I woke up around 4:00 PM, slid into my brown-and-tan velour sweat suit, and was on my way to take Felicity her picture. Before I left, I tried Ruby on her phone again, but couldn't reach her. I even held Jabbar's business card in my hand and thought about calling him. I didn't feel the need to open up a can of worms, though, so I dropped the card in the trash.

Since Felicity's apartment on Olive Street was a thirty-minute drive from my loft in downtown St. Louis, I rushed to get the picture to her by six. I'd thought about what had happened earlier, but nothing could help the disappointment I felt for having sex with her so soon. I felt terrible, and the only explanations that I had for my actions were Jabbar and my loneliness, which had obviously gotten the best of me.

When I arrived at Felicity's place, she stood on the wooden staircase waiting for me. She told me the elevators were broken, so I had to haul up six flights of stairs to get to her apartment. She offered to help, but I told her she would only be in the way.

She held the door open, and when I walked inside, I saw

Annette on the plaid sofa, looking at the plasma TV on the wall. Felicity directed me to the brass easel she'd gotten, and I placed the picture on it.

Annette turned to look at the picture. "Brandon, that has got to be the most beautiful picture I've ever seen. You actually made the wench look good."

"Forget you, Annette," Felicity said, smiling. "It looks good because he had something *good* to work with."

"Now, now, ladies. Don't y'all start no fighting up in here."

"Never," Annette said, and then stood up to get a closer look at the picture. She quickly pulled her long shirt down to cover her big butt, and then looked at Felicity. "Girl, weren't you nervous taking off your clothes in front of Brandon?"

"Just a little." Felicity looked at me. "Brandon made me feel comfortable, though."

"Like I do all of my customers," I added. "If you'd like to, Annette, I can paint one of you too."

"Let me do a bit of working out first. The last time I checked, my thighs were too thick and my midriff area needed some work. I don't have a man right now, so that'll give me some time to work on my physical appearance. A naked picture of me would probably scare a man away."

I quickly spoke up because even though Annette was thick, she reminded me of Jill Scott and was very attractive. "Woman, don't be so hard on yourself. It's the inside that counts. I think you're the perfect size, and I would love to paint a picture of you just as you are. Plenty of men love women with a little meat on their bones, and I don't mind saying that I'm one of them."

"Ya see, now I see why Cassandra was so in love with you. A charmer you are, but baby, you can say that mess all you want. Men are not looking at my fat butt going, 'Ohhh, I bet there's something so wonderful inside of her just waiting to come out.' Trust me, they're looking at me thinking, 'That bitch know she needs to lose some weight.'"

"I don't understand why you're being so hard on your-self," I said. "That's crazy."

"She's always downing herself like that. I told her she's a beautiful woman, but she ain't trying to hear it."

"No, I'm not, especially coming from a woman who re-sembles a young Vanessa Williams. Let's face it; you got it and I don't." Annette picked up her purse. "You have a won-derful time with Kurt tonight. As for you, Brandon, I'll come see you when I kick off about thirty or forty pounds, okay?"

I chuckled and kissed her cheek. "Okay. If you say so, An-nette. Take care. And whenever you're ready, just let me know."

She nodded, said good-bye to Felicity, and jetted.

Felicity quickly grabbed my hand and walked me down the hallway to her bedroom. I thought she wanted to fuck again, and after seeing how sexy she looked in her thigh-high dress, I was all for it. When we got to her room, though, she opened a box with a watch inside. I felt disappointed that she'd taken me to her room just to see the watch.

"So, what do you think? Do you think Kurt is going to like this?"

I looked at the Movado watch and nodded. "Like it? He's going to love it. It's really sweet of you to go all out like this for your anniversary. I hope he appreciates it."

She closed the box. "Yeah, well, I guess it's the least I can do after what—"

"Hey, forget it. Let's just pretend that sex between us never happened. I was wrong for taking advantage of you and—"

"You didn't take advantage of me. We had fun, and it'll be our secret. "

"Cool, but you didn't tell Annette, did you?"

"Of course not. Annette is the walking *National Enquirer*, and I don't want anyone to know what happened between us."

"Same here," I said, turning to leave.

We walked toward the door. Standing in front of it, she wouldn't allow me to exit. She gave me a seductive stare and lightly touched the side of my face. All of the guilt that I felt still didn't stop me from leaning in for another sweet kiss like the ones she'd given me earlier.

As we smacked lips, I wrapped my arms around her waist and gathered her ass in my hands. She returned the favor, and when she unzipped my pants, I lifted her against the door and straddled her on my hips.

We were about to indulge ourselves in another sex session, but there was a hard knock at the door. Felicity's eyes widened, and I could feel her heart race against mine. I lowered her legs, and as the banging became louder, we stepped away from the door. I wiped my lips and quickly zipped my pants. Felicity straightened her short dress.

"Who is it?" she asked.

"It's me, baby," Kurt answered.

"Here I come," she yelled. She pointed her finger and whispered for me to go into the bathroom.

She didn't have to tell me twice. Kurt was a professional weightlifter, and the thought of us getting busted made me nervous. I went into the bathroom and shut the door.

I heard Kurt talking, and listened to Felicity tell him I was in the bathroom. She made up some lie about why I'd stopped by so he wouldn't be suspicious. A few minutes later, I flushed the toilet, washed my hands and made my exit. While he talked to Felicity, I saw Kurt leaning against the kitchen counter.

"Hey, Kurt," I said, smiling and walking up to him.

"What's up, Brandon." He reached out and tightly gripped my hand. "How's everything going?"

"It's been okay. Just trying to take it one day at a time, that's all."

"That's all you can do. I can't even imagine what you've been going through, but stay strong, all right?"

I nodded. "I will. I most definitely will."

"If there's anything me or Felicity can do to help, let us know."

Felicity cleared her throat and walked over by the picture. She unveiled it. "Baby, look. Look what Brandon and I created for you."

Kurt took slow steps toward the picture and he examined it with a puzzled expression on his face. He placed his fingertips on his chin and rubbed it. "Mm, mmm, mmm." He smiled and then looked at me. "Now, how did you get so lucky? I thought this beautiful woman was for my eyes only."

I struggled to smile at Kurt, knowing that he'd probably want to kill me if he knew I'd done a whole lot more than just look at his woman. "Naw, you're the lucky man, Kurt." I felt in my coat pocket for my keys and hurried to the door. "You two have a nice evening."

"You too," Felicity said, opening the door for me. "And I'll be in touch."

I could've slapped myself for pursuing Felicity again. Kurt had been nothing but cool with me and had let me borrow money from time to time. Stupid me, there I was all hyped up and ready to fuck his woman again.

I hurried to my car in a daze. As I pulled the handle to open the door, I felt something heavy pound on the side of my face. The blow was so powerful that I blacked out for a few seconds. When I came to, a brotha with a dark mask covering his face tossed me on the hood of my car and went to work on my ribs with his fists. After he punched me in my mouth a few times, I tried to fight back, but I had no strength to do so. He was too strong, and once he kicked between my legs, I fell to the ground on my knees then rolled onto my back. Blood gushed from my mouth. My attacker bent down over me.

"Compliments of Jabbar," he said in a deep voice, and then laid a handkerchief on my chest before running away.

I lay on the ground and held my side in pain. One of Felicity's neighbors, who had seen the incident, came over to help.

"Man, are you all right?" he asked. "I didn't get a good look at the person who attacked you. Do you want me to call the police?"

I shook my head and managed to maneuver myself over to my car and open the door.

"I . . . I'm cool. Don't bother to call the police."

"Are you sure? This neighborhood is getting worse by the day, and—"

"Look, thanks for your help, but I said I'm all right."

The man watched as I got in my car and sat in the driver's seat. He shook his head in disgust and walked away. My whole body throbbed with pain, and I dropped my head on the steering wheel. I used the handkerchief to wipe the blood from my mouth then I started the car and cautiously drove home.

My apartment building's manager, Mr. Armanos, saw me struggling to the door. He ran up to help.

"Say, are you gonna be okay?"

"Yeah, I'm cool," I said, still holding my side. "If you would just get the door for me, I'd appreciate it."

"Ya sure you don't need a doctor or the police?"

"I'm positive."

Mr. Armanos took my keys and helped me inside. My legs were aching, so I limped to the couch and took a seat.

"I think you really need to call a doctor," he said.

"I'll be fine, Mr. Armanos. Just close the door behind you on your way out."

Mr. Armanos scratched the side of his head, but didn't say

another word. When he left, I put my feet on the couch and lay back. I was stiff and could barely move. I could taste the blood in my mouth and spat it out in the handkerchief that was still in my hand.

I closed my eyes tightly and thought about that mother-fucker, Jabbar. What in the hell did he have against me? That fool was with my woman. I should have been the one to send somebody to kick his ass.

I rubbed my face to soothe the pain and started dreaming about Cassandra. We stood closely together, holding hands, but just as I leaned in to kiss her, I was awakened by a knock at the door. I wasn't in the mood for company, so I lay silently on the couch.

When I heard Ruby's voice, I yelled back at her. "Just a minute, all right?" I sat up, and that's when I realized that the vision in my left eye was blurred.

When I opened the door, Ruby's arched eyebrows scrunched in. She had a puzzled look on her face. She came in, tossed her long, stiff blond weave to the side and placed her hands on her hips.

"Brandon, what in the hell happened to you?"

I closed the door and limped back over to the couch. "I got jumped."

"Jumped? By who?"

"Shit, I don't know. He said he was one of Jabbar's boys."

"Hmph, ain't that a bitch. You need to see a doctor. Let me take you to the emergency room."

Ruby ignored the mention of Jabbar's name. No one seemed to want to talk about this guy. This shit was starting to drive me crazy. "Look, Ruby, I'm not going to the emer-gency room. I'm not going anywhere but right here."

"Don't be so damn stubborn about this. I'm taking you to the doctor right after I call the police." Ruby walked over to my phone and picked it up.

I hurried off the couch and snatched the phone away

from her. I didn't trust the police, and I sure as hell wasn't going to the hospital so they could call them. "Don't! Please. I'll be fine, all right?"

I laid the phone down, and she gave me a hard stare. "Brandon, why don't you get yourself together? I've been calling here to check on you, and you won't even answer your phone. Trust me; I know you're hurting, but Cassandra wouldn't—"

"Yeah, yeah, yeah, whatever. What the hell ever, Ruby. I'm sick and tired of hearing about what Cassandra would or wouldn't want."

Ruby stepped back, looking shocked. She blinked her eyes, and her fake eyelashes fluttered. "Now, I know those harsh words didn't just come out of your mouth. What in the hell has gotten into you?"

I walked back over to the couch and plopped down. Ruby followed and sat in a chair next to me. When my eyes started to water, I covered them with my hands and then rubbed my face. As I held back my tears, I gripped my hands together and looked at Ruby.

"Who was Jabbar to Cassandra, Ruby? Please tell me."

Ruby sighed, folded her arms and scooted back in the chair. She looked at me with her dark brown bugged eyes, and then lifted one skinny leg on top of the other. She patted her leg and fidgeted around with her three-inch long fingernails.

"I truly didn't want to be the one to tell you this . . . but," she said sternly, "I want you to get on with your life after this, okay?"

I nodded.

"Jabbar was Cassandra's lover. She met him roughly over maybe . . . maybe two years ago. I told her several times that he was no good for her, but she wouldn't listen. I reminded her of what a wonderful relationship she had with you, but she told me that even though she loved you, there was something missing. After a while, Jabbar started coming around the family more, and, uh, she told us it was over between the two of you."

I strongly disagreed. "What? We never broke up! I've always been with her since day one. I don't know what in the hell—"

"Listen, I'm just telling you what she told me. When you called and told me about the engagement, I was shocked. And so was everybody else. We thought you had lost your mind. And then, when Cassandra wound up dead, of course, everybody thought you did it."

"Ruby, come on now. How in the hell could anybody think that when y'all knew how much I loved Cassandra?"

"That's just it. Everybody thought you were upset about the break-up and it drove you to kill her."

"But we never broke up! We were still together when she was killed!"

"Trust me; I know. And the only reason I know that is because Cassandra called me the day before she was killed. She told me how much she loved you, but said that she was in a dangerous situation with Jabbar and couldn't get out."

"Did you tell that to the police?"

"Yes, I did. I told them everything, but with Jabbar being a police officer, I don't think they're going to do much about him. If anything, you'd better get yourself together and get your story straight. The police questioned me, and it seems as if they're trying to point the finger at you. They asked me a lot of questions about your relationship with Cassandra, and I really didn't have much to say, other than she loved you and you loved her."

"That's fucked up. But that's why I didn't want to call the police after what happened tonight. I don't trust them, and after everything I told them that horrible day, they still took me to the station and questioned me. They need to be questioning Jabbar."

"I mentioned what Cassandra told me about him, but they paid me no mind. You know how the police are. They all stick together."

Ruby opened her purse, pulled out a cigarette and some aspirins. After she lit the cigarette, she shot the aspirin to the back of her throat. I looked for an ashtray and slid it over to her.

"Thanks." She blew out the smoke. "I know this is hard for you to swallow, but I wouldn't be here if I didn't believe in you. I know there's no way you would've done such a horrible thing to Cassandra."

"That means so much to me, Ruby. I just wish this bad-ass dream would go away."

Ruby and I spoke more about the police, and then she helped me to the bathroom. I sat on the tub while she dabbed my face with warm water and a towel. I pulled my shirt up and saw the bruises on my side. Ruby suggested again that I go to the emergency room, but I declined.

Since I refused to change my mind, she drove to a nearby store. When she came back, she had bandages to wrap my stomach and a sling for my left arm, which I could barely move. She pulled out a black patch for my eye, and we both laughed.

"Do you really think that's necessary?" I asked.

"Come on, now." She pulled me close to her and put the patch over my eye. "Just leave it on until it heals. I hate to see such a fine man all messed up like this."

I smiled and let Ruby put the patch over my eye. "Jabbar's friend really fucked me up, didn't he?"

"Yeah, he did quite a number on you. But that motherfucker's gonna pay."

"You got that shit right. And soon."

I thanked Ruby for everything, and before she left, I gave her a hug. She said she'd be back to check on me, and having very little support, I was glad to have hers. I missed my family a lot, but my mother had told me when they moved that if things didn't work out for me in St. Louis, not to come running my butt to her and my dad's home in Alabama. I knew she didn't mean it, but I was determined to get through this without leaning on them. I'd been so out of it lately that I hadn't even called to tell them about Cassandra's murder.

I did intend to focus on what Ruby told me about Cassandra's dangerous situation with Jabbar. Until now, it didn't even dawn on me that he could be the one responsible for her murder.

CHAPTER 4

For the next few days, I didn't do much at all. I was too embarrassed to show my scars, so I stayed in and didn't go anywhere. I thought about calling Felicity to keep me company, but I figured her and Kurt were probably still enjoying their anniversary, even days later. Yes, I was bothered, but it served me right for dipping in a relationship that I had no business being in.

I was thinking about Jabbar, so I got up and looked in the trash can to find the business card I'd thrown away. When I found it, I picked up the phone next to me and dialed his number. When a man with a husky, masculine voice answered, I asked for Jabbar. I was on hold for a while before Jabbar picked up.

"You got me," he said.

"Jabbar?"

"That's what I said, didn't I? Who is this?"

"It's Brandon. Cassandra's man."

"Yeah, I know who you are. I've been waiting for your call."

"After putting one of your animals on me, I'm sure you were waiting."

"I don't know what you're talking about. What animal?"

"Hmm, I figured amnesia would kick in. Either way, it's time that we talk."

"I agree. You tell me when, where and what time. I'll be there."

"Tonight. Meet me near the Metro link at the Convention Plaza stop around seven o'clock."

"I'll be there," Jabbar told me then hung up.

It was still early, so I dabbled around on some canvases in my art studio and cleaned up the mess I'd made of Cassandra's picture the other night.

As I took some of the trash to the Dumpster, Will was on his way up to see me. I almost dodged him because I didn't want to be bothered, but he'd already scoped me as I made my way back to my door. I held the door open so he could come in.

"Damn, man, what happened to your eye?" he asked.

"I had a fight," I said, closing the door behind him. He followed me back to my studio and took a seat on one of my stools.

"A fight? With who?"

"I didn't catch his name. Some brotha jumped me as I was leaving Felicity's crib."

"What were you doing at Felicity's crib?"

"I painted a picture of her and she wanted me to drop it off at her place."

"Aw. But did you at least win the fight? And why in the hell would somebody jump you for no reason?"

"Man, it's been some crazy stuff going on. I'll tell you more about it later, but I got this police officer on my back about some bullshit with Cassandra."

"Is he the one who fucked you up like that?"

"Nah, one of his partners did. I'm gon' handle it, though."

"Don't get ya ass in no trouble, man. It might be best that you fill me in on what's going on so I can help you figure this shit out."

"Will, I just don't want to get you involved right now. You know the police questioned me about the murder, and Ruby told me they questioned her too. They've been asking questions about me, and I'm not really sure where they're trying to go with this."

"I don't know what the hell to say. The police need to stop questioning you and go find the real motherfucker behind this shit."

"I couldn't agree with you more. Did you get a chance to talk to Antwone yet?"

"Yeah, I did. He didn't know nothing, though. He said if he found out anything, he'd fo' sho' let me know."

"That's cool. In the meantime, I'm starving. Do you wanna go grab a bite to eat somewhere? I'm supposed to go chat with Aunt Ruby about something later, so—"

"Aw, that's cool. I'm game for whatever you are—as long as you're paying."

I slapped Will on the back of his neck and we jetted.

Will and I hung out all day. I convinced him to get his hair cut, and while we were at the barbershop, I got mine trimmed as well. Even though I didn't want to get all G-ed up when I met Jabbar, I damn sure wanted to let him know that I had it going on just as much as he did. He wasn't a bad-looking brotha, and since we seemed to have a lot in common—nice physiques, chocolate-colored skin, goatees—I understood Cassandra's attraction to him. I could tell he was much older than I was, but since Cassandra was five years older than me, I guess his age wasn't a factor to her.

Once Will and I left the barbershop, I took him to one of his baby mama's houses. He invited me to go inside with him, but when he knocked on the door for Lakita to open it, she wouldn't. She yelled outside for him to get the fuck away from her door and threatened to call the police if he didn't.

He looked at me in disbelief as we stood on the broken-down porch. "See, man, this the bullshit I be talking about! I be fucking around with some crazy bitches. When I tagged that ass the other day, she was cool. Today, the bitch got a new attitude."

I didn't say one word until we got in the car.

"And I guess you haven't called her since the other day either, huh?"

"Call her for what? She knew damn well I had something to do because I told her."

"Will, you can't be referring to women as bitches and think they're going to be available for you whenever you decide to stop by."

"Man, fuck her. I was just looking for a place to lay my head since my mom's still tripping with me."

I was quiet because I knew where this conversation was going.

"Brandon! Did you hear me?"

"Yeah, I heard you."

"Then come on, bro, please. Within a month, I promise you I'll find another place to stay. Let me chill at your place for a while, a'ight?"

I hesitated for a moment. "Okay. One month, Will, and that's it. You can sleep on the couch, and if you don't clean up after yourself, your ass is out! Not only that, but your cigarettes ain't welcome, and neither is your marijuana."

"Damn, you drive a hard bargain. Now, if you wouldn't mind taking me to my mom's place so I can gather my things, I'd appreciate it."

I gave Will a hard and disgusted look.

When we got to his mother's place, her look was even more disgusted. Her tone toward him made me want to go off, but I stood closely by the doorway and waited for him to gather his belongings.

"Nigga, all you do is run in and out of here! You don't give me no damn money. Maybe you should take your ass somewhere else to live."

"Mama, shut up. I get tired of hearing it. How I'm supposed to give you some money when I don't have none?"

"Then get your lazy, trifling tail a job. Work never hurt nobody. You act like you disabled or something."

"How you gon' tell me to work and you haven't worked since the eighties? Like mother like son, right?"

While they continued to go at it, my eyes searched the tiny apartment, which was too small for the both of them and reeked of piss. After cursing at Will like she was crazy, his mom walked into the filthy living room looking like a cracked-out Diana Ross in *Lady Sings the Blues*. Her nightgown was a dingy gray, though it clearly had been white some time ago, and her dry, powdery lips showed evidence of a woman on crack. She sat on the couch and shot daggers at me with her glossy red eyes.

"Brandon, why don't you have a seat until that nigga get his shit?"

"That's okay. I'm cool, Miss Jacobs."

She tooted her lips. "What, you think you too good to be in the projects or something? I'on even know why Will still fooling with you. Since you got your li'l uppity girlfriend and model for them Polo people, you don't even come around here no mo'."

I knew the crack cocaine made her mistake me for Tyson Beckford, but I kept quiet. She took a few puffs from a cigarette and tooted her lips at me again. She yelled for Will to hurry it the fuck up, then turned to me.

"Boy, do you know where I can get some good stuff? The stuff they got around here don't do shit for me no mo'."

"No, ma'am," I said, looking straight ahead, attempting to ignore her.

"Uh-huh. That's the uppity motherfucker in you speaking. You know damn well where the good stuff is in this neighborhood. Hell, before yo' mama and daddy moved, they used to distribute to people around here, but look at ya now. Got yo' li'l modeling gig going on and things sho' nuff change, don't they?"

"I'm not a model, and what my parents did was their business. I'm just glad things worked out for me, and I'm not complaining."

When Miss Jacobs saw that she couldn't intimidate me, she got up to go rush Will out. He hurried out of his room with two huge duffle bags on his shoulder.

"You make sure you don't bring yo' lazy ass back here. Do you understand?" she yelled in his ear.

"G'on somewhere, Mama. Get your high ass away from me, please!"

She gave Will a hard shove in his back, and he dropped his bags and grabbed her throat. "Why don't you leave me the fuck alone? I don't ever wanna come back to this hell-hole again!"

A look of raging anger covered her face, so I ran down the hallway to pull him away from her. After he released her neck, she gagged and took deep breaths.

"The Bible says to honor your mother and father, nigga! Don't you ever put your hands on me like that again!" She rushed into her room to get something, but before we could see what it was, Will and I jetted.

No sooner had we got in my car than she chased after it and threw something that hit the trunk.

"Damn, dog," I said. "Your mom is out there bad!"

"I told you," Will said, laughing. "But you didn't believe me. Crack is whack, man. She all fucked up."

"She didn't used to be like that. What in the hell happened?"

"I'on know. She's been like that for as long as I can remember."

"Bullshit! When we were growing up, your mother was hooked up. She had money, good looks, everything."

"Bro, sadly, that was many, many years ago. I don't know what to say about her now, but I damn sure ain't never going back to that place again."

"I can't say that I blame you."

We laughed again, and when we got back to my place, I dropped Will off and told him I'd be back later.

It was almost 7:00 PM, so I hurried to meet Jabbar at the Metro link near Convention Plaza. When I got there, I was actually a bit early. I paced back and forth on the pavement, and my thoughts were racing. What would Jabbar reveal to me? This was a man who was sleeping with my fiancée, and the man who sent someone to attack me. I had no idea what was about to happen next.

The Metro link came to a halt and I moved out of the way as crowds of people stepped off. Finally, the crowd cleared and I spotted Jabbar. We made eye contact, and he nodded. Since he didn't get off the train, I made my way onto it. The doors closed and the Metro link took off. Jabbar took a seat on one side and I sat on the other side, directly across from him. I checked him out in his police uniform and noticed his gun by his side. He observed me casually dressed in my light tan jacket and jeans, and then looked down at my brown leather Timberlands that matched my outfit well.

"So," I said, "now that I know who you are, do you mind sharing with me how well you knew Cassandra? And while you're at it, tell me why in the hell she said she was in a dangerous situation with you."

He snickered. "Brandon, don't play games with me. I know you're responsible for what happened to Cassandra, and I'm going to make sure that you serve major time for what you did to her."

"Spare me the bullshit, Jabbar. I loved her, but I got a feeling you already know that."

He winked and smirked. "You're right. But, just maybe, you loved her too much. You loved her so much that you couldn't stand the fact she was in love with another man. She wanted it over with, Brandon, and that's why you did what you did to her. We were in love, but you just couldn't leave well enough alone. Had you just moved the fuck on, she and I could be together right now. Punks like you make me sick. Like I said before, you gon' do your time, and that's a promise I plan to keep."

"And I promise you that I intend to get to the bottom of this, and soon. Now, you can play this role with me all you want to, but we both know the truth. Cassandra was afraid of you, and before she was killed, she made that clear to someone close and dear to her."

The Metro link stopped and several people got on. I was glad because this conversation between Jabbar and me was over. I watched him as he leaned his head back on the seat and closed his eyes. As the Metro went through a tunnel, the tracks made a loud screeching noise. My body shifted around from the swift movement.

"Brandon," Jabbar whispered. "You have no idea what you took from me. You will pay with your life, and I hope like hell you don't think you're going to just walk away from this." I could see his eyes open as he stared at me on the partially dark transit. "When Cassandra told you she wanted it over with, why couldn't you just let her be, huh?"

I got angry with Jabbar for playing this game with me, and I refused to let it go any further. I hopped up, stood over him, and gritted my teeth.

"She never told me she wanted it over, motherfucker! Nor did she ever tell me she wanted to be with someone else. All she ever told me was how much she loved me, and that's all you need to know. Now, stay the fuck away from me. Do you understand?"

Jabbar stood up, and several passengers backed away from us. We stood face to face, and when the Metro link stopped, I got off and stared eye to eye with Jabbar until the transit pulled away.

Upset with our conversation, I sat on a bench and rubbed my face. I didn't know what the hell was up, but I finally got my answer. They were lovers, and it seemed as if Jabbar cared for her as much as I did. Maybe he was the one so obsessed with her, and he found out about me and wanted her dead. He definitely had the know-how to cover up a murder, and blaming me was an easy outlet. He seemed determined to put me away, and his anger showed that he wasn't going to give up.

I sat for damn near another hour racking my brain, and when it started to rain, I got soaking wet. I waited for the next Metro link to come so I could take it back to my car.

By the time the Metro came, I was drenched. I took a seat close by the entryway, and my heart raced furiously. I began to soak in my tears. An elderly black lady reached over and gave me some Kleenex, then asked if I was okay. I nodded, but was ashamed to look up.

When the Metro made another stop, I hurried to get off. I put my hands in my pockets and walked quickly to my destination.

Within moments, I was near the cemetery where Cassandra was buried. I started to jog as rain poured down on me. By the time I approached Cassandra's gravesite, my drenched clothes clung to my body. I dropped to my knees, and they started to sink. I wanted to be with her, and I desperately wanted to see her face again. I even wanted to hold her. I gathered the soggy mud in my hands and squeezed.

"Baby, why?" I sobbed. "Why'd you leave me like this? Tell

me what in the hell was going on with you! Didn't I make you happy? Didn't I?" I cried while rocking back and forth on my knees. "Please, give me some answers. I need to know." The thunder made a loud crackling sound and my entire body jumped. I knew that I wouldn't get an answer, but I begged for them. I yelled into the ground and used my fingers to rake and dig into the mud. I took deep breaths, and when I started to feel as if I'd lost my mind, that's when I snapped out of it and fell flat to the ground. I rolled over and looked up at the dark sky. I blinked several times, and as the rain heavily poured on me, I watched the lightning break dangerously through the clouds.

For a while, I lay quietly, and then lifted myself from the muddy ground. Mud covered my clothes, and I stood up to let the rain wash some of it off. I made my way back toward the Metro link to take it back to my car. When the Metro came, I got on and stood close by the entrance because a look of fear covered many of the passengers' faces. Little did they know, I wasn't a threat to anyone. I'd lost a huge part of my life, and the pain I experienced was unlike no pain I'd ever had before. All I wanted was my woman back, and if I couldn't have her, then I yearned to know why she was taken away from me.

When the Metro link stopped at Convention Plaza, I headed to my parked car. Not surprisingly, all four of my tires were flat. I didn't have to figure out who'd done it. There was no doubt that Jabbar had plans to make my life a living hell.

My cell phone was in my glove compartment, and having very little cash on me, I called Felicity to see if she'd come get me. She still hadn't paid me for the picture yet, so I was sure she'd come for me. When I called, though, she sounded as if I'd woken her.

"I'm sorry to wake you, but I kind of got myself in a jam. Will you come help me?"

"Sure, Brandon. Where are you?"

"I'll be near the parking garage on Sixth Street. Hurry, okay?"

When I heard a horn and looked up, it seemed as if I'd been out for only a few minutes. I saw Felicity in her silver Infinity. I'd fallen asleep with my head resting on the steering wheel. I got out of the car and locked my doors before heading to her car.

"Brandon, what is going on with you? Why are your clothes dirty like that?"

I dropped my head against the headrest and lowered my eyelids. "Because I'm losing it, Felicity. I'm losing my fucking mind."

"No, you're not," she said, driving off. "You're not losing your mind, and we'll talk more when we get to my place. Until then, lay back and relax."

I went back into a deep sleep until Felicity nudged my shoulder to wake me. I looked up and saw that we were parked outside of her apartment.

"Come on, Brandon. Let's go inside."

Thinking about the last beat-down I'd taken while at her place, I looked around to make sure no one was lurking in the shadows this time. I followed behind Felicity, and when we got inside, she gave me a towel so I could take a shower. No hesitation on my part, I went into the bathroom to clean myself up.

I must have stayed in the bathroom for at least an hour. It took forever for me to remove the mud that was matted in my hair and caked on my body. I finished up and wrapped a towel around my waist, then left the bathroom.

Felicity called my name, and when I went into her bedroom, she was lying naked underneath black satin sheets. Several candles lit up the room, and two bottles of wine were in an ice bucket on her nightstand. She motioned with her index finger for me to come to her.

With the pain of losing Cassandra, plus the heartache of learning that she had another lover, I was definitely in need of some of Felicity's sexual healing. I removed the towel from my waist and made my way to the end of the bed. I slowly pulled the sheets off Felicity's body so I could get a look at how sexy it was. She laid her head back on the pillow and widened her legs. I crawled on the bed and eased between her shapely legs. She wrapped her legs around me and we stared into each other's eyes. She traced my thick lips with her finger, and I slowly sucked it into my mouth; then I lowered her hand so she could feel how hard I was.

She smiled. "Before you ask, Kurt is out of town. He won't be back for two weeks, so I'm yours if you want me."

"Too bad for him," I said with a smile.

I separated her legs farther apart and made my way inside of her. Excited, she pressed her nails deeply into my butt, and the harder she squeezed, the harder I grinded. I got more aggressive with my strokes, and the feeling was so good to me.

"Da . . . damn, I'm loving this," I moaned. "You just don't know how this makes me feel."

Felicity's chest heaved in and out. "How about exactly how I feel? Keep fucking me hard, Brandon. I love the way you slam your dick into this pussy."

I slammed my dick harder, and Felicity reached for the bottle of chilled wine on the nightstand. She opened the bottle and let the wine flow down her breasts. I held them together and slurped between her breasts, while licking her hardened, tiny nipples. Loving how she squirmed around and fucked me down below, I took the wine from her hand and pulled my dick out from inside of her. I poured the remainder of the wine between her legs and sipped the wine as it flowed between her coochie lips. She took deep breaths and shouted out loudly, pounding her fist on the bed. Her legs trembled, and she rubbed my head until she calmed herself.

Felicity reached for the second bottle of wine and unscrewed the cap. She straddled my hips and turned up the bottle to her mouth. I reached for the bottle and gulped down the wine while rubbing her ass and touching her insides.

I started to feel a bit dizzy from the wine, so I lay back on the bed. Felicity leaned forward and put the bottle on the nightstand. She took my right wrist and held it tightly with her hand. When she reached for a rope, already tied to her headboard, I tried to rise up but couldn't.

"What are you doing?" I asked as she tied the rope around my wrist.

"Shhh," she whispered. "We're about to have more fun."

She reached for my left wrist and tied it to the headboard as well. I watched as she got up and went to the end of the bed to tie my ankles to it. Felicity straddled my lap again and rubbed her hands up and down my chest.

"Now," she said. "Does this seem familiar to you? Either you can pretend I'm Cassandra, or you can be glad that you're sharing a moment like this with me."

On many occasions, Cassandra and I specialized in sexual bondage. It was obvious she'd told Felicity about it. I was bothered that she'd shared our intimate moments with her cousin, as I felt as if that was a secret only she and I shared. I wondered who else she'd spoken to about what we'd done.

Just for a moment, I allowed Felicity to have her way with me. She lowered herself, sucked me deeply into her mouth and tightened her jaws. When I got tense, she removed my goods from her mouth and put her pussy to work on top of me. Her insides felt "juicilicious" and warm, and though I yearned to touch her body, I couldn't. I wanted to caress her ass in my hands, but I couldn't do that either. Bottom line, she was fucking me well, and there wasn't anything I could do but lay there and enjoy her pleasantly good torture.

After a while, I lost it. Felicity's actions were so much like Cassandra's, and I was wishing like hell that she was her. In the past, Cassandra would tie me up and joyfully ride me until I came. I'd tie her up too. She didn't believe in us making passionate love. She always required me to fuck her hard, and fuck her well.

"Damn, baby! Stop this," I yelled as I tried to pull my arms and legs from the ropes. I couldn't handle Felicity's aggressiveness, and my thoughts of Cassandra were too much. When Felicity stopped, I was angry and relieved that it was over.

Felicity leaned forward and whispered in my ear. "Tell me, was it her or me that you were thinking about?"

I hesitated to answer, because I didn't want to hurt Felicity's feelings. Truth is, my mind wouldn't allow me to think about anything but Cassandra. I was missing her like hell. I was so upset about her murder, and realized that I would never, ever have the true feeling of our sexual encounters again.

"It was you I was thinking of," I lied. "Nobody else but you."

Felicity smiled and reached for the ropes on my wrists and untied them. Then she scooted down and unloosened the ones tied to my ankles. As soon as I kicked the ropes away from my feet, I hurried to turn her on her stomach. I used my body weight to hold her down, pulled her hands apart and tied her wrists tightly to the bed, as she'd done mine. She tried to stop me, but it was only fair that she allowed me to play her game as well.

"Brandon, stop!" she yelled. "You're hurting me! The ropes are too tight."

I ignored Felicity and lowered myself to tie her ankles.

Afterward, I stood at the end of the bed and looked at her. She turned her head slightly to the side.

"Did you hear me, Brandon? I said the ropes are too tight. Would you please loosen them?"

I folded my arms and spoke in a soft tone. "Cassandra liked them tight. So, since you wanna fuck me like she did, then I'm sure you can bear the pain. From now on, if you want to have sex with me, be yourself. Trying to be someone else upsets me."

She nodded, and my pipe entered her from the back. Since I was in control, I took deep, long strokes inside of her that made her body jerk and caused her to release painful moans.

"This . . . this hurts, Brandon, but feels so, so damn good," she said, squeezing her eyes shut. "How do you make it feel this good?"

I ignored Felicity, and as we released our energy together, Felicity smothered her face in the pillow and screamed. I hurried to untie her. Exhausted, my sweaty and tired body remained on top of hers. The room was silent, but when we both heard a noise, our heads turned. I thought it was Kurt, but Felicity listened in and confirmed that it was her neighbors upstairs.

Sex between us had been off the chain, but I was afraid that Kurt would find out and seriously hurt me for sexing his woman. I couldn't help myself, though. She was filling a void that needed desperately to be filled. At this point, I didn't see our sexual escapades coming to an end any time soon.

CHAPTER 5

It was a voice that sounded like Cassandra's. *It's over, Brandon. I'm sorry, baby, but I've been seeing someone else.* I tightened my eyes and broke out in a sweat. "No!" I yelled. "I don't want this to be over!" My body jumped, and as I felt my head move from side to side, I quickly sat up. Several times, I blinked and widened my eyes to see where I was. I was still lying naked in Felicity's bedroom.

I realized I'd been dreaming. When I looked to my side for Felicity, she wasn't there. I released a deep sigh and moved to the end of the bed so I could get up. I thought about my dream, during which Cassandra had told me it was over. My meeting with Jabbar had stirred up major feelings inside of me, even though it wasn't the first time that somebody had mentioned Cassandra saying it was over between us. Ruby said the exact same thing. Was it possible that Cassandra had lied to them? Why would she do that? Maybe she wanted Jabbar to think it was over. But if she wanted to be with another man, all she had to do was tell me.

I tried to shake off the dream because up until recently,

my previous dreams were always about how happy we were together.

As I sat on the bed, I heard Felicity on the telephone in the other room. I quietly crept to the door, and when I cracked it open, I could see her on the couch with the phone pushed up to her ear. From the way she smiled, I could tell Kurt must have been on the other end.

I tried not to eavesdrop on their conversation, so I closed the door and made my way back on the bed. The room was slightly dark, and as the guilt I felt for sleeping with Felicity started to affect me again, I rubbed my temples and re-played the entire night in my mind. Felicity knew how and where to touch me. Not only that, but she'd mastered how to ride me. As for my favorite position, she knew that during a good ride, I desired to have my nipples sucked. I guess I couldn't trip because if Cassandra had ever discussed my way of loving with Felicity or Annette, I'd for damn sure shared some of our intimate moments with Will. He couldn't be-lieve the things I'd told him we'd done, but Cassandra was such a creative woman and had taught me the art of sex so well.

When Felicity came back into the room, I was still sitting on the bed, gazing at the wall. She turned on a lamp and straddled herself behind me. She wrapped her arms around my waist and laid her head against my back.

"How long have you been up?" she asked.

"I just woke up. What time is it?"

"It's almost three o'clock in the morning. Kurt called to check on me."

"He must have sensed something wasn't right, huh?"

"No. He's always checking up on me. Ever since I caught him cheating on me, he thinks I'm out for revenge."

I turned my head to the side. "So, how many times has he cheated on you?"

"Plenty of times. And before you ask, I stay because I love him."

Felicity removed her arms from around me. She scooted back on the bed and sat against the headboard. I did the same, and we sat next to each other.

"Loving him is cool. But why do you put up with a man who cheats on you? Is this something that the two of you just do to each other?"

"No, it's not like that, Brandon. I can't speak for him, but I've stepped out on him twice in this relationship. We've been together for a long time, and considering the times that he's cheated on me, I feel little shame. I stay because I know he loves me, and he takes very good care of me financially."

There was silence as I thought about Cassandra being unfaithful to me. I wanted to know her reasoning. It couldn't have had anything to do with me being unfaithful, because I wasn't. As for finances, she had money and didn't need mine or anyone else's. Jabbar's sex or money couldn't have been enough to turn her away from me, and there definitely had to be something else.

"Brandon, I will never understand what Cassandra saw in Jabbar," Felicity said as if she had read my mind. "She had everything with you. One day, she, I and Annette talked about it, but—"

"I don't know what she saw in him either. I did everything possible to make her happy, and I truly thought she was. But . . . but what is it that she said about him and me? If you know something, please tell me."

"Really, she never said much to me, but I'm sure Annette knows more. The . . . he . . . ." She paused.

"Stop beating around the bush, Felicity. What is it?"

Felicity hesitated again and touched my hand. "One of the last things she said to me was that she was in love with two men—one she said that she hated to love, but she couldn't help herself. I knew she was talking about Jabbar, but she also said . . ." She paused again.

"What, Felicity?" I yelled. "Tell me what else she said!"

Felicity let out a deep sigh. "She . . . she also said that she regretted telling you that it was over."

"But she never told me it was over! I swear to you that she never said one word to me about leaving me to be with someone else."

"Well, she told me that she did. That's why we all—some people thought you killed her."

"Do you really think I killed her?"

"No, Brandon. Honestly, I think Jabbar had something to do with it, but the question is, why? From what Cassandra told me, she wanted to be with him because he was an already established man. She felt more secure."

"Bullshit, Felicity! What did she mean by established? I . . . I was trying to do—"

"Brandon, don't get upset. I'm just telling you what she told me and Annette. No doubt, she loved you, but it seems as if she needed so much more than just good sex."

"But I gave her everything," I said, feeling hurt. "Aunt Ruby told me somewhat the opposite of what you're saying. She told me Cassandra feared Jabbar."

"Maybe she did. But she never said that around me. I'm just telling you what—"

I pulled the covers back and started out of bed. Felicity grabbed my hand.

"Brandon, don't—"

"Felicity, look. I'm sick of this shit, and I don't know where all this mess is coming from. Cassandra never said anything to me about feeling unfulfilled in our relationship. I gave her all that any man could give to a relationship and she knew it. I didn't have much money, but that didn't stop me from showing her respect, being faithful to her, and loving

her like she deserved to be loved. Tell me what was so fucking wrong with that!"

"Nothing at all. But there was a part of her that felt like
she had to take care of you. You never made nearly as much
money as she did, and when you started going from one job
to the next, I think she got frustrated."

"Frustrated! She was the one who encouraged me to start
my own damn business. I quit those jobs because she liked
my artwork and bragged about it to other people. Until I got
on my feet, she knew times would be tough for me. Damn it,
she knew it! So why in the hell she would talk behind my
back like that puzzles the hell out of me!"

"Brandon, you don't have to explain yourself. I know how
much you loved her, but sometimes that's just not enough."

"Well, then, I guess it wasn't," I said, walking toward the
door. "Do you mind if I wash my clothes so I can go?"

"I already washed them for you. I put them on top of the
dryer in the kitchen. If I hurt your feelings, I'm sorry. You
don't have to leave so soon, and I'd rather you wait until late
morning to go."

"I'm ready to go now. I need my money for the picture
and then I'll call a taxi to drive me back to my car."

With a disappointed look on her face, Felicity walked with
me into the kitchen. She gave me some of my money in cash,
and the rest she wrote out to me in a check. I frowned, and
the wrinkled lines on my forehead were visible. When the
taxi came, I didn't even say good-bye. I slammed the door
and left.

CHAPTER 6

By the time I'd gotten my car taken care of, it was almost noon. I went back to my place and was more upset when I got there. Will had the whole place lit up with his funky socks and was crashed out on the living room couch with his mouth wide open. Evidently, he'd fried some chicken because the bones were beside a plate on the table. From a distance, I gazed and the messy kitchen, and noticed cigarette butts and blunts in an ashtray. I was pissed about my conversation with Felicity, but I didn't want to take my anger out on Will; however, when I noticed a burn hole on my couch, I shook his shoulder to wake him.

He opened his eyes and wiped the saliva from the corner of his mouth. "Damn, man, what you doing? I was sleeping good and dreaming about Beyoncé. I ain't slept that good in ages."

"Why have you been smoking in here? And why do you have your leftover food on my table?"

"Brandon, please. You starting to sound like my moms." He stood up, scratched his head, and then picked up the plate from the table. "I only had a few cigarettes, man. Don't you understand that my nerves are bad?"

"No, I don't," I said, following him toward the kitchen. I looked around and almost lost it. Grease was everywhere on the stove. The thawed chicken that he hadn't cooked was still on the counter, and wasted Kool-Aid was dried on the island. "Will, I can already tell this ain't gonna work out. I told you that I didn't want—"

"I know what you said, and I planned to clean up today. I got tired, man. I stayed up waiting for you, and when you didn't show, I fell asleep."

"Whatever. I want my place cleaned, now! And please do something with those funky socks."

"Negro, those are your funky socks that you're smelling. I just washed mine the other day." After he dumped his plate in the trash, he put it in the sink. We both walked toward the living room and I pointed to the couch.

"What's up with that hole in my couch, Will?"

"I . . . I don't know. I didn't do it."

"Well, who else did it?"

He shrugged. "I'on know, but it wasn't me."

"Look, I'm not your mama, okay? It ain't like I'm gonna turn you over on my knee and spank your ass. Just 'fess up and stop lying. If you did it, take responsibility for it."

Will looked at the hole and touched it with his finger. "It's tiny."

"I don't care how tiny it is. I have a no smoking policy in my place, and if you want to smoke, take yourself, your blunts and your cigarettes outside."

"Deal. And . . . and I'm sorry about your couch." He picked up his socks from the floor and sniffed them. "I'm sorry about these funky motherfuckers too. By day's end, your shit will be back to normal."

"Thank you. And if we ever have this problem again,

you're out of here." I headed off to my bedroom. Before I reached the door, I turned around and asked, "Did anybody call?"

"Yeah, a few people did."

"Who?"

"I'on know. I didn't ask."

"If you're not going to ask, then don't answer the phone."

"Cool. But I think one of the callers was Ruby. She asked where you were and I told her I didn't know. Anyway, where were you all night?"

"Out. I had car trouble so I stayed out until somebody came to help me fix it."

"Damn, it took all night? You should have called me. I would have come to help."

"On your bike, huh?"

"Nigga, I'm gon' get me a car. You can bet your last dollar that I will."

I turned away and walked into my room. Since I didn't get much sleep at Felicity's place, I lay back on the bed to rest my eyes. I couldn't sleep, so I reached over to the phone and started to dial Ruby's phone number. She was the closest person to Cassandra, and I needed to know so much more than she told me the other day. I wanted closure with this, and I knew Ruby was the only person I could trust not to lie to me.

Just as her phone rang, I heard Will call for me. I hung up and headed for the living room. Two detectives stood by the door.

"Can I help you?" I said, moving closer to them.

"Brandon Fletcher?"

"Yes."

"We were wondering if you'd come down to the station with us to answer a few questions."

"Questions about what?" I asked. I was pissed about being questioned again, but I had a feeling that Jabbar had sent them over. All I could do was tell them the truth, and since I knew I had been very honest about what had happened, I wasn't fearful.

The officers looked at each other. "We want to question you again about the murder of Cassandra White."

"I already answered plenty of questions before."

"Well, now we have some more for you."

I cut my eyes and walked off to my room to get my jacket. This shit was so unnecessary, but hopefully they'd get off my back and go find the real killer. Will asked if I wanted him to go with me, but I insisted he stay and clean up my place like he said he would.

No sooner had I gotten to the station than Detective Banks was all over me. He insisted that all of the evidence pointed to me.

"Well, if it does, sir, then arrest me. You know darn well you ain't got nothing on me. I'm innocent, and it's time you all focus on the real killer."

Banks slammed his hand on the table in front of me. "Why focus on somebody else, motherfucker, when we got you?"

"I'm sorry, motherfucker, but I'm not your man!"

He balled up his fist and punched me hard on my face. I jumped up, and when I darted toward him, the other detective grabbed my arms and put them behind me. He put handcuffs on me and slammed me down on a chair.

"Sit your punk ass down, fool!" he said. He looked at Detective Banks. "Boss, why don't you finish your business with this animal and turn him loose? We'll get'im. I promise you that something will show up soon." He glared at me and left the room.

Detective Banks pulled up a chair and placed his foot on it. He was a tall, dark man with beady eyes and a very intimidating look. When he stared at me with his yellowish eyes, my mind flashed back to the day I was beat down after leaving Felicity's crib. If I had to put some money on it, I'd bet that he was the one who jumped me.

"Mr. Fletcher," he said calmly, "for the record, I want you to walk me through the day you found Cassandra's body. When you're finished, you can go. Before you go, though, I want you to take a look at these and think hard about that day." He opened an envelope and pulled out some pictures. He slammed them on the table in front of me and spread them out. They were pictures of Cassandra's bruised and lifeless body, showing the slash on her throat. Unable to look at them, I gasped and took a hard swallow. I looked away and tightly closed my eyes. The day I found her was still fresh in my memory.

"Please put them away," I said, feeling as if the words could barely get past the lump in my throat. A tear rolled down my face. "If you put them away, I will tell you, for the last time, exactly what happened."

He put the pictures back inside the envelope and straddled the chair next to me then pulled out a cigarette and lit it. When he offered me one, I shook my head. He blew the smoke in my face and smiled. I looked at the gaps in his teeth and coughed from the smoke.

"Would you mind taking these cuffs off me?"

"I'll take them off once you get finished with your lies. The longer you wait, the longer we gon' be here."

I knew his statement was true, so I started with the story I had told them before. "Cassandra and me had plans that day. We were supposed to have lunch and go pay for the dress she'd picked out for our wedding. When I called to tell her I was on my way to get her, she didn't answer. I figured she must have gone to the cleaners because when we spoke earlier, she said that she wanted to have some things cleaned. When I got to her place, though, her car was there. I . . . I stopped to get roses, and when I went to the door, I put them behind my back. I noticed that the door was already opened, so I pushed on it. That's when I saw her . . . her lying in a puddle of blood." I paused for a moment. "It was horrible. I didn't even recognize her until I pulled her up to my chest. I panicked and tried to get her to breathe. She . . . she was gone, but I didn't want to accept it.

"I laid her body down and rushed over to the phone to call the police. Before they got there, somehow, I . . . I blacked out. Seeing her that way just did something to me, and I was losing it. When the officers got there and asked me what happened, I told them the exact thing I just told you."

Detective Banks clapped his hands. "That was a remarkable story. But you know what, Brandon? It doesn't sound too convincing."

"Well, I don't know what else you want me to say. I already told you everything."

"So you stayed with her until the cops came, right?"

"Yes, I did. I held her in my arms and I blacked out."

"Yeah, yeah, yeah, but if that's the case, then how did the flowers get into her bedroom? You did bring the roses to her house, didn't you?"

"Yes."

"Then how in the hell did they get on her bed? While thinking of a lie about that, why don't you tell me how the blood on the bottom of your shoes was tracked throughout the entire place if you supposedly stayed and held her in your arms?"

"Man, I don't know. I was so out of it that maybe I did go into another room. I must have gone into her room to use the phone and then laid the roses on the bed."

"But you used the phone in the kitchen that is adjacent to the living room, where you found her body, didn't you?"

"Yes, but I remember walking around to make sure nobody was there."

"Negro, you just told me you walked in, saw the body, called the police, went back over to her and blacked out!

Don't play games with me! You walked in, cut her the fuck up because you'd lost her to another man, and then walked around the house to find any evidence that you'd left. Those damn flowers you bought were to kiss ass. She didn't want you anymore, and you got angry, didn't you?" His spit sprayed in my face as he yelled at me.

"No, I was not angry," I said. "We had our day already planned—"

"You damn right you had the day already planned! It is quite odd that this wedding you're talking about, nobody knew about it. Her mama didn't know, her daddy didn't know . . . nobody knew, Brandon!"

"That's because we wanted to keep it a secret. Cassandra said she wanted to wait before telling—"

"Cassandra was in love with another man, Brandon! When are you going to get that through your thick fucking head?" He chuckled, and when the door opened, he turned his head. I wasn't surprised to see Jabbar walk in. He stared me down and then looked at Detective Banks.

Detective Banks stood up and cut his eyes at me. He patted Jabbar on the back and left the room. Jabbar stood close by the door and folded his arms. He displayed his waves when he removed his Inspector Gadget hat and held it in his hands.

"Brandon, I'm sorry to tell you this, but it's not going to get any easier for you. Let's end this today, all right?"

"If you all don't have any evidence against me, then I'd like to get the hell out of here. I'm not afraid of you, Jabbar, and if you think that you're going to put this bullshit off on me, you're crazy. Cassandra was afraid of you, not me. She made that publicly known to a lot of people, and before you go trying to convict me, I suggest you work on trying to clear your own damn name. If I'm not being released right now, I'd like to make a phone call to my attorney."

He rubbed his goatee and snickered. "Fool, you couldn't even pay your own bills. Your woman had to do that for you. Now, how in the hell can you afford an attorney? A public defender is more like it. And you'll soon need one."

"Whatever. And like I said, if you're finished with me, I'd like to go home."

Jabbar called the detective who had previously cuffed me back into the room. After he took off the handcuffs, he nudged me toward the door. Jabbar bumped my shoulder, and we gave each other a long, hard stare before I left.

When I got to my car, the front window had been smashed. This shit was getting ridiculous. I felt as if I was fighting a battle with the police that couldn't be won. I knew they were up to no good, but what was I going to do about it? If I went back inside to complain, they'd all just laugh at me.

At this point, I started to feel hatred for Cassandra for being involved with such an asshole. I seriously thought shit was tight between us, yet she had told Jabbar how broke I was. The only way he could have known that she'd paid my bills was if she'd told him. "Damn her," I yelled and punched my window on the driver's side of the car. I let off more steam and punched it repeatedly. I didn't stop until it cracked, and when I saw blood dripping from my knuckles, I opened the car door and got inside.

I sat for a while with my head down, and then started my car. The pain from the cuts on my hand hurt badly, so I pulled over to the curb and got out. I searched the trunk for a towel, and when I found one, I wrapped it tightly around my hand.

As I drove down Grand Avenue, I turned to make a stop at Ruby's house, which was nearby on Compton Avenue. When I pulled up, I saw Cassandra's mother's car parked out front. I really didn't want to go inside because I knew she was still bitter about what had happened and would want some answers. I was tired of trying to explain myself. Besides, they should have known better than to feel as they did, especially after how well I treated Cassandra.

Instead of going inside, I reached for my cell phone and dialed Ruby's number. She answered in laughter.

"Hey, Ruby, it's me," I said.

"Brandon?"

"Yes."

"Boy, I've been trying to get in touch with you. Where have you been?"

"I've had a lot going on, Ruby. I'm parked outside of your house, but I see Vivica's visiting with you."

"Hold on," Ruby said. I could tell she moved into another room. "Listen, Vivica is leaving in a few minutes. Give us about ten minutes and then come back."

"Is she still upset with me? I mean, the other day she called to apologize, but—"

"She's okay, Brandon. I think she still has questions, like we all do."

"I understand. I'll wait until she leaves, and then I'll come back."

"Ten minutes," she said again, and then hung up.

I drove to White Castle on Kingshighway to get something to eat. While I sat in my car eating, a police officer parked next to me. I figured he was going to question me about the cracked windows, but he didn't. At this point, I had so many bills to pay with the money that Felicity had given me for the picture. My car insurance had just expired, so the windows would have to be put on the back burner.

By the time I made my way back to Ruby's house, Vivica was driving off. I waited until she drove down the street, and then went to the door and knocked. Ruby opened the door and reached out to give me a hug.

"I can see the stress written all over your face, Brandon."

"No doubt," I said, and then removed myself from her embrace. "Do you mind if I use your bathroom? I have a nasty cut on my hand that I want to wash off. I would've taken care of it while I was at White Castle, but the cops came. They've been tripping with me, and—"

"No explanation needed, Brandon." Ruby looked at my hand. "How'd you manage to do that anyway?"

"I'll tell you what happened once I take care of it."

I went to the bathroom and closed the door. The bathroom reeked of a foul odor, and Ruby had her lace bra and girdle hanging over the shower rail. The bathroom itself was filthy. The old fashioned white tub was lined with dirt, and the toilet had stains for days. You'd never think Ruby lived like she did because of the way she carried herself. She wore name brand clothes and wouldn't be caught seen without a designer purse clutched to her side. Her weaved-in braids were always in tact, and she kept her nails neatly manicured. But it wasn't my business how she lived. And besides, I'd always felt comfortable around her. Cassandra spoke well of her, and knowing how much she loved and trusted Ruby, over the years I'd grown to do the same.

I washed the dried blood from my hands, and as I dried them, I looked in the mirror. Ruby was right; stress was written all over my face. I had small bags underneath my eyes and they had a tint of red to them. Since my head was banging, I opened the medicine cabinet to look for some aspirin. It was like searching for a needle in a haystack because Ruby had multiple bottles of medication in the cabinet. Cassandra said that she'd had some serious issues after her husband was killed in the war, but damn! I realized that if I didn't get myself together, I would probably wind up in the same condition.

I reached for the bottle of Tylenol and opened the container. There was only one left, so I popped it into my mouth. I put the empty container back into the cabinet and closed it. I took one last look in the mirror and then reached for the light to turn it off. Suddenly, I felt queasy. The bathroom felt too hot, and my palms started to sweat. I turned the light back on, and a vision of Cassandra's face was directly in front of me. My heart raced and I backed into the door. My eyelids were getting heavy, and I felt as if I was getting ready to black out again. It had only happened once before, and that was the day I'd found Cassandra's body. I took deep breaths while looking at her, and then tightly closed my eyes. When I opened them, she was gone. My heart was still racing fast, and the bathroom felt like it was on fire.

When I came to, I saw a blurred vision of Ruby fanning me with a church fan. She called my name, but it was hard for me to respond. My eyes shifted, and I realized that I was still on the floor in the bathroom. Ruby helped me off the floor and walked me over to the couch in the living room. She held a glass of water in her hand and spoke in a panicky voice.

"Brandon, baby, drink some water. Relax and drink some water."

I took a few sips then sat up. "What happened?" I asked.

She sat next to me. "I don't know, baby. You tell me."

"The . . . the last thing I remember is seeing Cassandra in your bathroom. Before that, I'd taken a Tylenol for my headache."

Ruby took her hand and placed it over mine. "Brandon, those weren't Tylenol that you took. Boy, don't you know better than to mess around in my medicine cabinet?"

"Then what was it, Ruby? I thought they were Tylenol."

"You thought wrong. The pill you took, well, it was a pill I take to help me sleep better. It doesn't make you hallucinate, though, so I don't know about you claiming to have seen Cassandra."

"Well, I did. She was right in front of me. I swear."

"Brandon, I think it's time that you saw a doctor. I'm really worried about you. I heard a loud thud, and when I went into the bathroom, you were laid out on the floor. I know losing Cassandra was hard on you, but you're letting her death consume your mind. Now, we're all upset about what happened, and the only thing we can do is let the police do their job."

"But they're after me, Ruby. They've been hounding and sweating me like I'm their only suspect. I don't know what to do!" I yelled.

"Before you do anything, you've got to see about yourself. You're a handsome man, and I've never seen you look so worn and tired."

"I'm trying," I said, knowing that what Ruby said was right.

I stood and rubbed my hands together. I thought about my ordeal at the police station as I looked at her. "Aunt Ruby, you said that Cassandra told you she feared Jabbar, right?"

"Yes."

"Are you sure you told that to the police?"

"Yes, I did. But when they asked Jabbar about it, he denied it and told them she had no reason to fear him. He talked about how much love they had for each other, and another officer vouched for Jabbar and told me I was a liar."

"Ruby, you gotta help me get to the bottom of this. Is there anything else Cassandra told you that can help me clear my name?"

"Brandon, I'm sorry. Cassandra was a very private woman and you know that. When I'd ask about you, she told me everything was okay. Up until a few days before her death, that's when her story changed. She did say she was forced to end it with you because she was afraid of what Jabbar would do."

"This shit is crazy," I said, sitting back on the couch next to

Aunt Ruby. "Just please believe that I'm innocent. I don't care about anybody else believing in me, but you've got to. Okay?"

Ruby placed her hand on the side of my face. "Brandon, I know there ain't no way you would've hurt Cassandra like that. But you've got to let this go before you make yourself sick. If you don't, you'll be an easy target for the police, and we definitely don't want that to happen."

Ruby stood and pulled me up with her. She gave me a tight hug, and I wrapped my arms around her waist.

"Thank you so much," I said.

"You're welcome. Now, either you can stay here for the night and relax, or you can take your butt home. Bingo is tonight, and after that, I'm gonna go get my swerve on at May's Lounge around the corner."

"You know you be partying, don't you? For a woman in her fifties, you don't look a day over twenty-one."

She laughed and so did I. It really wasn't meant to be a joke because Ruby did look good for her age. I just hoped that if she met somebody tonight, she didn't have the guts to bring him back to this jacked-up place she called a home.

Either way, I left Ruby's house feeling a bit better. My headache had chilled, and I knew it was time for me to take it easy. It felt like I was on the verge of going crazy, and there was only one thing that could save me now. I had to find out who killed Cassandra before it pushed me over the edge.

I was relieved to get home, until I heard the loud music. When I walked inside, Will was working the vacuum cleaner on the area rug that covered the hardwood floors, while rapping 50 Cent's lyrics out loud. He didn't even hear me come in, so I walked over to the outlet and unplugged the vacuum cleaner.

He was startled, but smiled when he saw me. "So, how'd it go at the station?" he asked.

"The usual questions, questions, and more questions. They ain't got nothing on me, man, 'cause there ain't nothing to get."

"I feel for you, Brandon. But I told you to let me in on what's been happening so I can help a brotha out."

"Will, there ain't much I can do, and it's time that I took Ruby's advice. She told me to move on, and that's what I'm gonna do."

"Well, good for you. 'Cause I'm sho' sick and tired of seeing you down in the dumps. Whatever Ruby said, I must thank her."

We slammed hands together and Will bragged about how well he'd cleaned up the place. Before giving him props, I inspected the place, and I had to give Will some credit. It was rather clean.

"See, I told you that you didn't have nothing to worry about. And to show you a li'l appreciation, I'm gonna cook us dinner tonight."

"Negro, please. You know how to fry chicken—so what? I'm sure your cooking skills don't go beyond that."

"Are you crazy? Man, I'm the king of the kitchen. Since moms never cooked, I had to learn how to do it my damn self. Tonight, though, I'm gonna put together some pork chops smothered with onions and gravy, some mashed potatoes, and some homemade buttermilk biscuits."

"And how are you supposed to put this together and the only damn thing in my fridge is some hotdogs and bologna?"

"I was hoping that you had about twenty or thirty dollars I could borrow. I'll hook up dinner for us and use the rest for bus fare so I can go look for a job tomorrow."

"Yeah, I knew it was something," I said, reaching into my back pocket. I gave Will thirty dollars and told him to make it stretch.

He snatched the thirty bucks from my hand. "Thanks. Now all I need is the keys to your car."

I cut my eyes and tossed my keys to him. "Make sure you hurry up and get a car. Since you moved in with me, mine ain't gon' be used as no taxi cab."

"Never," he said with a grin and left.

Having a little quiet time to myself, I stripped naked and ran some bath water. I sank my body deeply into the tub and leaned back. I closed my eyes, as the thoughts of making love to Cassandra roamed around in my mind. The last time we made love was at her place. Her Jacuzzi tub was big enough for both of us, and we had the water near boiling hot. The bathroom was filled with steam, and I could barely see her. But I could definitely feel her. She worked her pussy on me and worked it well. Since she liked it rough, I spanked her ass hard and stuck my fingers into her backside. She said my touch was painful, but asked me to go deeper. We both enjoyed the everlasting hours of wild and crazy sex.

The phone interrupted my thoughts, but I wasn't about to get out of the tub to get it. I washed up and chilled in the soothing water for a while longer.

Nearly thirty minutes later, I dried off and wrapped the towel around my waist. I went into my bedroom, and when I checked the caller ID, I saw that the call was from Felicity. Feeling bad about leaving her the way I did and about how we were using each other for sex, I called her back.

"Hey, Felicity. It's me, Brandon."

"Hi. I thought you were trying to avoid me. I called your place several times to check on you."

"No, I'm not trying to avoid you. I got some heavy things on my mind, that's all."

"I wanted to apologize for what I said to you earlier. It wasn't right for me to share those things with you, and that's why I didn't want to. I figured you would get mad at me, but—"

"I'm not mad at you. I'm mad at myself for being so stupid."

"Brandon, don't be so hard on yourself. When you're in love, sometimes it's hard for you to see the truth."

"True. I appreciate everything you've done for me lately, but . . . but I don't think it's a good idea if you and I keep using each other for sex."

Felicity was quiet for a while. Finally, she spoke. "We're not using each other, Brandon. I've enjoyed our time together. I thought you did as well."

"I do. Well, I . . . I did. It's just that I can't stop thinking about Cassandra when I'm with you; especially the way you—"

"I know what you're going to say. Cassandra told Annette a lot of y'all's business, and she told me. I was just trying to make you feel at home, that's all."

"That's cool, but it's not working out for me. I've found myself thinking more and more about Cassandra, and I'm trying to get over my hurt."

"Brandon, I can't make you continue this if you don't want to. So, it was good while it lasted, and I guess this is good-bye."

"I guess so," I said.

Felicity didn't say another word before she hung up. I held the phone in my hand, feeling disappointed that our time together had come to an abrupt end. But I knew it was necessary. I couldn't go on being with her but thinking about Cassandra. I don't know what she was feeling, but I felt she was using me to get back at Kurt. I guess it really didn't matter anymore because we'd both agreed to end it.

I slid on my white Calvin Klein briefs and went into my studio to dabble a little. It was the only thing that kept my mind off my troubles, and I hoped that tomorrow would bring me nothing but peace.

CHAPTER 7

I was more than full from Will's gourmet cooking last night and was too lazy to get up in the morning to do anything. It wasn't like I had much to do but sit around and paint my life away anyway. I definitely had to find a job because all I had was the three grand Felicity gave me, minus the minor splurging I'd done. Before she'd given me that, I only had twenty-five dollars in the bank. Cassandra had said she'd help me with this month's rent, but so much for that. If anything, in order to stay on top of the rent, I knew I had to give Mr. Armanos this month's plus next month's rent. My utilities would take up the rest of the money Felicity had given me, and I knew that relying on Will to help me was a big mistake. He hadn't offered me a dime, and barely mentioned finding a job. I was damn mad about it too, but there was no need for me to sit around and do nothing.

Today was a new day for me, and since it was Monday, I woke Will and asked if he wanted to go job searching with me. Last night, I scoped the *St. Louis Post Dispatch* and applied for two jobs online. The art museum required me to apply in person, so I got dressed up in a suit that Cassandra had bought me and was ready to go. I thought Will would be ready too, but when I walked into the kitchen, he was slumped over in the chair, holding his stomach.

"Fool, what's wrong with you?" I said, placing my briefcase on the counter.

"I'm sick, man. My stomach is tore the fuck up."

I tooted my lips. "I knew you were going to come up with an excuse."

"Nigga, it ain't no excuse! I've been in and out of the bathroom all night long."

"Well, grab yo' ass some Pepto Bismol and let's go."

"I'll go next time. I don't feel up to it today. Besides, with two brothas riding around in an Acura with smashed windows, we for damn sure will get stopped by the police."

"Yeah, I guess you got a point. In the meantime, will you call Antwone for me and see if he knows someone who can hook up my windows for me at a discount?"

"Now, that I can do. Just make sure you don't let nobody bust them again. It's a shame what those cops did, and when I say it's time to shake, rattle and roll on them fools, I mean it."

Will held his stomach and hauled ass back to the bathroom.

Since I didn't have much experience, I searched for positions that pertained to what I knew best—art. The art museum was hiring tour guides, so I went there first. The position only paid $9.50 an hour, but I couldn't complain. It was better than nothing, and I was sure I'd meet many customers who were interested in purchasing paintings from me.

When I arrived, I found out that they were giving interviews on the spot. I was given an application to fill out, and I sat down to complete it. I waited patiently for the interviewer to call my name, and it was at least another fifteen minutes before a thick white lady with round glasses came out and shook my hand.

"Hi, I'm Jennifer. Jennifer Carlson."

I reached for her hand and shook it. "Brandon Fletcher," I said. "Nice to meet you."

"Well, come on and follow me," she said with an upbeat attitude. She was perky as perky can get, and I could tell by the way she looked at me, she already liked me.

Once we were in her office, she closed the door and asked me to have a seat. Her office was pretty nice, with antique furniture and expensive drawings and paintings covering the walls. I sat in a tall wooden chair with a velvet cushion. It was extremely comfortable and put me at ease.

"So, Mr. Fletcher . . ."

"Brandon," I said. "Feel free to call me Brandon."

"Okay then, Brandon it is. By looking at your application, I can see that you haven't worked for quite some time. Is there any reason why?"

"Yes, Ms. Carlson, actually there is. I've been working from home. I'm fascinated with art, and the jobs that I had prior to my decision to work from home were not pertaining to it. I've been doing well on my own, but now, I'm looking for a way to express my talents even more. I want to meet more people in this business, and hopefully learn some more things about the creativity of art that I don't already know. Working for the museum could be a good start for me, and something tells me that you might be a good teacher."

Jennifer smiled. I could tell I was already working her over. She asked more about my experience with art, and wanted to know if I knew more about the history of it. I did, and when she gave me a brief quiz, I answered the questions correctly. My responses were thorough, and she couldn't do anything but smile after each response.

Nearly an hour later, she wrapped up the interview. She offered me the position, and of course, I accepted. Before I left, she gave me a tour of the facility. She stopped and introduced me to another tour guide, who was touring a group of elderly people.

"Evelyn, this is Brandon Fletcher. He's going to be one of our new tour guides."

"Oh, really," Evelyn said, checking me out in my black suit. "It's nice to meet you. I'm sure Jennifer will assign me to show you the ropes, so I look forward to seeing you."

"Likewise," I said, holding my hand out to shake hers. She was awfully gorgeous for a woman with a hair cut as short as mine. Her tall, slim body fit well in the navy blue pants suit that Jennifer had already told me was the required uniform.

Evelyn said good-bye and continued on with her tour. I tried to focus on the rest of my tour with Jennifer, but Evelyn's curvaceous hips and sexy voice had me in awe.

After Jennifer finished with our tour, we headed back to her office. She gave me some paperwork to complete and told me to bring it back to her as soon as possible. Of course, she wanted me to have a drug test completed, and then stated that she'd have to run a police check on me as well. I was worried about that because I wasn't sure if Jabbar had fabricated something on my record. I had never been arrested for anything, and as far as I was concerned, my record was all good. I promised Jennifer I'd get the paperwork back to her soon.

On the way to my car, I looked at the windshield and saw that the police had given me a ticket. I'd been running my mouth so long with Jennifer, I forgot to go outside and put some change in the parking meter. I snatched the ticket off my windshield and stuck my key in the door to unlock it.

"That happens all the time," I heard a voice say. I turned and saw Evelyn. With her arms folded in front of her, she stepped up to me.

"Yeah, well, that was my fault. I was so excited about getting the job that I forgot to come back and check the meter."

"St. Louis isn't the place to forget about the parking meter. Once your time is up, the police will surely get you."

We both agreed and laughed.

"So, tell me, Evelyn, do you like working for the museum?"

"It's okay. It pays the bills, so I can't complain. How about you? If you don't mind me saying, you look as if this might be a step down for you. What brings a man who could easily be a model, drives a nice car, and wears an expensive suit like the one you have on, to a place like this?"

"Woman, don't you know it's hard out here for a black man?" I chuckled. "We have to take what we can get until we can do better, right?"

"I guess." She smiled. "And nobody knows your situation better than you."

I nodded and Evelyn waved good-bye. She gave her hips an extra swish from side to side, which had my attention. Before she went inside, she turned and said she'd see me next week.

Finally, I felt as if things were looking up. Since Cassandra's death, I'd been catching hell, and getting a job was just a start. I couldn't wait to get back to my place and throw my new job up in Will's face. Maybe my finding a job would encourage him to do the same.

However, when I got back to my place, I found my thoughts to be short-lived. Will was in his usual place—on the couch, watching TV, with food in front of him. He had the nerve to be watching *As The World Turns* and was all into it.

"So, how did the job search go?" he asked, munching on some Doritos.

"Quite well. I got a job, and if you had gone with me, maybe you'd have one too."

"Fool, ain't nobody trying to give me a job. You and me on two different levels. I mean, look at how you're dressed. You clean up well, my brotha. If I put on a suit and tried to look like that, anybody would see straight through me."

"There you go with another one of your excuses. I really don't care what you do, but whatever it is, you got one month to do it here. After that, bro, you got to go."

"I'm gon' get up tomorrow; I promise. I ain't wearing no suit, but I'm gon' go fill out some applications tomorrow."

"Yeah, whatever. In the meantime, did you get a chance to call your boy Antwone?"

"Uh-huh," he said, gazing at the TV.

"Well, what did he say?"

"Shhh . . . cool out. Once my soap go off, I'll tell you. It'll be off in about five minutes."

I shook my head and walked off to my bedroom. A few minutes later, Will came in and told me that Antwone said to bring my car by later on today.

"Then let me change clothes so we can go," I said.

"Naw, fool. He told *me* to bring it by later. Not you."

"And why not me?"

"Because he know you, but he don't know you like he knows me. I've known him a lot longer than you, and he trusts me. He said for a hundred bucks he'll fix both windows for you."

"Man, don't play no games with me."

"Okay, fine. To hell with your windows, chump. I'm trying to do you a favor."

I thought about it, but I really didn't have any other choice. "Take the car, Will. And if you don't come back with my shit fixed, I'm gonna hurt you."

"Ooooh, I'm shaking like a leaf. Just give me the damn keys."

I tossed the keys to Will, gave him a hundred dollars, and he left. I pretty much trusted him, but I didn't really know Antwone that much to trust him. If anything, I hoped he didn't play me, because I sure didn't have a hundred dollars to lose.

I felt good about my new job, and it was just what I needed to help with my rocky financial situation. It gave me a chance to be around what I loved so much, art, and I planned to seek out as many people as I could about paintings.

I changed into my gray boxer shorts and sat at the kitchen table to complete the W2 forms that Jennifer had given me. Will had turned down the heat, so I walked over to the thermostat and turned it up. My feet were cold, so I grabbed a pair of white socks from my drawer and put them on.

As I headed back to the kitchen, there was a light knock at the door. I tiptoed to the door, fearing that it was Mr. Armanos asking for the rent. I had enough to pay him, but most of the money Felicity had given me was still in the bank. When I looked out the peephole, I saw Felicity. She looked as if she'd been crying, so I rushed to open the door.

"Hey," I said, moving aside so she could come in.

"Hi," she replied, looking down at the floor. She walked over to the couch and took a seat. I sat next to her and rubbed my hands together.

"Are you all right?" I asked.

At first, she didn't say anything. Then she started to cry and covered her face with her hands.

"Felicity, what's up?" I said. I placed my arm around her shoulders.

"Kurt and I had an argument about his baby's mama. We argue about her a lot, and I'm sick of it. She calls me looking for him, and I don't think it's appropriate for her to call my apartment. Her attitude is horrible, and I don't care if she's calling about his son or not. She has his cell phone and home phone if she wants to reach him."

"Do you think he's still seeing her?"

"I don't know. He says he's not, but it's hard to believe a man who I don't trust."

"Nothing should surprise you when it comes to Kurt, Felicity, but you've cheated on him too. What's the big fucking deal?"

"Maybe I'm just getting tired of the whole thing. Our relationship is by no means perfect, and it's not going to get any better if he continues to take up for his baby's mama."

I gave Felicity a shoulder to cry on, but a part of me had no sympathy for her. She was confused, and I wondered if it was how Cassandra might have been, trying to juggle two men.

Once Felicity calmed down, she walked back to my studio with me.

"Were you painting before I stopped by?" she said, looking at the picture I'd started to paint the other day.

"No. Actually, I was filling out some papers for a job I got today."

"So, you decided to go back to work, huh?"

"Yeah, it was long overdue. Since Cassandra's been gone, if I haven't learned anything, I now know how stupid I was for depending on somebody else's income."

"I'm proud of you, Brandon. I admire you in so many ways, and I can't express how lucky Cassandra was to have you."

"I'm starting to feel like she didn't feel that way. The more people I talk to, the more and more shit is coming to the light. I feel like such a fool, Felicity. You just don't know."

"There's no reason for you to feel like a fool. If anything, you wasn't the fool, she was."

"You got that right," I said.

I looked at the picture in front of me and picked up the paint and brush from the floor. I started painting, and Felicity sat quietly next to me and watched. As she saw me getting into it, she headed for the lights and dimmed them. I knew what she wanted to do, but I didn't want to.

"Let's not go there again, all right? We agreed that this was over, and I'd like to just remain friends."

"But I need you, Brandon. Just like you needed me. I'm going through something too, and I need you."

I grabbed her hands, which were already massaging my chest. "I don't want to keep doing this, Felicity. Don't my thoughts of Cassandra bother you? Give me time, okay?"

"How much time do you need?" she asked while lowering her hand. She pulled my dick out from inside of my boxers and rubbed it. It was stiff, and when she noticed the attention it gave her, she straddled my lap and looked into my eyes.

"I like the way you fuck me," she said. "Take me to your room and do what you wish."

Something clicked in my head, as her voice surely sounded like Cassandra's. She'd always ask me to do what I wished; I was sure that Felicity knew that and knew it well.

Either way, I moved her off my lap.

"No!" I yelled. "What is it that you don't understand about the word *no?*"

"I understand the word, but not when you don't mean it. You really don't mean what you say, do you?"

I moved away from Felicity and started to work on my picture again. She ignored my actions and began to remove her clothes. She was down to her white silk bra and panties, along with her black pointed-toe stilettos. She took the paint and brush from my hands and placed them on the floor. It took everything I had to look away, but I did. She grabbed my face. When she leaned forward and placed her lips on mine, I snatched my face from her grip.

"What did I say, Felicity? Why aren't you listening to me?"

She gritted her teeth. "Because you don't mean it!" She smacked me hard across my face and waited for a response.

The force from her smack quickly turned my head. I couldn't believe what she'd done, and my reflexes made me

jump up from my chair and grab her hair. I pulled it tightly—
so tightly that her head leaned far back.

I was seething with anger because this chick just wouldn't
go away. I was in no mood to think about Cassandra, and I
knew that was going to happen if I gave in to Felicity. "What
in the fuck do you want from me?"

"I already told you, didn't I? Or do you have a problem
comprehending?"

"So, you want me to fuck you?" I released her hair. "Fine!
If that's what you want me to do, then I'll do it!"

I hadn't made a move, so she smacked me again. "Then
stop your whining, bastard, and just do it!"

Before I knew it, I pushed Felicity backward and she fell
onto the canvas I'd been working on. The canvas cracked,
and she sat up on her elbows, widened her legs, and gave me
a devilish grin. No doubt, she had successfully raised my
pulse, and now, she'd have a chance to enjoy what Cassandra
liked so much about me.

As Felicity sat still, I stared her down and wiped the sweat I
felt forming on my forehead.

"So, you like it rough," I said with a devious smile.

She nodded. I looked at her flat, sweaty stomach as it
moved in and out from the deep breaths she took. I looked
between her legs and noticed her already moist panties. I
pulled my boxers down and kneeled in front of Felicity. My
hands went to her hips, and I pulled her panties down to her
ankles. She kicked her panties off with the heels of her shoes
as I unlatched her bra from the front and watched it fall to
her sides. I held her breasts in my hands and roughly massaged them. While nibbling on them, I reached down and
rubbed my fingers between her legs.

She seemed excited by my touch, and placed her legs high
on my shoulders. Her moans got louder, and when I lowered
myself to taste her insides, she used the back of her heels
and fingernails to rake my back. Her heels began to hurt, so

I held her legs together and pressed them close to her chest. I teased her with the head of my dick, but she quickly made her way on top of me and seductively looked down at me on the floor. She grinned and tightly stretched her panties across my mouth. This was all so familiar to me, so I went with the flow.

"I got a feeling that you're bullshitting around with me, Brandon. You wouldn't be holding back on me, would you?"

I moved my head from side to side.

"Then what are you waiting on? There's no need for us to make love to one another if we aren't in love."

She lowered her panties from my mouth and placed them beside me. I pulled her face toward mine and gave her a hard, wet kiss. We smacked lips for a while and then backed up so we could remove ourselves from the floor. I stood tall in front of her and held my hands around her neck. I rubbed my thumbs against her lower jaw and placed my lips on hers once again.

Our kissing became intense, so I backed her up into the wall behind us. I lifted her legs and she straddled my hips. When I inserted myself, I started off slowly, but soon tore into her. I pounded her so hard that her head and back banged against the wall. From the gleeful expression on her face, I could tell she was enjoying herself. She grabbed tightly around my neck and held on for dear life.

I carried Felicity to my bedroom while she straddled my hips. I moved her back on the bed and grabbed her arm to turn her on her stomach. I was in control, and I opened her butt cheeks and found myself another hole.

"No," she said, gripping my sheets. "I can't take it like that."

"Yes, you can," I said. I pulled the back of her hair and jerked her head back. "Cassandra loved it like this. I can't believe you don't want it like this too."

Felicity strained to talk. "But . . . but I enjoy it so much better the other way. Please give it to me the other way," she said.

I gave off a soft snicker and pulled out. She didn't know what she'd gotten herself into, so I walked over to my closet and pulled out two extension cords, some candles and a blindfold. When I turned to look at Felicity, she looked nervous. She scooted back on the bed and eyeballed the items I had in my hand. I placed the candles on my nightstand and lit them. I then turned off the lights and sat on the bed next to her. I held the extension cords and blindfold in my hands.

"What are you gonna do with that stuff?" she asked.

"Don't you know? I think you already know, don't you?"

Felicity's worrisome look made me uncomfortable. So, instead of me taking control, I turned it over to her. I pulled up a chair beside the bed and sat in it. I reached out to give the extension cords and blindfold to her.

"Here," I said. "Tie my hands and legs with the cords as tightly as you can. Then place the blindfold over my eyes. After you do that, the game begins. I want you to ride me until you get tired. If you allow me to get loose, then I take control. Trust me; you don't want that to happen."

Felicity got off the bed. First, she covered my eyes, and then she placed my hands behind my back to tie them. The cord was tight on my hands and even tighter on my ankles as she tied them to the chair. She'd done as I had asked, and straddled herself on top of my lap to give me a ride. My dick was already hard, so she jolted up and down on it. She kept at it, and then turned herself backward, used the floor for leverage, and rode me in an even better position.

I grew hungry for Felicity and damn near went crazy because I couldn't touch her. I was wiggling my hands to untie them from the extension cord, but was unsuccessful. And just as I was about to let loose inside of her, she rose up. I heard her footsteps next to me, and then she leaned down and whispered in my ear.

"This might burn a little, but I'm sure you can stand the pain."

I felt the hot wax from the candle running down my chest. I pressed my lips tightly together so I wouldn't scream, but when she poured the wax on my dick, I went crazy.

"Damn you!" I yelled out loudly and released the sound of sizzling bacon. "Sssss . . . that fucking hurts!" I leaned forward, struggling to pull my hands apart.

Felicity held my goods in her hands, and I could feel the cool breeze from her mouth blowing on my dick. She licked up and down it. I reached for the back of her hair and yanked it; then I removed the blindfold from my eyes and watched the extension cord drop to the floor.

"That's enough," I said. I stood up and pushed her back onto the bed. When I got on the bed with her, she reached out to smack me. I caught her by the arm and held it down tightly. I pinned her other arm so she couldn't move. I was highly aroused by all of this, and my hard thang pressed against her. I worked it inside while continuing to hold her arms down tightly, and lowered my head to bite her nipples. I intended to hurt her just as much as she'd hurt me.

As soon as I reached for the extension cord to tie her, I'll be damned if I didn't hear Will calling my name. I smacked Felicity hard on her ass and told her to get underneath the covers. I knew Will all too well, and I was positive that he was headed in my direction.

Sure enough, he came in and hit the light switch. I was turned sideways, lying next to Felicity so he wouldn't see her face. The cover was over both of us, and I turned my head to look at Will.

"Man, do you mind?" I said. "I'm kind of busy."

Will looked at the candles, and then at the extension cords on the floor. He scratched the top of his head. "Uhhh, so it's like that, huh? I . . . I just wanted to tell you that the windows are all good."

"Thanks," I said. "Now, do you mind?"

Will didn't say another word as he closed the door on his way out. I looked at Felicity and smiled.

"You have no idea how he just saved you."

"Oh, yes I do. From the look in your eyes, I pretty much had a gut feeling about what would happen to me next."

"Or maybe you knew what to expect because Cassandra told you. If not, it's almost like you were watching us every time we had sex or something."

"Or maybe we all have something in common."

I pulled my head back and gave her a puzzled look. "What do you mean by that?"

"I mean, haven't you come to your senses yet, Brandon? How could I know so much about you and Cassandra if we weren't somehow involved?"

"Are you telling me that you and Cassandra were lovers?"

She placed her nail in her mouth and bit down on it. "That's not what I meant, Brandon. With all of the investigations going on, I know sooner or later the truth is going to come out. Only a few times did she and I and Jabbar get together.

"One night, at a nightclub, I introduced them. Jabbar had big plans for us. I didn't think things would get serious with her and Jabbar, and once they did, I backed off. Again, I was only involved because of my on-again-off-again relationship with Kurt. Jabbar was the other man I'd been seeing, and—"

I was speechless. This bitch was playing serious games with me. Why in the hell hadn't she told me that she and Cassandra had both been fucking Jabbar? I knew Cassandra was a sexually adventurous woman, but never did I think she'd be involved in a threesome. I felt set up, and I didn't know Felicity's motive.

"Get out of here, Felicity. This shit is done. For all I know, you and Jabbar probably trying to set my ass up!"

"The sex between Jabbar and me only lasted for a month.

I haven't talked to him in quite some time, and he's made no attempts to contact me."

"You just saw him at the damn funeral! You were kissing his ass and talking to him then. Stop lying to me, Felicity, and get the hell out of here!"

I yanked the covers back and got out of bed then grabbed my robe from the closet and put it on. Felicity hadn't moved, so my voice got stern.

"Now, Felicity! If you say one more word without moving your ass off my bed, it's gon' get ugly up in here."

"Brandon, please don't—"

I raised my voice. "I said get out!"

"Would you listen—"

I reached for her arm and snatched her off the bed. "Get your clothes and leave here, now! Don't force me to kick your motherfucking ass!"

I opened the door, and with my cover wrapped around her, Felicity stepped into the living room. When Will saw that Felicity was the person in the room with me, his eyes bucked.

I followed her into my studio and watched as she put on her clothes. She stood across the room from me and tried to explain.

"I was lonely, Brandon. Kurt and I had problems, and—"

"Fuck you and Kurt, Felicity. The two of you deserve each other. This shit is crazy. I don't trust a word you say. My gut is telling me to run, and run fast."

Felicity didn't have anything else to say. After she slid her shoes on, she walked tearfully out the door.

Will sat on the couch in a daze. He looked at me with his mouth hanging wide open.

"Man, you have got to tell me what's going on. Were the two of you just in there fucking? And what was all the yelling about? You look angry as hell."

"I am. And for the record, we've only been screwing for a few weeks. " I made my way to the kitchen and Will followed.

"Where . . . when did all this shit take place? And why were you mad at Felicity?"

"I was mad because the bitch is a liar. Plus, she just told me she'd been fucking the police officer who's been investigating me."

"Well, calm down. It couldn't be that serious between y'all, unless you've been fucking her longer than you told me."

"Don't go judging me. You don't even know what the hell I've been going through!"

"Maybe I don't, but that's because you acting all secretive and shit, like you got something to hide. So what you've been fucking Felicity? Did you feel like you had to keep it a secret from me? We boys, Brandon, and I thought you felt cool talking to me."

"I do, but I was embarrassed to tell you that Cassandra had been seeing another man. Jabbar. The same police officer that Felicity just admitted she'd been fucking, and the one who's been investigating me. Man, it's been one big mess, and I got a headache from talking about it."

"So Cassandra was seeing someone else? I tried to warn you, dog, but you shouldn't be embarrassed about it. Like I said, move the hell on and be done with it. Hell, we've all been played, and yo' ass should have never felt exempt."

I slammed my hand against Will's and we left it at that.

He opened the fridge, picked up the milk carton and guzzled down some milk. He wiped his mouth and swiped his hand on his pants. "So, do you want to go check out your car?"

I gave him a disturbed look and snatched the milk carton from his hand. "The next time you want some milk, get a glass. My car, hopefully, you got it taken care of for me."

"I said I did, didn't I? I'm a man of my word, and you can always count on me."

"Yeah, right. I wish I could count on you for some money. And it would be nice if you'd drop some funds on a brother right about now."

"I got your back. Give me another week, and I'll be able to give you a li'l somethin' somethin'."

I cracked up.

We sat around for the rest of the evening playing cards and talking. He questioned me about the wild sex I enjoyed, but I told him that he couldn't even imagine some of the things that Cassandra had taught me. I told him just how rough and intense our sex had been, but was reluctant to talk about some of the toys we used in the bedroom. Will's mouth was already wide open, and I didn't want him to think that Cassandra's and my relationship was based on sex alone.

I felt good about my discussion with my best friend, but after what Felicity had told me, I felt betrayed—betrayed by a woman I had loved dearly, who had not given the same kind of love in return. I was ready to put everything behind me and distance myself from her friends, her family, and from the past. I was looking forward to my new job, and to making another connection with a new woman who had definitely gotten my attention.

CHAPTER 8

Monday was here. I'd taken Jennifer my paperwork last week, and was delighted when she called me on Friday and told me everything checked out. Since I'd only been questioned about Cassandra's murder, nothing showed up on an official police record, so I was cleared to start work.

Will never did get around to looking for a job, but I hadn't kicked his ass out yet. He did keep his word on getting my windows fixed, and he sat around all day screening my phone calls for me.

Felicity had called several times since she broke the dreadful news to me about her "play time" with Jabbar and Cassandra, but I hadn't spoken to her. It was obvious that the only idiot there seemed to be was me. I'd been a sucker, but I would not be a sucker anymore.

The police seemed to have backed off, and I was damn glad about that. Aunt Ruby called and said the last she'd heard, they didn't have much else to go on. She promised me that she'd make them keep at it until the person who was responsible was put behind bars. But I was bitter now, and

didn't have the same enthusiasm to find Cassandra's killer as
I'd had before.

I had an uneasy feeling about Jabbar, but that was based
on Aunt Ruby mentioning Cassandra's fear of him. Somehow, that just didn't add up to me. There were too many lies
being told, and everybody I talked to had a very different
story. Everything went back to Cassandra's conflicting words,
and I hated to admit that I was in love with a woman who
seemed to have lived a double life. I needed to accept the fact
that I'd been played for a fool, and a huge part of me felt no
guilt for trying to move on.

I arrived fifteen minutes early for work. As soon as I
walked in, I saw Evelyn talking on a payphone. She immediately ended her call and headed my way. I hoped that she admired the way I looked in my navy blue suit and white
starched shirt. My low cut had been trimmed, along with my
thin beard and goatee. She gave me a flirtatious smile, and
the look of satisfaction was all over her face.

Evelyn went to Jennifer's office with me and we waited
outside until Jennifer ended her call. I couldn't help but notice Evelyn's constant stares.

"Is everything okay?" I asked. "You keep looking at me like
something is wrong."

"No, everything is fine. Really fine, but . . ." She paused.

"But what?"

"The earring. It kind of makes you look like a playa.
You're not a playa, are you?"

I laughed. "No, I'm not a playa. I intended to take it out,
but I forgot." I reached for the earring and removed it.

Jennifer invited both of us into her office. She laid out our
schedule, which required me to be at Evelyn's side for the
entire day. I surely didn't mind, because I liked being in the
company of a mature woman, and she appeared to have her
shit together.

For the first few hours, I followed behind Evelyn as she gave three tours. Two of them were with children from a nearby elementary school, and the other was a group of elderly people from a nursing home. I admired the way Evelyn knew what she was talking about, and I took notes about some things that I, as an artist, didn't even know about the paintings on display. Evelyn had observed me taking notes, and complimented me on paying attention.

By noon, we walked to Talaynas for lunch. The people in the restaurant knew her well, and she introduced me to the workers as one of her friends.

"Friend," I said. "I've already stepped up, haven't I? This morning I was just a co-worker."

Evelyn chuckled. "Why do men always try to make something out of nothing?"

"Because we pay attention to a lot of things as well. Sometimes, women don't give us the credit we deserve."

"Yeah, right. The only things men pay attention to when it comes to women are the shapes of our backsides and the wideness of our mouths."

I laughed and denied it. "For some men that might be true, but not for all men."

"Really," she said, folding her arms. "And what makes you so different, Mr. Brandon Fletcher?"

"You'll have to see for yourself."

She tapped her fingernails on the table. "How old are you?"

"I'm thirty-one. How about you?"

"I'm forty, but I'll be forty-one next month."

"You look awfully good to be forty. And that ain't game I'm running on you, either."

She smiled. "I hear that all the time, so I know it's not game on your part. I appreciate the compliment. And feel free to keep them coming."

The waiter brought our food to the table. We conversed a while longer, and when it came time to pay the bill, she offered. I declined Evelyn's offer and paid the bill in full.

"Thank you for lunch," she said as we walked back to the museum.

"You're welcome," I said as I tried to get up enough courage to ask her out for a date. "Uh, Evelyn, would you maybe like to have dinner sometime in the near future? No hurry, but whenever you can get around to it."

"Honestly, Brandon, I'm kind of seeing somebody right now. We're dealing with some issues, but I expect for us to work through them."

"Oh, that's cool." I was disappointed. "But if it doesn't work out, you know where to find me."

She told me that she'd keep me in mind, but my feelings were a bit bruised. One thing I hated was to be rejected by a woman. She probably didn't even have a man, and that was her way of letting me down easy. If she was trying to play hard to get, then I intended to play the same game with her.

By day's end, I stopped by the break room to say good-bye to Evelyn and Jennifer, who had been sitting in there yakking. I told Jennifer I was prepared to work on my own, and Evelyn looked kind of shocked. I guess she figured I wanted to be as close to her as possible, but after her earlier rejection, I intended to keep my distance.

"Do you think you're ready to tour on your own?" Jennifer asked.

"Yes, I do. I took some good notes, and I'm one who many might consider a fast learner."

"Jennifer, I allowed Brandon to give the final tour of the day and he did pretty good," Evelyn weighed in. "Just don't forget to ask the visitors if they have any questions."

"Thanks, and next time, I won't forget. You ladies have a good evening, and I'll see you tomorrow."

On the drive home, I slid in a Wallace Roney CD and listened to some jazz. When my cell phone rang, I looked at the number. It was Aunt Ruby. I wanted to distance myself from Cassandra's family, but I felt bad not answering Aunt Ruby's call because she was the only one who believed in my innocence. I turned down the music and answered.

"Brandon," she said in a panic. "Can you come by my house to see me?"

"Yeah, sure. What's going on?"

"Just come and I'll tell you."

"Okay, I'm on my way."

By the time I made it to Ruby's house, she was already at the door waiting for me. When I walked in, I followed her to the kitchen, where she immediately sat down and fumbled around for a cigarette. She opened a container of pills and popped four of them into her mouth. I placed my hand on top of hers.

"Ruby, will you tell me what's going on? Calm down and tell me."

"Brandon, the police have been questioning me about Cassandra's murder."

"What!" I yelled. "Why in the hell would they question you?"

"Because she had a healthy life insurance policy, and guess who the sole beneficiary is."

"You?"

"Yes. A long time ago, she asked me to sign some papers, but I forgot about them. Her lawyer had been trying to contact me, but I'd gotten my number changed. He said he'd been sending me letters in the mail, too, but last week was the first time I got a letter from him. I went to go see him, and that's when he told me about the money. Ever since then, those detectives been bugging me. They won't leave me alone, Brandon, and I'm really worried."

"But if you didn't do nothing wrong, Ruby, then what do you have to worry about?"

"My nerves, Brandon. They're bad, and the money . . . the money makes me nervous."

"Well, popping those pills for damn sure ain't gonna help you. You're in the same situation as I am with the police, but they're grasping at straws. Everybody knows how close you and Cassandra's relationship was. She looked up to you more than she did her own mother. I think it's going to take more than just speculations to convict either one of us."

"I know you're right, but I'll be glad when all of this is over. Vivica is upset with me about the money, and I told her if Cassandra leaving me the money upsets her that much, then she can have it. She claimed it wasn't about the money, but I know better."

"That's crazy. Vivica has no right to be upset with you, and Cassandra did what she felt was right." I didn't know that Cassandra had an insurance policy, but hell, there were a lot of things I didn't know. It did surprise me, though, that Cassandra would make Ruby her sole beneficiary. I knew she had issues with her mother, but I thought her relationship with her father was cool. For Ruby to claim she'd forgotten about signing the policy, that seemed a bit untrue. I tried not to judge, but like everything with this case, some shit just wasn't adding up.

"I guess you're right," she said. "If Cassandra didn't want me to have the money, she never would've asked me to sign those papers."

I stayed with Ruby for a while. She seemed unstable, and her hands were shaking like a leaf. When she suggested having a séance, I knew it was time for me to go. Witchcraft and that voodoo shit was the name of her game, and after what happened to me the last time I was at her place, I was anxious to leave.

The pills she'd taken made her drowsy, and she started nodding off at the table. I wanted her to get some rest, so I walked her into her bedroom and laid her down. I stayed with her until she fell asleep, and pulled up the covers to keep her warm.

On my way out of her stuffy and musty bedroom, I lit a strawberry candle on her dresser and turned off her light. I headed to the front door, and when I opened it, I heard a voice call my name. It didn't sound like Ruby's voice, but I walked back into her room. I turned on the light, but she was still sound asleep.

I quickly turned my head to the side, and my heart began to thump fast. There was a shadow behind me, and when I turned around, there was nothing there. I thought about the last incident that had taken place in her house, and I hurried to the front door to leave. When I pulled on the door, it wouldn't open. The voice called my name again, and this time when I turned around, a vision of Cassandra stood before me.

"What is it!" I yelled in a panic. "What are you trying to tell me?"

A strong breeze kicked up, and I panicked even more. I pulled on the door handle again, but it still wouldn't open. I shook the door so hard that the glass broke.

"Damn!" I yelled out loudly and dropped down to pick up the glass.

I heard another voice call my name, but this time it was Ruby. She came up from behind and placed her hand on my back.

"What happened to my glass?"

I took deep breaths. My palms were sweating, but not as much as my forehead. "I'm sorry. There is something going on with your house, Ruby. Every time I come here, she . . . she tries to make contact with me."

Ruby looked at me like I was crazy. "Cassandra's gone, Brandon. Why don't you take a few of these pills I got and go lay down for a while."

"No, that's all right. I . . . I need to go home. Your door got stuck, and when I tried to open it, I couldn't. I pulled harder and the glass broke."

Ruby put her hand on the doorknob and turned it. The door opened easily. She looked at me again, and then at the glass on the floor.

"Look, don't worry about the window. I'll get somebody—"

"It's my fault, so I'll make sure I pay for it. In the meantime, do you have some cardboard? I'll put up the cardboard until I get somebody to come over and fix it."

"Yes, I have some cardboard, but in this neighborhood, that window needs to be fixed tonight."

"Right now, I don't have any money on me. I promise you that I'll have it fixed tomorrow."

"Well, I'm not gonna wait until tomorrow. You'll never catch me up in here 'sleep with no broken window. A friend of mine, Clarence, can fix it. Why don't you get a broom and dustpan to pick up the glass while I go call him?"

Even though I was anxious to get the hell out of there, sweeping up the glass was the least I could do. Ruby walked into the other room to call Clarence, and I headed to the kitchen to get the broom and dustpan.

Though I didn't really want to, I waited at Ruby's house for Clarence to come. I wanted her to know how sorry I was about her window, and I truly was. But as soon as Clarence arrived, I told Ruby I'd bring her the money tomorrow then I jetted.

It was almost 10:00 PM and I was exhausted. The visions of Cassandra made me feel as if I was losing it, and after I paid Ruby her money, she didn't have to worry about me visiting her house again. It gave me the motherfucking creeps, and it was best for me to stay away.

I'd hoped when I got home that I'd be able to relax, but as always, with Will being there, things couldn't go that smoothly. This time, he had company, and the music was turned up rather loud. I didn't even sweat him because I was in no mood to embarrass him. I spoke to his guest, Stacie, and went straight to my room and closed the door.

I hurried out of my clothes and got in the bed. Unable to sleep, I tossed and turned, reliving the crazy things I'd seen at Aunt Ruby's place, and didn't fall asleep until nearly five o'clock in the morning.

CHAPTER 9

It was almost noon, and work was going along pretty well. I'd kind of kept my distance from Evelyn, but I noticed her desperately trying to get my attention. I thought it was funny how women operated. It seemed as if they were more interested in you when they knew you weren't interested in them. If you showed them the least bit of attention, of course, that was a big mistake.

As for Will and me, things weren't working out in my favor—not that I expected them to. He had no intentions of finding a job, and I didn't have the funds to take care of him and me both. And even if I did, I for damn sure wasn't taking care of a grown-ass man who didn't want nothing out of life but some ass from the ghettofied women he'd been seeing, and to lay up and do nothing all day.

Several times, he'd invited Stacie over and kept me up with all the outrageously loud fucking they'd been doing. When I brought the issue to his attention, he had the nerve to tell me to buy a pair of earplugs. I couldn't believe how selfish he was, especially since I'd allowed him to live with me rent-free and eat whatever he wanted from the fridge. If that wasn't enough, I'd let him use my car—a car which was on its way to being repossessed if I didn't come up with three car payments soon. He for damn sure didn't have any money to help, and unfortunately for him, he had to go.

The situation with Aunt Ruby was getting more and more complicated. She called and said the police took her in again for questioning. Since her attorney was with her, the detectives weren't as aggressive with her questioning as they had been before. They thanked her for coming in, and told her they'd be in touch.

Honestly, I felt that Ruby was innocent, but who knew? I'd also thought Cassandra was faithful to me, and look how that turned out. Nobody could be trusted, and I knew that the love of money often made people do crazy shit.

I still wondered if the police had even considered Jabbar. He hadn't sicked any of his animals on me lately, but something told me they weren't finished with me yet. They seemed to be on to something with Aunt Ruby, and it felt kind of good not to have the police knocking at my door. The sensible thing to do was to sit back and wait for all of this to play itself out.

As always, I got to work at least fifteen minutes early. I went to the break room to get a cup of coffee, and then sat at the table to read the newspaper. Soon, Evelyn came in with a bag of donuts in her hand. She put the bag in front of me and sat in the chair beside me.

"Here," she said. "I bought you some donuts."

"Thank you," I said, and then opened the bag to get one. I reached for a twisted glazed and put it in my mouth.

"I knew you'd go for the biggest one in the bag and leave me with the little one," she griped.

I chewed the donut and swallowed before responding. "I thought you said that you bought *me* some donuts. You didn't say nothing about you."

She laughed as she walked over to the coffee machine. When she sat back down, she grabbed my newspaper.

"I was still reading that," I said playfully. "How you gon' just take my paper?"

"The same way you just ate my other donut."

I smiled and tried to snatch the paper away from her. She moved it away, and before I knew it, the paper was in pieces from us pulling it back and forth. Jennifer walked in and saw us playing around with each other.

"Now, now, children," she said. "Let's get to work and cut out all the playing."

"Good morning, Jennifer," I replied while picking up the paper from the floor. Evelyn said hello too, and after Jennifer spoke, she put her lunch in the refrigerator and left.

Evelyn and I picked up the rest of the paper and threw it in the trash. I thanked her for the donuts again and headed out of the break room to get to work. No sooner had I reached the door than Evelyn called my name.

I turned. "Yeah, what's up?"

"Before you go out there, you might want to know that your fly is unzipped."

I looked down at my zipper, and sure enough, my bad boy was damn near poking through my pants. "Thanks for noticing." I winked and then zipped my pants.

The day moved by quickly. I gave twelve tours, and was exhausted from all of the day's excitement. One kid was sick and vomited everywhere, and when I tried to show a film to another group of students, I couldn't get the projector to work. Rushing to leave, I went into the break room to get my coat. I reached for the keys in my pocket and found a note inside. It was from Evelyn, and implied that she was ready for dinner whenever I was. Her home and cell phone numbers were written down for me to call. I chuckled, realizing that my standoffish approach had worked.

I was interested in having dinner with her, but I also wanted to take it one day at a time. I'd been deeply hurt by what Cassandra had said to others and what she'd done behind my back. But I couldn't let my hurt stop me from meeting other people and pressing on with my life. I stuck the note back into my pocket and jetted.

When I got home, I happily jogged up the steps to my apartment but stopped short when I noticed the door was slightly open. I pushed on it and saw that my place was in shambles. My couch had been ripped, papers were scattered everywhere on the floor, and one of my TVs was busted. As I made my way to the kitchen, I saw that it was just as bad. Spilled milk covered the floor, broken plates were everywhere, and a note with a knife stabbed into it was on the kitchen table.

I snatched up the note, which read: I HAVEN'T FORGOTTEN ABOUT YOU, PUNK! I put the note back down and went toward my studio. When I walked in and saw the condition it was in, I could have died. I dropped to my knees and covered my face with my hands. All of my canvases had been broken up, and many of my pictures had been shredded to pieces. Paint was splattered all over my hardwood floors, and the word *sucker* was painted in bold red letters on the wall.

My entire body was numb, and I couldn't even move to go see the rest of my place. To me, it didn't even matter because they'd fucked with my livelihood. My chest felt tight, and I grabbed it. Tears welled in my eyes. Just when I thought things were starting to look up, this happened. The only way for this shit to stop was for me to do something about it. I rushed up, grabbed the note from the table, and headed to the police station.

There were two officers on duty at the front desk. One was sitting in front of a computer, and the other was on the phone, smacking on some gum. They both saw me, but neither offered to help. I knocked on the window to get their attention. The officer who was on the phone put the caller on hold.

"What?" he said rudely.

"I need to file a complaint."

He ended his call and walked up to the window to assist me.

"What did you say?"

"I said I would like to file a complaint against another police officer."

"What's the officer's name . . . badge number or something?"

"Jabbar."

"What's his last name?"

"I don't know."

He snickered. "Son, how are you going to file a complaint and you don't even know the officer's name?"

"I don't know it, but I'm sure you do. All I know is that he works here."

He turned his head to the other officer. "Say, Jeb! Do you know an officer Jabbar?"

The other officer didn't even look up. Just shook his head and continued to look at the computer monitor. I could only imagine what he was so engrossed in.

"Look!" I yelled. "I need to file a complaint because this officer has been harassing me. I was brought here for questioning about my girlfriend's murder, so I know he works here."

"You need to lower your voice, son. If you've been questioned about a murder, that's not harassment. We have a job to do, and we're gonna do it."

"Then do your damn job and direct me to someone who can assist with me filing a complaint."

He walked away from the window and took his time getting some papers. He slid them underneath the glass divider and directed me to a bench in the corner.

"Have a seat and fill out the information. When you're finished, let me know, and I'll have someone come out and speak to you about your complaint."

I took a seat and struggled with completing the form. I couldn't tie any of the incidents that had happened to Jabbar, and I knew completing the forms would be a waste of time. Still, I wrote down what had happened to me that day, and explained how the person who had jumped me made it clear that it was "compliments of Jabbar." I also mentioned that Jabbar and me disliked each other because of our relationships with Cassandra. I hoped that someone saw the connection, but I seriously doubted it.

Once I finished, I knocked on the window to get the officer's attention. Now, he was enjoying whatever was on the computer monitor with the other officer. I slid the papers underneath the glass.

"Thank you," he said from a distance. "There's no one in to speak to you right now, but someone will give you a call in a few hours."

"Would you mind making a copy, so I can have one for my record?"

"Sorry, but the copy machine is broke. If you want a copy, you'll have to get your own."

I grabbed the papers from underneath the glass and went to a nearby Quik Trip to make a copy of the report. Whenever some serious shit went down between Jabbar and me, I wanted evidence that I'd made an attempt to do something about it.

When I got back to the police station, I slid the papers back underneath the glass and tapped the window again. I showed the officer my copy.

"I got my own copies. If you disregard my complaint and don't pass it on to the appropriate person, just know that somebody's blood will be on your hands. I'll be waiting to hear from someone soon."

The officer picked up my papers and looked through them. "Thank you, sir. Have a nice day."

Honestly, I think the officer got a kick out of the whole damn thing. As I was speaking, he smirked and didn't seem to take my concern seriously. I wouldn't be surprised if I didn't hear from anyone.

I realized if I intended to pursue this bullshit with Jabbar, I had to make it my business to know a little more about him. I hadn't spoken to Felicity since I'd thrown her out, but she'd been calling like crazy, trying to explain her position. I listened to several of her messages, begging me to understand her side of the story and forgive her for making plenty of mistakes. Yes, a part of me believed that she was working behind close doors with Jabbar, but I wasn't sure. I felt it was good to consult with your enemies, and knowing more about Jabbar would benefit me. Felicity was the only person I knew who could feed me more information about him.

When I arrived at her place, I heard laughter inside. When Felicity opened the door, she didn't say one word, but widened the door so I could come. Annette was sitting in a chair in the living room, chomping down on popcorn.

"This is a surprise," Felicity said. "We're watching movies. Is there something—"

I didn't feel comfortable speaking around Annette. "Maybe this isn't a good time," I whispered to Felicity. "Can I give you a call tomorrow? I really need to talk to you about something."

Annette stood up and rolled her eyes at me. I wondered what was up with her. When I spoke to her, she didn't speak back. She reached for her purse. "I'm going to get our pizza," she said, ignoring me and focusing her eyes on Felicity. "It should be ready by now. What kind of soda do you want?"

"A Pepsi will be cool," Felicity responded. "And while you're out, pick up something sweet."

"Something sweet like what?"

"Like some candy or cake . . . anything. Just as long as it's sweet."

Annette walked past me and left. I looked at Felicity.

"Tell me that you didn't tell her about us. Please, tell me you didn't."

"Well, uh, I sort of—"

"Damn, Felicity! Do you know how that makes me look?"

"Brandon, what's the big damn deal?" she said, walking away. "What we shared is over and done with, so why do you care about who knows about us?"

"I can't believe you just said that. There are plenty of people who care about what happened between us. Everybody around here pointing the finger at me, and she's got to be wondering if I loved Cassandra so much, then what in the hell was I doing fucking you? Telling people about us might make me look guilty."

"Yeah, well, the only person I told was Annette. The last time I came to you, I explained to you how lonely I was. She's a close friend of mine, and has been the only person I could talk to."

"So, did you tell her about you and Cassandra?"

"Hell no! I don't want her putting my business out there like that!"

"But it's okay if she put my business out there, huh?"

"Brandon, you are overreacting. Annette doesn't care about us having sex. She's upset because you threw me out for telling you the truth."

Felicity's phone rang, and she hurried to her bedroom to get it. I stood in the hallway for a minute, and then walked back to where she was. Whoever was on the phone, she kept their conversation to a minimum. I walked into the room as soon as she hung up.

She plopped down on her bed and picked up a hairbrush

on her nightstand. "So, you never told me why you're here," she said, brushing her hair back.

I slid my hands into my pockets. "I wanted to ask you a few questions about Jabbar."

"No, Brandon. Every time I try to tell you anything about him or Cassandra, you wind up getting angry with me. I've learned my lesson, and now, I'm staying out of it." She headed for the door.

I reached out my arm and blocked her from leaving the room. "Listen, I'm sorry for the way I treated you, but you have to understand how I felt. I promise you I won't get mad anymore about anything you tell me."

"Well, there's not too much more I can tell you. I pretty much told you all there is to know."

"For starters, would you happen to know Jabbar's last name?"

"It's Booker. Why?"

"Because I didn't know that. When I got home today, my place was a complete mess. I think Jabbar and his crew broke in and fucked it up. I went to the police station to file a complaint, and I didn't even know the damn fool's name."

"Well, it's Booker," she said, moving my arm. She went into the living room and sat on the couch. I followed and took a seat on the arm.

"Is there anything else you want to know?" she asked.

"Yeah, there's plenty. But can you tell me something, anything that will help me get this joker off my back?"

"Something other than he's a freak in bed like you are? I really don't know what else to tell you other than that. I only knew him on a sexual level, nothing more and nothing less. Since Cassandra's murder, I haven't heard from Jabbar. Yes, I saw him at the funeral, but I wasn't the one all up in his face. I told you that my encounter with him only happened a few times."

"Felicity, you've got to know something. Was there anything that Cassandra said to you about him that's just not clicking at this time?"

"Brandon, I'm sorry. I can't tell you what I don't know. Again, sex is my only connection with Jabbar, and I swear that there has been no other connection between us."

I was disappointed, but saw no reason to continue the conversation since she wasn't giving up any information. "Thanks," I said, heading for the door. "If you remember anything, call me."

"Sure."

By the time I reached my car, my cell phone was vibrating in my pocket. When I answered, Felicity said, "You could have given me a hug or something."

"I wasn't in the mood."

"Well, when do you think you might be? You left so fast that I didn't get a chance to talk about us. The last time we were together, you were about to show me some things I hadn't seen before. Would you come back so we can talk?"

"Not today," I said. I had no intentions of ever having sex with Felicity again. I didn't want to hurt her feelings, though. "I'll call you next week."

"Sure you will. But if I come up with anything about Jabbar, I'll call you."

"Please do," I said and hung up.

When I made it back home, Will was already there, cleaning up. He was trying to straighten up the living room, and gave me a serious, concerned look as I walked in.

"What the hell happened in here?" he asked.

"Somebody trashed the place. I'm sure that you don't have to ask who had something to do with it."

Will shook his head. "Brandon, you really need to do something about RoboCop. When are you gonna do something about this bullshit?"

"I'm trying. Today I went to the police station and filed a complaint. I'm waiting on a follow-up phone call."

He laughed. "You're kidding me, right?"

"No, I'm serious. I got the complaint papers right here." I reached in my pocket and handed my copy to Will.

"Don't waste your time, fool. I mean, it's really time to do something about it. That asshole needs to be put in his place."

"Yeah, well, I know he do, but I don't want to be in any more trouble than I'm already in. He's waiting on me to do something stupid so he can have me arrested. I gotta be smart, and I'm not going to play that stupid game with him."

"I guess you're right," he said. "But we got one hell of a mess to clean up, don't we?"

"Yes, we do. I'm gonna change my clothes and get started. If you wouldn't mind, I need a favor."

"What's that?"

"Would you get started on my studio? That's the most important thing, and I can't stand to look at it."

"Don't worry. I'll get to it right now. As long as you got the kitchen, I got the studio all taken care of."

I smiled and walked into my room. It wasn't as bad as I expected it to be, but they'd pulled several pieces of my clothing from the closet and cut them up.

Will and I had been at it for hours. By the time we finished, I was so worn out that I couldn't even get up the next day and go to work. Besides, my dream about Cassandra wouldn't let me sleep. It seemed as if, for some reason, she'd been making her presence known. Maybe she was upset about me sleeping with Felicity, or she knew that I'd been trying to forget about the past and move on. Whatever her message was, it caused me to wake up in a major sweat and rush to the bathroom and throw up. I called Jennifer and told her I was ill. My excuse was a migraine headache, and I promised her I'd be back to work the next day. She told me to get well and said she'd see me soon.

As for Will, I guess he must have felt sorry for me. When he woke up, as tired as he was, he put on some clothes and went on a job search. He said he'd catch up with me later and assured me he'd have a job whenever he got back.

I had hoped to talk with an officer about my complaint, but by four o'clock in the afternoon, I hadn't heard from anyone. I refused to follow up at the station, and there was no doubt that it was time to take this matter into my own hands. Jabbar was about to wish that he'd never met me, and that he'd never messed around with my woman.

CHAPTER 10

The next few days were kind of tough for me. Even though Will cleaned up my studio as best as he could, there were still haunting memories of what had been done to it. The many containers of paint had stained the floor, and since I didn't have any money until payday to buy some white paint for the walls, the word *sucker* in red continued to stare at me.

Normally, when I wanted to relax, I'd go in my studio to do so. Since there were no canvases for me to paint on and no paint to paint with, I was bored. I'd given Mr. Armanos $2400 for two months' rent, and I really didn't have much left to splurge with. I did, however, plan on buying some new art materials as soon as I got my first check.

Though I hadn't intended to, I was out of work for three days. I couldn't get past the damage that had been done to my place, I couldn't stop thinking about my fucked-up financial situation, and the fact that no one had followed up from the police station truly angered me. I didn't have the strength to work, but if I wanted to make any money, I knew I'd better get my butt back to work and fast.

I thought about asking Ruby for some money, but the last

time we spoke, she seemed to be losing it. She was talking crazy, and when I asked her what was wrong, she said that she was still worried about the police. I was worried for her, and worried for myself as well. I figured Jabbar was aware of my complaint by now, and it was going to cause continuous problems for me.

The following day, I got up early and headed for work. Will had gotten a job at a burger joint around the corner, and he insisted it simply had to do for now. I wasn't mad at him for settling, but if he was going to take a job at a burger joint, he could have done that a while back. It sure would have helped me. But I had to start looking out for myself.

Will wasn't expected at work until two o'clock in the afternoon. I woke him up and told him I was on my way out. He said he'd holla at me later on that night when he got off.

Before going to work, I stopped by Krispy Kreme and bought Evelyn two donuts. I hadn't responded to the note she left in my pocket, so she probably thought I'd forgotten about her. I hadn't, but I had so many other things on my mind. She didn't seem like the type of woman to accept a brotha with a bunch of baggage, and I didn't want to bring her into this chaos I was already in.

My stop at the donut shop delayed my arrival at work. As soon as I got there, I rushed to the break room to clock in. It was one minute until clock-in time, and the clock stamped my timesheet just in the nick of time. Evelyn came rushing in to beat the clock as well, so I moved aside for her to stamp her timesheet.

"There was a bad accident on the highway," she said. "Did you get caught in traffic too?"

"No," I said. "Instead, I got caught up at the donut shop." I placed the bag in her hands. "Here. I was thinking about you this morning, so—"

She smiled and looked inside the bag. "Thanks, but I'm

on a diet. Since you didn't take my invitation for dinner, I figured maybe I needed to check my weight or something."

I laughed. "Woman, please. You know darn well that your body got it going on. If you don't want to eat them, give them to me. I'll eat them."

She held the bag close to her chest. "You Indian giver. On my lunch break, I'm going to have the pleasure of wearing out these donuts. And if you ever get a chance to see me naked, I don't want to hear your mouth about how my butt is too big."

My mind left me for a second, and I visualized her being naked. I couldn't believe what she'd said. She was definitely showing a different side of herself. I guess that previous relationship she mentioned wasn't working out.

"So . . . so, now I might get a chance to see you naked, huh? If that were the case, I would've bought those donuts for you a long time ago."

"A phone call would've gotten you anything you wanted. But since you didn't have time to call—"

"Oh, trust me, I intended to call. Something just came up, that's all."

"I'm sure *she* did. Whenever you get *her* all taken care of, you have my number."

Evelyn headed for the door, and I didn't say one word. It was in my favor that she at least thought there was someone else occupying my time. And even though there wasn't, she would never know.

At the end of the day, I caught up with Evelyn and told her I'd see her Monday. Since today was payday, I had mega shit to do, but I wanted to talk to her before I left.

"Hey, Brandon, listen," she said, standing by the exit. "Why don't you let me cook dinner for you tonight? That's if you're not too busy."

"I would love to, but I have a lot of things to take care of tonight. How about tomorrow night?"

"Tomorrow night it is. If anything comes up, please call so I can make other arrangements."

"Will do. But I'm sure I'll see you tomorrow."

Excited about her offer, I headed to my car and jetted. I stopped by the bank to cash my check, and then headed for the nearest Hobby Lobby so I could buy my art supplies. After taxes, I didn't bring home much, so I had to be careful to put some aside for my bills. Truthfully, I had no business in the store splurging on art materials because I was already parking my car a block away from my house so it wouldn't get repossessed.

Unable to control my obsession with art, I spent nearly four hundred bucks trying to get some of the items back for my studio. The rest of the money had to be put aside, with hopes that Will would be able to kick me out a li'l somethin' somethin' too.

I tried to fit all of the canvases in my car, but I couldn't. I had to drive home and ask Mr. Armanos if I could use his beat-up old truck that was barely working. He let me use it, and when I got back, I asked if he would help me take the canvases up to my apartment.

As Mr. Armanos made his way to the door, I asked if he'd seen anyone hanging around my place. He was always lurking around, and if anybody had seen anything unusual, I knew he had.

"Yeah, that friend of yours been coming by a lot lately."

"I know about Will, but have you seen anybody else? I'm asking because somebody broke into my place the other day and trashed it." I unlocked the door and we both went inside. I knew how protective he was of his property, so I was sure the damaged floors would make him just as angry as they made me.

"Whatta hell happen?" he asked as we entered my studio.

"This is what somebody did. Paint stained the hardwood floors, and I'm gonna have to replace the entire floor."

"Yeah, you certainly are." He looked around the room and shook his head. "I . . . I remember seeing two well-dressed men the other day. I was taking out the trash, but didn't get a chance to see where they were going."

"Did they look like police officers?"

"Possibly."

I got excited. "Mr. Armanos, do you have any tapes from Monday? Will the tapes show their faces?"

"No, no I don't have no tapes. I use the cameras to see if anything suspicious is going on. If I notice something suspicious, I always call the police."

"Damn," I said. "In the future, will you keep an eye on things for me? The only reason I didn't call the police is because I think they're trying to cause problems for me about Cassandra's murder. If I can catch them in action, then I'll be able to press charges."

He nodded. "That's a shame. Your girlfriend was nice and sweet. The two of you loved each other, and I always seen you together. I'll keep my eyes on things, but you hurry up and get that floor taken care of."

"I will, Mr. Armanos. I promise you that I will."

My next few hours were spent painting my walls and fixing one of my many wooden easels that had been broken. Around eleven o'clock, Will strolled in, looking beat.

"Man, I am not cut out for this work bullshit," he said, sitting on the windowsill. "I almost got fired for fucking up so badly."

"Fired? From a burger joint? Come on, Will, how difficult can that be?"

"For your information, Negro, the restaurant business is the hardest place to work. It's fast-paced and if you can't keep up, then you got to go. Today was pretty bad, and I don't think I'm going to make it back there tomorrow."

I cut my eyes at Will. "You got fired, didn't you?"

He laughed. "Hired one day and fired the next. Man, me and that fucking manager couldn't get along. I ain't gonna be bossed around by no damn body, and that's a fo' sho' thang."

"Damn, Will. Sometimes you gotta kiss a little ass. Not a lot, but just a little. I would bet some money on it that you got fired over something stupid."

"If you call yelling at me and talking down on me like I'm a nobody stupid, then you go right ahead. The man disrespected me, he didn't appreciate my four hours of work, so therefore, he lost me."

"Four hours? You were only there for four hours?"

"Yep. After I left, I stopped by Stacie's house. Since my time is running out with you, I'm working on another place to stay."

"Your time has run out with me, especially since you can't keep no job. I need some help, man, and bad."

"I got your back. As soon as I get a steady job, I'm gonna kick you out a li'l somethin'."

Yeah, right, I thought. It was obvious that Will couldn't even take care of his damn self, let alone help me when I needed him to. There was no doubt that he had to go, and friend or not, I had to stop being passive about the situation.

I was overly excited about dinner with Evelyn that night. Trying to get my attire together, I searched in my closet for my blue blazer and stone washed jeans. It was kind of chilly outside, so I found my ribbed turtleneck and shined my leather loafers.

By five o'clock, I was all ready to go. Will was trying to stay on my good side, so he mentioned that Stacie was coming over and he was going to borrow some money from her. Since I was on my way out, I told him that was cool. I encouraged both of them to have a good time, and I jetted.

Evelyn gave me directions to her crib, but before I went there, I stopped by a store and bought her a rose and a bottle of wine. I didn't have much money, but damn, she didn't have to know it. The way I looked and dressed, it was hard for anybody to tell I was actually broke.

From the outside, Evelyn's house looked pretty nice. It was a ranch-style home made of brick. The bay windows gave the house an elegant look, and so did the neat landscaping. I knocked, and she opened the door with a bright smile. Her low haircut was neatly lined, and it gave an awesome view of her pretty, round face. Wearing very little makeup, her natural skin looked flawless. She had an apron tied around her tiny waistline, and her curvy hips made me lick my lips. She invited me inside and I looked around.

"You have a beautiful home," I said, admiring the high vaulted ceilings, the exquisite paintings that covered the off-white eggshell walls, and peach-colored L-shaped suede sofa in the living room.

"Thank you," she said. "Can I take your jacket?" I pulled it off and handed it to her. "I'm just about finished with dinner. You can come on back to the kitchen until I get everything finished."

After she hung my jacket in the closet, I followed her into the kitchen. The aroma in the kitchen was delicious. I saw two plates with porterhouse steaks, potatoes, mushrooms and onions, smothered in a creamy sauce. Evelyn opened the oven and pulled out a homemade peach cobbler with its juices boiling over the side.

"Can I help you with anything?" I asked before taking a seat.

"Nope," she said. "All I have to do is put my dinner rolls in the oven and everything will be ready. If you would like to pour us some of the wine over there on the counter, you can."

I was so anxious to get to the door that I'd left the rose and wine in the car. Embarrassed, I stood up.

"I forgot something in my car. I'll be right back."

She gave me a hard stare. She was so damn pretty to look at, but I couldn't figure out what the evil look was for.

"Evelyn, did you hear what I said?"

"Look, Brandon, if you want to go out to your car and call one of your little girlfriends, don't do it on my time."

I smiled, wondering where in the hell that came from. "I'm sorry if you think that's what I'm going to do, but if you must know, I forgot the bottle of wine I bought for you in the car. When you mentioned wine, it jogged my memory."

"Hmm, I'm sure a man like you always keeps wine in his car, don't you?"

"No, I don't."

I hurried to my car as I thought about Evelyn's comments. She obviously had some trust issues with men, so I tried like hell not to trip. I grabbed the rose and picked up the bottle of wine. On my way out, I'd closed the front door behind me and had to knock again. This time, I had both items in my hand.

Evelyn opened the door, looked at me, and couldn't help but smile. I gave the rose to her, and displayed the wine.

"I hope you like white wine. And since I made a special trip to the store to purchase this for you, if you like red, going back to the store would be no problem."

"White wine is fine. No need for you to go back to the store, okay?"

We both laughed as I followed her back into the kitchen. I filled our glasses with wine and sat at the table, admiring the hell out of Evelyn until she got ready to sit down with me.

She dimmed the lights in the kitchen, lit the candles on the table, and sat directly across from me. Wanting to be close to her, I pulled my chair up beside her.

"Now, why are you coming over here?" She grinned. Her dimples made my heart flutter.

"Because I want to be close to you while we eat. You got a problem with that?"

"As a matter of fact, I do."

"Why? Because you're nervous about me being this close to you?"

She turned her head away and teased her short hair with her fingers. When she looked at me again, she was smiling. "Yes, I'm very nervous about you being this close to me. I . . . I don't like a lot of attention, and besides that, I'm shy."

"Woman, please. Tell that to somebody else. And if you were shy, you never would've said what you said to me the other day."

"And what did I say to you the other day?"

"You know . . . about taking off your clothes for me."

"I said no such thing," she said, raising her voice. "My exact words were, 'if you ever see me naked.' That's what I said."

"But how am I going to see you naked if you don't take off your clothes for me?"

Again, she turned her head and looked away. "Can we please change the subject? This talk is making me very uncomfortable, especially for a first date."

"Relax," I said, placing my hand over hers. "I promise you that I won't bite." I picked up her hand and kissed it. She inched it back. "Damn, you really are shy, aren't you?"

"I told you I was. Did you think I was lying?"

"But you seem so relaxed and confident at work. The way you carry yourself, and—"

"And when you put me in a room alone with a fine young

man who resembles Tyson Beckford, I can't handle it. I can't get my thoughts together, and . . . Damn, did I take the dinner rolls out of the oven?"

"I don't think so," I said, looking over at the oven.

Evelyn hurried out of her chair and opened the oven. The smoke poured out as she pulled out the pan of burnt dinner rolls. I got up to help, but she told me to move back. She placed the hot pan on top of the stove. I placed my hand over my mouth and tried to clear my throat.

"I am so sorry." She coughed while fanning the smoke. "If you need to, go outside and get some fresh air."

"I . . . I'm cool," I said, still coughing.

She looked at me and laughed. "See, this is what I was talking about. All that crazy talk made me forget about my darn dinner rolls."

"I could care less about those dinner rolls. I'm a bit hungry, so do you mind if we get back to dinner?"

Once Evelyn cracked a window to clear the smoke, we went back over to the table. I pulled out her chair for her and then kept my chair next to hers.

I was enjoying dinner, and Evelyn seemed to as well. She laughed a lot and talked a bit about her rocky relationship with her ex. She didn't trust him, and apologized to me for the previous comments she'd made. I had trust issues with people too, so I understood. I didn't mention Cassandra at all, and kind of beat around the bush when it came to my past relationships. I couldn't deny, though, that Evelyn had put a smile on my face that hadn't been there for a long time.

Before Evelyn got up to clear the table, I leaned in and gave her a peck on the lips.

"Thank you for dinner," I whispered. "It was delicious."

"Anytime, Brandon," she said, our eyes still locked together. She looked at my wet, soft lips and leaned in for another kiss. This time, our tongues intertwined and we smacked lips for a while longer. When I got more aggressive with my kiss, she backed away.

"Now, that was a kiss," she said, and then lightly touched her lips. "Before you leave, make sure you give me another one of those."

"Oh, I plan to."

I helped Evelyn clean up the kitchen, and then we took our wine and glasses into the family room by the fireplace. Evelyn straightened the rug on the floor and we lay down next to each other. She took a sip from her wineglass and then placed it on the table. She lay on her back and looked over at me.

"What's on your mind?" I asked.

"Do you have to ask?"

"Well, what do you plan to do about it?"

"Nothing. I don't have sex with men on the first date, Brandon. I haven't been a teenager for a very long time, and I've learned after many years that you can't give yourself to a man just like that. So, I can sit here and think about sex with you as much as I would like to, but tonight, this is as far as it goes."

"I respect that. If I told you I wasn't thinking about having sex with you, I'd be lying. But I respect a woman who knows what she wants and sticks to it."

Evelyn was quiet for a minute. She rose up, took another sip from the wineglass, and put it back on the table.

"You're a mystery to me, Brandon," she said, lying back again. "I really and truly can't figure you out. During dinner, do you know that you avoided a lot of my questions?"

"If I did, maybe I didn't want to elaborate on the subject. Don't take it personal, but I have a problem opening up to people, especially if I don't know much about them."

"Now, that's fair. I'm the same way, but what I really want to know is why you don't have a steady lady friend."

I didn't feel comfortable talking about my past with Cassandra, and I knew my explanation wouldn't be acceptable. I didn't want to scare away Evelyn with the level of drama in my life, so I left the subject alone. "I just haven't found what it is that I'm looking for in a woman."

"What is it that you're looking for?"

"Honestly, I don't know that either. I guess I'll know what it is whenever I find it."

"See, those are the kind of responses I'm talking about. You're never direct and to the point. But I guess it's a game you young men play."

"Listen, Evelyn. My age has nothing to do with what kind of man I am. It's just a number. Don't forget that, okay?"

She didn't respond as she looked at her watch. To me, that was my cue, so I stood up to leave.

"Well, I'd better get going," I said.

"Yeah, I guess so."

"Hopefully we can do this again soon. Next time, I'll cook dinner for you."

"I am a very picky eater, so it better be good."

"Trust me; it will be."

Evelyn walked off to the hallway closet and got my jacket. She handed it to me, and we made our way to the door. I wrapped my arm around her waist and dropped my eyes to her lips. We kissed, and as she felt my hardness press against her, she touched my chest and backed away.

"Goodnight, Brandon."

"Goodnight," I said, making my exit.

On the drive home, I couldn't stop thinking about Evelyn. I was considering a serious relationship with her. She exemplified the stability that I looked for in a woman. Maybe this was a turning point for me, and I wanted to get to know her a little better. I wanted to have sex with her, and I hoped that the next time we got together, she'd be ready.

CHAPTER 11

On Monday, I couldn't wait to get to work to see Evelyn. For the past couple of days, I'd been thinking about her a lot, and the thought of seeing her again was heavy on my mind. When I got to work, however, she was nowhere to be found. I waited around for her in the break room, but she didn't come in. I already had a tour scheduled, so I hurried to clock in and then got to work.

Finally, during lunch, I saw her on the payphone, just as I was on my way out to get a bite to eat. I whispered to her and asked if she wanted to go with me. She shook her head and continued on with her conversation. I thought maybe I'd gotten my hopes up too high, and even though her coldness had an effect on me, I left.

When I got back a little more than an hour later, I saw her sitting in a parked car with another man. She seemed to be all smiles, and when I looked her way, she turned her head. This situation had me all fucked up, and it was obvious that I'd read more into our date. She wasn't my woman, so how could I be mad about her seeing another man?

For the rest of the day, I avoided her. I saw her before I left and gave her a quick wave. She waved back and gave me the fakest smile I'd ever seen.

In reality, I was pissed, but she'd never know it. How could I have been so wrong about her? Was I rushing things? She did tell me she was involved with somebody, but she also mentioned that the relationship was rocky. Was she just as confused as I was about dating?

When I got home, I was pleased to see that Will wasn't there. I pulled off my clothes and changed into a sweat suit that was a bit more comfortable. Wanting to relax, I had plans to work on a painting, but not before I checked the messages on my phone.

Ruby had left a message for me to call her, but I couldn't make out what she'd said. When I called her, her mouth was moving so fast that I still couldn't understand her.

"Ruby!" I yelled. "What's going on."

"I . . . I just got back from the police station," she sobbed. "Brandon, I think they're gonna try to pin Cassandra's murder on me."

"What! How can they do that and they can't build a case against you?"

"That damn Jabbar is making up all kinds of stuff about me. He keeps bringing up Cassandra's life insurance policy and says that it gave me motive."

"Look, take it easy. Tomorrow I'm gonna go talk to some people that might be able to help. Until then, don't worry yourself too much. Stay focused."

"All right, Brandon. You be careful too, okay?"

"I will," I said and then hung up.

This thing with Jabbar had gone too far. How in the hell was he able to keep getting away with it? He was definitely barking up the wrong tree. He seemed determined to blame anybody, and Ruby was falling for his stupid game. I had to get with Antwone and his boys quick to see if they'd help me settle this shit.

When Will came in, it was almost nine o'clock. I was still painting in my studio, and he strolled in with his hands in his pockets. He pulled out four hundred dollars and gave it to me.

"Well, I'll be damned." I smiled. "Is this for me?"

He scratched his head. "Yeah, man. I asked Stacie for a loan, and she gave it to me. I went back to that burger joint and asked for my job back. I'll pay her back whenever I get my first check."

"Why the change of heart? I thought you wasn't up for kissing ass."

"I'm not, but I need some money. I can't be living with you and expect not to pay nothing. I know you've been struggling your damn self, so if I call myself a friend, it's only fair that I contribute."

I nodded and we slammed our hands together. He took a seat on a stool and cleared his throat.

"Now, since I'm gon' be contributing and everything, can I ask you for a favor?"

"Somehow, I knew this was too good to be true. What's up?"

"Can I chill at your place for a while longer? I know I've already overstayed my welcome, but I really don't have no place to go. I stopped by to see my moms today, and she was out there so bad that it made me sick. The last thing I want is to go back and live with her."

"Will, I don't mind you staying here, but man, I need some help. I can't keep taking care of you when I can't even take care of myself. No doubt, if you want to stay here with me, you will have to keep a job and keep some kind of money coming in. All right?"

"You got a deal. From now on, I'll do what I can."

"That's all I ask. In the meantime, now I need a favor."

"Anything."

"I . . . I need somebody hurt. Badly hurt."

"Who and why?"

"Jabbar. He won't stop tripping with me, and he's been causing Aunt Ruby some problems too. I know you're cool with Antwone and his boys, and you mentioned y'all rolling on some fools before. I wondered if you could get him to do a li'l damage for me."

"Antwone and his boys gon' want some money. And for a cop, they might want even more."

"Well, whatever they want, let me know. Somehow or some way, I'll get it."

"I'll give him a call tomorrow. I'd hate to see you get involved with those fools, but I agree that Jabbar needs to be dealt with."

"No doubt," I said. "No doubt."

At work the next day, I completely ignored Evelyn. She didn't say much to me either, and since I was waiting to hear from Will, I wasn't tripping off her too much. Right before lunch, I walked right past her as if I hadn't seen her. She called out my name and I turned.

"What's up, stranger?" I said.

"Nothing much. I wanted to know if you had plans for lunch."

"Yeah. I got plans to go to McDonald's and grab me a quick bite to eat. How about you?"

"I had plans, but I cancelled them. Would you like to go to my house for lunch?"

I looked at my watch. "Fifty-five minutes ain't long enough for lunch at your house."

Evelyn smiled and moved closer to me. "You must have something else in mind. I was strictly talking about grabbing a sandwich and heading back to work."

"Nah, I'll pass. But if you'd like for me to bring you something back from McDonald's, I will."

Evelyn shook her head, so I turned to leave. She was so full of shit, and I didn't have time for it. If she thought I was going to act like a desperate fool who couldn't wait to fuck her, then she was sadly mistaken. Already, she'd been playing the same games as Felicity, and if Evelyn was still with her man, why in the hell was she sweating me? It brought back memories of Cassandra, and I was starting to feel as if all women were worthless.

The line at McDonald's was too long. My stomach told me to wait, but my legs encouraged me to take a seat. I went with the flow of my stomach and waited almost fifteen minutes in line just for a Big Mac and fries.

I found a table and removed my jacket before taking a seat. I'd barely put two fries in my mouth before I looked up and saw Jabbar walking in with another officer. I didn't want him to see me, but since I couldn't stop staring, his eyes finally met with mine. He grinned, said something to the other officer, and headed my way.

"Well, well, well," he said, sliding into the booth with me. "I guess punks got to eat too, huh?"

"Yeah, they do," I said, smacking hard on my fries. "I guess it was time for your punk ass to eat, and that's why you're here too, right?"

He snickered. "Real cute, playboy. Not only was your comment cute, but your complaint against me was the most hilarious thing I've ever read."

"Well, I'm glad you got a chance to see it. It's good to know that the fat motherfucker who took it didn't let me down. Now, if you don't mind, I'd like to eat my lunch in peace. I'm sure I'll deal with you in another place, on another day, and possibly, at another time."

"Brandon, I don't understand why you're so bitter with me. Yeah, I took your woman from you, but that's because she needed a man and not a boy. I've been keeping my eyes on you, and I can't believe that you turned to a woman like Felicity. You can keep on tagging that because she ain't ready for a real man. In the meantime, you should be grateful that I haven't made you my prime suspect for murder anymore. I'm after the real killer, and if I were you, I'd wake up and face reality."

"I've already faced reality. Reality is Cassandra never left me for nobody. She had a man who loved her a lot, but I guess that wasn't good enough. She never said that it wasn't, and I'm dissapointed that she thought you had something else better to offer.

"As for Felicity, if you've been watching me, then I'd say you're speculating about us. Unless she's told you herself that we've been involved, and that's always a possibility too. I think you know how much of a liar she is, and in case you didn't know it, that's free advice I'm offering to a man like you, who's been dead wrong about everything."

Jabbar sucked his teeth. "You . . . you are really more ignorant than I thought. Even though I don't have to, I'm gon' let you in on a secret. I know for a fact that Cassandra wasn't killed by you, and she for damn sure wasn't killed by me. When you open your eyes, you'll see that her killer has been playing your dumb ass like a fiddle. I've been playing you too, but that's because I don't like your ass and you were fucking my woman.

"The next time you talk to Ruby Dee, you tell her I said hello. Let her know that I'm coming for her, and tell her that the warrant is only days away. When I close this case, I want a personal apology from you. If you loved Cassandra like you say you did, that shouldn't be too hard, should it?"

I really didn't know what to say, so I shoved my food into a bag and left. I walked back to work, feeling awkward about Jabbar's news. It was good to know that he no longer viewed me as a suspect, but what kind of evidence did he have against Aunt Ruby? Maybe I was overlooking some things about her. Did I trust her? Was she capable of killing Cassandra? Jabbar seemed serious about what he'd said. What if his intentions all along were to simply find the person who had killed Cassandra?

Work dragged on, and I couldn't stop looking at my watch. I was in the break room waiting until my last tour at three o'clock. When Evelyn came in, I pretended to be occupied by watching the TV in the far corner of the room. She noticed my attitude and stood in front of the TV so I couldn't see.

"Okay, tell me what's wrong with you. I can tell you're upset with me about something," she said.

"Upset? I'm not upset with you about nothing."

She moved away from the TV and took a seat next to me. "You're such a liar. Why don't you tell me what your attitude is all about? If you don't tell me, I can't fix it."

"Evelyn, please. You think I'm some kid you can toy around with, but I'm not. Bottom line, I'm just not up for a bunch of games, and a woman your age should be ashamed for playing them."

She folded her arms defiantly. I must have touched a nerve. "Where do you get off telling me what a woman my age should or shouldn't be ashamed of? For your information, I haven't played any games with you. The only thing I've done is tried like hell to end my previous relationship before jumping into another one."

"Yeah, right," I said, looking away from her and back at the TV.

She grabbed my face and gave me a soft, wet kiss. I welcomed her kiss, but when I got more into it, as usual, she backed up.

"Now do I have your attention?" she asked. I didn't say a word. "Good," she said. "Why don't you come by my house tonight? I had a wonderful time the other night, and date number two might bring about bigger and better things."

"I'm looking for a guarantee that it will. If you can give me some type of guarantee, then you got yourself a date."

Evelyn stood up and leaned in closer to me. She placed her lips on my ear. "Satisfaction guaranteed, young man. Leave your tricks for your girls at home, and be prepared to make magic with a real woman. I hope like hell you perform like your eyes tell me you will; and if you don't, this old woman won't be ashamed to tell you it's lousy."

I moved my head back and looked into her eyes. "My dear, I never talk about it; I just be about it. All you need to do is provide me with a time, and since you're still working through some issues with your man, I hope this doesn't become a problem for you. You're not gon' back out on me and change your mind, are you?"

"You let me handle him. All you have to do is worry about getting to my place on time."

Before I could respond, Jennifer walked in and cleared her throat. Evelyn stood up straight and I picked up the newspaper in front of me, pretending to be occupied.

"Like Nelly always says, it's gettin' hot in here." Jennifer laughed while fanning herself. She looked awkwardly at Evelyn and me. "Listen, boys and girls, save the heat for later. I got people who need tours."

I scooted my chair back and we both headed for the door. Jennifer called out Evelyn's name, but both of us turned around.

"He's gorgeous, isn't he? Who could blame you for turning up the heat?"

We all laughed. As soon as we were out of Jennifer's sight, Evelyn gave me a pinch on my ass.

"All right, now. You don't want me to file a sexual harassment claim against you, do you?" I teased.

"If that's the case, then we both need to file one."

"Get out of here. I have never put my hands on you against your will."

"No, you haven't. But from day one, the way your eyes undressed me, and continue to undress me, I should've filed my complaint a long time ago."

I laughed again because there was no denying that. Evelyn walked off, but before she got too far, she turned and noticed me observing her. She shook her head and kept on walking.

No doubt, I was ecstatic about my progress with Evelyn. The way she made me feel was the same way I felt when I was with Cassandra. More than anything, Evelyn made me forget about the drama that was unfolding outside of work. I didn't have time to think about what Jabbar said about Ruby, but a part of me was worried about it being true. And Felicity? I knew she'd damn well been talking to Jabbar, so I couldn't wait to confront her about it.

After work, I rushed home to eat, shower and change. I hurried through the door, only to see Will and Antwone sitting on the couch, talking. Antwone quickly stood up and reached his hand out to shake mine.

"Long time no see," he said with a sneaky grin on his face.

"What's up, Antwone?" I took a seat on the couch with him and Will. "I guess Will told you I needed a favor."

Antwone stretched his arms on the top of my couch. He licked his thick, crusty lips and squinted at me with his nearly closed eyes. "Yeah, he told me, but before we discuss anything, I need to know how much money you're working with."

"I'll get you whatever you need. I just need this cop to be dealt with soon."

"How soon?"

"As soon as you can get to it."

"I can get to it tonight if you got the money. If not, then it's gon' have to wait until you get some money."

"Like I said, just tell me how much and I'll get it."

"First give me a name."

"Jabbar. Jabbar Booker."

Antwone leaned forward and gripped his hands together. He cracked a tiny grin. "Boy, you ready to dance with the devil, ain't you? Jabbar ain't nothing to play with, and he got a good rep on the streets. He tough, but a lot of people like him."

"I'm just ready to do what I gotta do, that's all."

"This gon' be a touch knock, so . . . a hundred G's will get the job done."

My mouth widened. "A hundred what!"

His voice dragged. "A hundred grand, nigga. Either you want him taken out or not. If not, then don't waste my time."

"Shit, that's a lot of money, Antwone."

His voice rose. "Do you have any fucking idea what's at stake for killing a police officer? Man, me and my boys don't do nothing like that for no petty change." He tapped Will on his chest. "What's up with yo' boy, Will? Is this nigga coo-coo or something?"

Will shook his head. "Nah, he ain't coo-coo. If he coo-coo, then I am too. That's a whole lot of money to me too."

Antwone laughed and stood up. He made his way to the door and held the knob. "Whenever you get the money, call me. I don't want to hear from you unless you singing a tune that sounds like a hundred G's. In other words, the tune you singing today don't sit right with me. Until it does, holla."

He opened the door and walked out.

I wasn't sure how to move forward, but I was incapable of coming up with a hundred thousand dollars. I could always ask Ruby for the money, but there was no guarantee that she'd even want in on this. And what if Jabbar was right about what he'd said at McDonalds? I didn't want to be responsible for hurting a man who was just trying to do his job. This seemed to be a problem for Aunt Ruby now, and maybe it was best that I stay the hell out of it.

CHAPTER 12

I was so anxious to see what Evelyn was working with. After I showered, I slid on my khaki pants, loafers, and my well-pressed navy blue button-down shirt. I splashed my face with Kenneth Cole aftershave and made sure my hair, beard and goatee were neatly trimmed. On my way out, I told Will I'd see him later and dashed to my car to make it to Evelyn's place by eight.

When I arrived, I was almost forty-five minutes late. I knew that was a no-no for a woman like her, and it proved to be true when she opened the door and gave me one hell of a look.

"I should make you turn around and take your butt right back where you came from."

"But you won't," I said. I stepped forward and wrapped my arms around her waist. I breathed in her sweet-smelling perfume and thought dirty things. Evelyn was like the Cassandra I'd met many, many years ago and had fallen in love with. In many ways—her classiness, her personality, her sexiness, and her knowing exactly what she wanted from a man— she turned me on. I didn't want to compare the two, but I had a hard time forgetting the reason I'd fallen in love with Cassandra from the beginning.

I hoped like hell that Evelyn would not turn out to be the Cassandra I'd known after her death. Somewhere down the road, things changed, and it could have possibly happened when she made a connection with Jabbar.

Evelyn's demeanor showed that she was still a bit bothered about me being late, and she tried to push me back, but my grip was too tight. "What makes you think that I won't make you leave?" she asked.

"Because you wearing nothing under this silk robe would be a waste, the scented candles you have burning in the living room would burn for no reason, and the wine that I'm positive you have chilling would have to go back to the store. You wouldn't put forth all this effort just to send me back home, would you?"

She removed my arms from around her waist and held open the door. "Try me," she said. "I have a serious problem with men who are late. I don't like to wait on no one."

Her stubbornness was driving me crazy, but I loved it. I pulled her away from the door and slammed it. I backed her against it and lightly rubbed my index finger between her breasts.

"Why you always being so mean to me? My feelings get hurt very easily, and you should be ashamed of yourself for being so cruel."

She gave me a wink and whispered, "Don't cry. I'll make it up to you."

Evelyn pulled my face to hers and placed her lips on mine. Before giving me her tongue, she teased me a bit with quick pecks, and then went full force into my mouth. I moved her robe aside and rubbed my hand on her silky smooth inner thighs. They were soft as cotton, and I found home when I touched her pussy. It was hairless, moist and warm. I separated her lips with my index finger and danced between them.

She groaned as we continued to kiss, and then she pulled my finger out from inside of her.

"Let's go to my bedroom," she whispered. Getting no reply, she took my hand and led me down the hallway to her room. The bed was big enough for us to do our work, and was neatly covered with paisley printed sheets and pillows. A cherry oak armoire was in the front of the room, and African art dressed the walls.

Before I could compliment the room, Evelyn dropped her robe to the floor and her body left me speechless. I inched my way back on the bed and sat in awe. I stared at her in front of me and reached for the top button on my shirt to undo it. One button after another, I took my time. I guess she didn't like that idea, so she stepped closer to me and laid me back on the bed. She straddled my lap and looked down at me.

"I thought you told me you were shy, didn't you?" I asked.

"Yes, I am shy. So shy that by the time I get back from making sure my front door is locked, your clothes better be off."

Evelyn removed herself from on top of me. I pulled my shirt over my head, and in no hurry, I stood to remove my socks, shoes, pants and briefs. When she got back, my pants and briefs were at my ankles. She got a glimpse of my long pipe and embraced me around my neck. We fell back on the bed and laughed.

"You were too quick," I said, caressing her ass in my hands. She straddled me again and let my dick rest against her warm pussy.

"No, you were too slow. If anything, you'll have to pick up the pace in a bit, okay?"

With her on top, I kicked off my pants and briefs from my ankles. Evelyn slid her wetness along the sides of my dick as it pointed in my direction at full attention. I closed my eyes and thought about what being inside of her would feel like.

"Ummm," she whispered. "I like what I'm feeling. Did you bring any condoms?"

My eyes went buck. "Uh, I . . . I normally—"

She rose up and went over to her dresser. I heard the package unravel and felt like a fool. Not having a condom showed irresponsibility on my part. I hoped it didn't mess up the mood.

Evelyn stayed down low and put the condom on me. My dick was like a rocket ready to explode. She jolted down on it and started to ride me slowly. I closed my eyes again and tossed my head from side to side.

Her strokes were cool, but I wanted more. There was too much silence, and her hands didn't know how to wander. Frustrated, I dug my fingers into her hips and pumped myself up inside of her. I could tell that she didn't like my rhythm, because at times, she wouldn't even move.

Since she didn't cooperate, I decided to take control. I flipped her on her back and spread her legs far apart. I placed one of them on my shoulder and leaned in close to her. This way, she got the full effect of me, and my effect started to show. I hit her with several deep strokes, and when her legs trembled, she was on the verge of an orgasm. She took deep breaths and wrapped her arms tightly around my neck.

"Ohhhh, Brandon! That feels so gooooood! Do it, baby! Do it again!"

I wanted Evelyn to come back for more, so I pulled out and lowered my face between her legs. I licked her from front to back and circled her clitoris with my tongue that still carried her juices. She rubbed my hair, and the room echoed with her screams.

"You are amazing!" she yelled. "But you've got to let me take care of you. Please let me take care of you."

I rose up and rolled my tongue across my lips to taste her. "I want it doggy style," I demanded.

With no hesitation, Evelyn got into position and I got behind her. I knew where I wanted to explore, but I didn't think she was ready for that yet. Instead, I teased her crack with my dick and swooped my way inside of her. She could barely keep still, and as I hit her walls from every angle that I could, I knew it was going to be hard for Evelyn to let something this good go.

When Evelyn decided to finally call it quits, we'd been sexing each other for almost two hours. Her body was stretched out on mine, and I rubbed up and down the small of her back.

"I'm getting too old for this shit," she said with a laugh.

"You need to stop complaining about your age. I happen to know plenty of women in their forties who can give many of these younger chicks a run for their money. Like I said before, age is just a number."

"Then why is my body so sore like this? I feel like I've been in a fight with the heavyweight champion of the world."

"That's because you were. It was a good fight, but you'll have to take that one as a defeat."

"I knew you were going to go there, Brandon. Now, I'm not afraid to give credit where credit is due, so . . . that was nice."

"Nice? I wasn't trying to be nice, nor do I intend to be in the future."

"Well, I like my loving given to me in a nice and gentle way. Tonight, you got a li'l rough, and those were the moments that you didn't get a response from me. Did you notice?"

"Yeah, I noticed. But sometimes I like to . . . to tear something up."

Evelyn cracked up. "Tear something up? Brotha, if you

didn't just tear into it, then I don't know what you did. Some
things you say are hilarious."

For the rest of the evening, I joked around with Evelyn
and kept a satisfactory smile on her face; however, I wasn't
playing about sex between us getting more intense. But I
wasn't going to rush things, because I enjoyed being with
her and didn't want to introduce my more kinky preferences
until she'd gotten used to me. Hopefully, this would lead to
something I could hold on to and treasure for a long, long
time to come.

The next day, as soon as I walked into the art museum, I
saw Evelyn standing by a window, looking out. Today, she
looked even better than before, standing in her black heels
and navy blue suit. Her jacket fit her waistline to a T, and the
tight skirt squeezed the curve in her ass. I visualized her
long, smooth legs on my shoulders just like last night, and I
couldn't help but want them there again.

As I got closer, she placed her fingernail on her lip and
folded her arm in front of her. She appeared to be in deep
thought, and I surely wondered what her thoughts were
about.

I had a surprise, so I stepped behind her and slid my arm
around her waistline. The rose I'd gotten appeared in front
of her, and I held up a bag from Krispy Kreme.

She smiled and took the rose from my hand. "Thank you
for the rose, but you can keep those donuts. I already had a
fruit cup for breakfast."

I slid my arm from around her and she faced me. "Are you
sure? And what makes you think there are donuts in the
bag?"

"What else could be in a Krispy Kreme bag but donuts?"

I shoved the bag in her direction. "Open it up and see."

Evelyn opened the bag and pulled out a small ice pack.
"An ice pack? What is this for?"

"I thought you could use it between your legs. Last night, I—we worked kind of hard, and you're the one who said your body was sore."

She poked her finger at my chest. "You, Brandon Fletcher, are quite nasty. Why don't you save the ice pack for later on in the week? By then, I'm sure we'll both need it."

"So, I take it that you're inviting me over again?"

"Of course. Only if you don't have anything else to do."

"Nothing. Nothing at all."

"Then I'll see you at seven. Not seven forty-five, but seven, okay?"

"Seven o'clock sounds good. Seven o'clock every day for the rest of the week sounds even better."

"Deal." She smiled. "Now, back off me. Jennifer is being rather nosy behind you, and we need to chill out at work."

Not concerned about Jennifer, I leaned forward and gave Evelyn a peck on the lips. She was shocked.

"Sorry," I said. "I couldn't help but kiss you because you're looking so damn sexy this morning."

Evelyn looked over my shoulder and didn't say one word. I knew Jennifer was close, so I walked away.

I couldn't wait to get home, grab a bite to eat and change. Will held me up a bit, as we sat in the kitchen and talked for a while.

"So, do you intend to get back with Antwone or what?" he asked.

"I'm not sure. I called Aunt Ruby, but she hasn't returned my calls yet. Getting rid of Jabbar will be in her best interest too, so maybe she'll go with the flow."

"I think that's a bad idea. Getting too many people involved will make shit difficult."

"Well, where else am I going to get a hundred G's from? I don't know of anyone else who got that kind of money but Ruby."

"Do what you wanna do, Brandon. I just hope this shit works out for the best."

"Me too," I said. I grabbed my keys from the counter and got ready to go. Will stopped me.

"Who's the lucky lady that's got you busting in at five o'clock in the morning?"

"A friend. Why?"

"I'm just asking. Lately you've been all giddy and shit, and it's good to see you coming alive again."

I nodded, and after Will gave me two hundred dollars, I thanked him and jetted.

He was so right about my new attitude, and I had Miss Evelyn to thank for that. She was something else, but I was worried about her other man on the side. She hadn't mentioned him at all, and after all of the hours I'd spent at her place, he hadn't called or come around. I was feeling so good about our relationship, and I hoped that he had no intentions of coming back on the scene and swaying her away from me.

CHAPTER 13

Evelyn and I had been having sex all week long. I was so into her that it was almost scary. What I could no longer have with Cassandra, I found it in her. She filled a major void, and the way she made me feel was unbelievable. I didn't give a damn about anything but making money and being between her soft legs.

Since we'd been at her place all week, I decided to invite her to my place. She'd mentioned coming to my place, and proving to her that I had nothing to hide, I asked Will if he would jet for the weekend and allow us some quiet time together. He agreed and said that he could chill at Stacie's place for a few days. I wondered why he wouldn't just move in with her, but I was almost afraid to ask, since he'd been kicking me out cash every now and then. The money he'd given me sure as hell helped. I used it to get my car payment back on track, and was able to put a small portion of my paycheck in the bank.

When Evelyn called to tell me she was on her way, it was a little after six o'clock on Saturday evening. My loft was sparkling clean, and burning incense killed the smell of Will's funky socks. Since he was a better cook than me, I'd asked him to dress up some pork chops before he left. I had those cooking in the oven, along with some steamed vegetables on the stove.

A few minutes later, there was a knock at the door. I had on nothing but a white apron that covered my bare muscular chest, and a pair of Sean John jeans. Pretending to be a gourmet chef, I opened the door with a wooden spoon in my hand. I was shocked to see it was Felicity. Since she sported a black eye and a frown on her face, I couldn't help but invite her in.

"More drama, I guess," I said with little sympathy.

She seemed embarrassed and held her head down. Her flower-print dress was torn on the shoulder, and a scratch was visible on her left cheek. "Brandon, I don't know what is happening to my life. Kurt ended our relationship, and Jabbar—"

"Jabbar what?" I asked. I closed the door and we both headed to the couch.

"He hurt me."

"And? I guess he would, since you told him you and I had sex." She rolled her eyes and couldn't even look at me. "Felicity, why did you tell him about you and me? You told me that you hadn't talked to him. I guess that was a lie too."

"I had to tell the detectives about us, because they took me in for questioning. In return, they told Jabbar what I said. Today, I was at the grocery store minding my own business, and he stopped me. We went to his car and talked, and when I shoved him back for trying to kiss me, he got angry and hit me."

"Look," I said, and then stood up, "I'm sorry about all of this, but I really don't have time for it. I don't know who or what to believe, but keep me out of this shit, please! You, Jabbar, and Cassandra played this fucking game, and now you have to deal with it. I'm truly sick of it!"

I walked off into the kitchen and Felicity followed. I stood at the stove and turned off the burner where I was cooking the veggies. Felicity tried to rub the side of my face. I grabbed her hand.

"No, Felicity! Don't touch me."

"Why are you so angry with me? I've been the only person who's been honest with you about everything."

I couldn't help but laugh at her joke. The only reason I let her in was because I thought Kurt found out about us and decided to kick her ass. But my company was on the way, and I wasn't trying to hear about Felicity's issues with Jabbar. "Unfortunately, I gotta wrap this up. Maybe I'll call you later so we can talk, but now is not a good time. I'm expecting company soon."

Felicity stared at me and wiped the tears that had fallen from her eyes. Now, I could see right through her. She was up to no good, and so much more about her didn't sit right with me.

"I can't believe how cold you've been toward me. I truly thought you cared for me, Brandon. I would have done—"

My voice got louder. "Felicity, go!"

She took a hard swallow, and clutched her purse close to her. "Before I go, can I please use your bathroom?"

"Sure. Do whatever. Just hurry it up."

She walked off to my bathroom and I glanced over at the clock on the wall. Thirty minutes had passed since Evelyn said she was on her way. I knew she would be here soon, and I didn't want any trouble.

I opened the oven and checked on the pork chops. They still weren't ready, and since Felicity was taking so long in the bathroom that I went to see what was up with her. When I got to the doorway, I was shocked. She stood crying hysterically, with a blade pressed against her wrist. Her opened purse was lying on the floor. I rushed in and snatched the blade from her hand.

"Damn! What in the fuck are you trying to do?" I yelled.

"I hate myself, Brandon," she sobbed. "Why is it that I'm never good enough for a man? Why?"

My heart raced. All I could do was wrap my arms around her for comfort. I guess her unstable relationship with Kurt, Cassandra's death, and Jabbar's abuse was a lot for her to handle. Not to mention my disrespect. I rubbed her messy hair back, and she continued to sob on my chest.

"It's all right. I know you've been through a lot these past few months, but you can't let this kind of stuff get to you. You're a beautiful person, Felicity, and don't let anybody tell you any differently."

My words calmed her somewhat. I walked her over to my bed, and as soon as we took a seat, she was all over me.

"Brandon, make love to me, please," she begged. "I'll do whatever you want me to do."

I couldn't believe that after what had just happened, all she wanted to do was have sex. I tried hard to have sympathy for her, and under the circumstances, I had to be careful not to hurt her feelings.

"We . . . we can't have sex right now, Felicity." I pulled her tight embrace from around my neck. She pulled harder, but when I heard a knock at the door, I got loose. "Please, stay here until I explain to my guest your reason for being here. And don't do anything stupid, okay? I promise I'll be back." Felicity didn't respond, and I rushed to answer the door.

Seeing Evelyn made my heart melt. She had on a short magenta dress that dipped low in the front and showed her cleavage. As always, her hair was perfect, her makeup was right, and her arched eyebrows made her face look even more beautiful. She made me want to break it down for her right there and I couldn't wait to feel what the night had in store for us.

She entered and tossed the scarf around her neck to the

side. Smiling, she showed me a tiny black bag she held in her hand.

"Pick your mouth up off the floor, Brandon. Since you're always bringing me something nice, I thought I'd do the same for you."

I took the bag from her hand. Before I could even explain the reason Felicity was there, she came from my bedroom covered in my satin sheets. Evelyn's smile vanished as she looked in Felicity's direction and then mine. It was evident that she was at a loss for words, and so was I.

"Brandon," Felicity said, "what is she doing over here?"

Evelyn wasted no time in turning around and reaching for the doorknob. I grabbed her hand and spoke softly.

"Please don't leave." I turned to Felicity and yelled, "Why do you keep playing these damn games with me? Bitch, are you crazy?"

Calling Felicity a bitch slipped, and Evelyn couldn't stand for much more. She gave me an evil stare.

"See, this is what I was afraid of. Handle your business with your *bitch*, and call me some other time."

"I wasn't no bitch before she got here," Felicity said. "You—"

I wanted to fuck Felicity up, but I had to stay close to Evelyn so she wouldn't leave.

"Do you really think I would've invited you over here if something was going on with her? Don't be foolish and believe what she's saying. I swear, there ain't nothing going on between us."

Felicity walked closer to us and grinned like the shit was funny.

"Whoever you are, Brandon is a liar. Him and I just got finished—"

I didn't let another word spill from Felicity's mouth. Before I knew it, I released my hand from Evelyn's and reached for Felicity. My hands went straight for her neck, and I squeezed it tight. We both fell back on the floor, and she squirmed around, trying to break my grip. My mind was gone, until I turned my head and saw that Evelyn had left.

I hopped up and ran to the door to see if I could catch her. I heard her heels moving down the steps and I went after her. By the time I reached her, she was already in her car, backing up. I stood, watching her leave, and desperately pleaded for her to stay.

"Hear me out, please!" I yelled. But she drove away, and I stood there, looking like a fool.

I gritted my teeth and went back inside to deal with Felicity. When I got back to my loft, there was no sign of her. I searched my rooms, but she was gone. She must have taken the back stairs to exit, and that was good for her, because I probably would have killed her.

I locked my door and headed for the kitchen. I'd already smelled smoke, and when I opened the oven, I saw that the pork chops were burnt to a crisp. I fanned away the smoke, reached for an oven mitt, and pulled out the pan. I threw the pan against the wall. My forehead was lined with wrinkles, and I snatched my keys off the counter, slamming the door on my way out.

When I arrived at Evelyn's house, I knew she was there because her car was in the driveway. I got out and banged hard on her door. She didn't answer, so I banged harder.

"Go away, Brandon. If you don't, I'll call the police."

"I don't give a damn about the police!" I yelled. "You've got to give me a chance to explain what happened!"

"I don't have to give you nothing. Just get off my property and stay the hell away from me!"

I ignored Evelyn and banged some more. When she didn't answer, I figured she had probably moved away from the door to go call the police. I kept turning the doorknob and pleading for her to open the door. It finally swung open.

"Have you lost your freaking mind?" she yelled.

I wiped the sweat from my forehead. "No, I haven't, but—"

She reached up and smacked the shit out of me. I lowered my eyelids and stood still for a moment. When I stepped forward, I slammed the door behind me. She slapped me again and stepped backward.

"Get out of my house!" she yelled.

I pulled the apron off my chest and moved forward again. "Slap me again," I said calmly.

She slapped me harder, glanced at my chest, and inched her way backward. I placed my hand on my silver belt buckle to undo it. I slowly eased the belt out of the loops on my jeans.

"Your smack wasn't hard enough, so do it again."

Evelyn looked down at the belt I held in my hand and appeared frightened. She eased her way back to the arm of the couch. I wanted to use my belt as a weapon, but instead, I pushed her back on the couch. She fell backward and quickly sat up on her elbows.

"If you hurt me—"

"I'm not going to hurt you," I whispered. I unzipped my pants and pulled them down. I tossed the belt over to the side and walked around to the front of the couch. Evelyn swung herself around, looked at my naked body, and stood up.

"You need to leave," she said, still full of anger.

I pushed her back on the couch again and leaned over her. I held my arms up and looked down at her.

"Why do you keep making this so difficult? I don't want nobody else but you. Felicity was upset because her boyfriend ended it with her. Now she's trying to make shit hard for me because we used to be involved. I told her you were on your way, but—"

I stopped talking because I saw the unconcerned look in Evelyn's eyes.

"I don't want to hear about you and your tramps, Brandon. Men like you think that women are fools."

Before she could say another word, I leaned in and kissed her with much pressure, and she bit down hard on my lip. She smacked me again, and when she shoved my chest, I grabbed her wrist.

"You don't give up," she said, trying to pull her wrist away.

Showing her that I wasn't going to give up, I released her wrist and dealt with her resistance. As she pushed me backward, I gripped the sides of her dress and pulled it up over her hips. She didn't have on any panties, and when I moved my face between her legs, she lifted my head and held it back.

"I don't want this," she said, struggling to keep my head from going between her legs. She tried to rush off the couch, but I grabbed her waist and pushed her back down. She pressed her hand against the side of my face to keep it turned. "You . . . you can't make me do this, Brandon. I want you to leave. Now."

I placed my hand over hers and wrestled it from against my face.

"Please stop this," I begged and tightly held her hands. "I know you've been through some shit, but I'm not him, Evelyn. Do you think I'm here to waste my time?"

"I'm not sure why you're here, but I'm not going to let you add me to your collection of women. And I'm not going to stand by and let you break my heart either."

"Never," I said, releasing my grip on her hands. I leaned down to peck her thighs, and since she let me peck them, I figured I was in business. I took it further and separated her pussy with the long tip of my curled tongue.

Her forgiveness became obvious. She got comfortable, widened her legs, and placed them on my shoulders. She raked her fingers through the waves in my hair and swayed her fingers across my back.

"You're soooo good at this," she moaned. "If you keep giving it to me like this, how can I resist you?"

I couldn't talk to Evelyn because I was busy. Once she broke off an orgasm, I stood up. I pulled her up with me and lifted her dress over her head.

"I'm sorry about what happened at my place. You have to know that's in no way, shape, or form how I treat women."

"I hope not, but like I said, please don't put me in your mess with your other women. I'm not the kind of woman who will put up with it for long."

I tossed Evelyn's dress to the side, and she sat on the couch in front of me. She held my goods in her hands, and for the first time, she gave me head. She massaged my ass and I held her head steady and focused. As I stood, my legs trembled. I got ready to come, and leaned her back on the couch while stroking her mouth at a slow rhythm. My buttocks tightened, and my body got weak.

Once I regrouped from my explosion, I carried Evelyn to her bedroom and apologized again for what had happened. I was glad that she'd forgiven me, and I don't know what I would have done to Felicity had she not. I expected her to continue on with her games, but the next time I saw her, I knew it was going to be ugly.

CHAPTER 14

I spent nearly the entire day with Evelyn. We ate breakfast, exercised, showered, watched football, and before I left, we had sex again. I was worn out, and if I didn't get a chance to get home and rest, I knew another sick call was coming soon.

I was glad to see that Will wasn't at home. That gave me a chance to get some sleep without any interruptions. I climbed into bed, and within seconds, I was out. I hadn't dreamed about Cassandra in a few days, but no sooner had I closed my eyes than there she was. She had a sad, disgusted, and hurtful look on her face that made me want to comfort her.

During my dream, I did just that, and when I asked her what was wrong, she told me I was a disappointment. She claimed I wasn't the man she thought I was, and she laughed about her relationship with Jabbar. Her laughter became louder and louder—so loud that it broke my sleep.

I jumped up and rubbed my eyes. I couldn't get back to sleep, so I reached over at five o'clock in the morning to call Ruby.

"Hello," she said in a groggy voice.

"Hey, Ruby. It's Brandon."

"Why haven't you returned my phone calls?" Ruby asked.

"I've been calling you a lot too, and I've left you several messages. Didn't you get them?"

"No, I didn't."

I wasn't sure why Ruby hadn't gotten my messages, but I'd left them almost every day. "Is everything okay?" I asked.

"No, it's not. Yesterday, the police came by with a search warrant. They tore up my house, and I couldn't stay there no more. Brandon, I think they're going to arrest me."

"Ruby, I'm confused. How can they arrest you and you didn't do anything?"

"It's a set-up, Brandon. They're gonna set me up. I can feel it."

"What about your attorney? You still have an attorney, don't you?"

"Yes, but he wants too much money. Besides, I don't think he believes my story. I'm trying to find a lawyer who believes I'm innocent and who ain't trying to break me."

"Ruby, do you want Jabbar out of the picture? If you give me some money, I can make sure that he never bothers us again."

Ruby was silent for a while before she said, "Getting rid of Jabbar ain't gon' solve my problems. Them other detectives are the ones who keep following me and coming by my house. If you're talking about killing that man, I can't believe you would suggest such a thing."

"Jabbar is the one trying to frame you, Ruby. I know that you want this mess over with, and I know a person who's willing to help. Aren't you tired of being harassed?"

"Don't be foolish, Brandon. I . . . I hate that man, but I plan to take my chances in court. Just be there for me, okay?"

"You know I will, Ruby. If you change your mind, please let me know. All I want to do is help."

"I know you do, but you're going about it the wrong way. Cassandra wouldn't want any of this, and at this point, all we can do is pray."

I agreed, and after Ruby made it clear again that she didn't want to have anything to do with my plan, we ended our call.

Monday was slow at the museum. Evelyn called in sick, so it was rather lonely without her. I called her house to check on her, but I got no answer. Before I left work, I called again, and she still didn't pick up. I was worried about her, and decided I would stop by her place.

My plans were cut short when I left work and saw Jabbar leaning against my car. He was dressed in casual attire, wore an Inspector Gadget hat tilted to the side, and dangled a toothpick from his mouth.

I slowed my pace and walked up to him.

"When is this shit going to stop?" I asked. "Don't you have another case or something else you can work on?"

He got off my car. "Brotha man, I'd like to go somewhere, have a drink with you, and chat."

I headed over to the driver's side of my car. "Please. I ain't got time to sit around and listen to more of your bullshit."

He gave me a stern look. "It's imperative that we talk. I have vital information that might be of importance to you. If you loved Cassandra, then you for damn sure would want to know."

I hesitated, and then unlocked the doors to my car.

"Get in," I said.

"Naw, I'll follow you to Maggie's Soul Food on Delmar. That way, once we're finished, we can go our separate ways."

I nodded and got in my car. After I drove off, I saw Jabbar following me in an older model white Lincoln.

When we got to Maggie's, I went inside, and he came in behind me. We were seated at a booth in the far corner.

"Della," he said to the waitress, "bring me the usual and grab something nice and strong for my friend here."

"I don't drink hard liquor," I said. "A Pepsi will be fine."

Della walked away, and Jabbar looked at me from across the table.

"Before I say anything out of line, I want to apologize to you for what I've been putting you through. At first, I thought you were the one who killed Cassandra, and I was only trying to do my job."

"Jabbar, you knew I didn't kill Cassandra. You wanted to fuck with me because you were involved with her too. I—"

"I loved her too, Brandon. I loved her, and I was angry because she wouldn't let you go. She kept telling me it was over between the two of you, but then I'd spy on y'all, and nothing about y'all's relationship showed me it was over. Right before her murder, she came to me and told me that she broke it off with you, and you were upset. I wasn't lying to you when I told you that she said it was over. I immediately put the blame on you for her murder and started my investigation."

Della came back over to the table with our drinks. After Jabbar gave her a tip, she walked away.

"How did you and Cassandra spend so much time together when she was with me most of the time?" I asked.

"Lies. She'd lie and tell you she was out of town, but she was with me. I went with the flow simply because I thought she'd end it with you. When my feelings got deeply involved, damn right I got angry. I almost fucked her up several times, and we started arguing a lot. She played the victim, and told Annette and her aunt Ruby that I was threatening her and she was afraid of me."

"What about Felicity? How is she involved in all of this?"

"Felicity ain't good for nothing but threesomes, sucking dick, and playing games. A few times, she . . . she joined in with Cassandra and me, but there was never nothing serious between us."

"But the other day, she came to my place sporting a black eye. She claimed you was the one who put it there."

"Yeah, right. Kurt's been kicking her ass around for being such a tramp. The other day, there was a domestic violence call that came from her apartment, and a close friend of mine told me Kurt caught her in the bed with somebody. He beat that ass, and she called the police on him. My partner made Kurt leave, and the rest is history."

I was shocked, but it was all starting to make sense. "Man, you have got to be kidding me. That bit—fucking slut has been playing games with me all along. I seriously thought we were cool, and I can't believe she's been stooping to such low measures. I don't understand why."

"Because the skeeza was jealous of Cassandra. She wanted you, she wanted me, but Cassandra had us both. Honestly, I think she had it out for all of us, but somebody beat her to it in Cassandra's case."

"So you don't think she had anything to do with Cassandra's murder? After what's been happening, I can put her at the top of my list."

"Nah, Felicity ain't smart enough to pull off nothing like that. She couldn't benefit from Cassandra's death like Ruby did."

I shook my head. "Jabbar, I'm not feeling this shit with Ruby. She loved Cassandra and would never do anything to hurt her."

"No doubt, but she loved money more. Ruby stood to gain half a million dollars if something happened to Cassandra. Her house was in foreclosure, she'd been on heavy medication since her husband died, and she owed a doctor who was writing her illegal prescriptions a fortune. The other day, we talked to him, and even though he didn't want to talk, to avoid being arrested, he told us that Ruby promised him fifty thousand dollars a few days after Cassandra was killed."

"It's hard for me to believe something like that."

"Why? Brandon, the woman has been off the rocker since her husband died. She calls herself a psychic and practices all kinds of crazy shit. And her house; it looks like something that came straight from the movie *Carrie*."

I couldn't help but snicker because Jabbar was on point with her house. "So, why are you telling me all of this? If you have such a strong case against Ruby, why hasn't she been arrested?"

"I'm still working on it, but I might need your help, especially since I've been suspended for a while."

"Suspended? For what?"

"Because of too many complaints, nigga."

I smiled. "A suspension serves you right. I hope you think twice before—"

"I'd become obsessed with finding the killer of the woman I loved. You can't blame me for that."

"I guess I can't, but I can't turn my back on Ruby. The only way I will help you is if I know for sure she's guilty."

"Okay, but don't blame me if she gets arrested. Soon! No doubt, she will, but in order to have a solid case, I'm looking for a confession. Think about it, and maybe you can get it for me. I'd appreciate it, and I'm sure Cassandra would too."

I took a sip from my watered-down soda, and Jabbar sipped his brandy. What he said was hard for me to swallow, but I couldn't deny that everything made sense. At this point, he seemed to be honest about his past relationship with Cassandra, and he didn't have anything to gain by telling me lies. If Ruby was responsible, she deserved to go to jail. I just couldn't see myself setting her up. But maybe I had to do what I had to do.

Jabbar placed his glass on the table and cleared his throat.

"I know you might feel as if you can't trust me, Brandon, but to prove to you that you can, I got more news for you. Besides, I feel kind of bad about what I put you through. Let's just say that I owe you one."

"What news?"

"You know the classy, fine woman you've been seeing is bad news. You need to watch your back. And since it would be a shame to see you hurt again, my tip will cost you nothing."

My heart dropped into my stomach. "Evelyn? Have you been seeing Evelyn?"

Jabbar snickered. "Brandon, you have so much to learn about older women. Many of them have mastered the game, and they know how to play men without us ever knowing it. I wish I was tagging that ass, because it looks damn good. But just a little FYI . . . a longtime boyfriend of hers has been sneaking in and out of the back door.

"Through my investigating you, I found out about him. He's five years older than her, has his own business, make lots of money, and he's damn hard to compete with. Don't get yourself into nothing you can't handle."

My heart was crushed, but I tried not to let it show. I knew Evelyn hadn't taken our relationship serious, and now I was hearing that she was using me. At least I knew now what kind of woman I was dealing with. It was up to me to end this before I hurt myself even more.

I took a hard swallow, finished up my soda, and reached my hand out to Jabbar.

"Thanks for the information. I'll get back with you if or whenever need be."

Jabbar slammed his hand with mine and gripped it tightly. "See you around, young blood. In the meantime, don't do nothing stupid like putting a hit out on me. I'm bound to find out about it. And you've got to stop trusting so many people."

He winked, and I let go of his grip. He was right. I couldn't trust no damn body. It had cost me too much hurt, and damn near could've given me many, many years in jail.

I thought about what Jabbar said as I drove by Evelyn's house to see her. Realistically, I was checking up on her, since she hadn't answered any of my earlier calls.

When I got to her house, I got the shock of my life. A brand new Mercedes SUV was in her driveway, and every light in the house was out. My stomach turned. It didn't take long for me to figure out that Jabbar had told me the truth.

I tightened my fist and reached for the handle on my door. I had one leg on the ground before I decided against going to her door. For one, she wasn't my woman and had made no commitments to me. Who was I to tell her who she could or couldn't date? All I was to her was some dick that her nymphomaniac ass had to have whenever she needed it.

I didn't want to make a fool of myself, so I headed home. It was late, and as I neared the door, I heard Will's loud voice inside.

I unlocked the door and pushed it open. Will was sitting on the couch with Stacie, and both of them turned their heads.

"If you're working as many hours as I think, that check should be fat," he joked.

"I stopped for a drink," I said in a slump.

"By the looks of your shirt hanging outside of your pants, I'd say a drink ain't all you had. Besides, the last time I checked, my partna don't drink nothing but soda and wine."

I walked farther into the room and tossed my jacket on the chair. "Well, I wish I had something strong and hard that could knock my ass out. I'm not feeling well."

He took Stacie by her hand and they both stood up. "Listen, we'll go chill at her place. The exterminators were there today, and—"

"Sit down, man. Y'all can chill here. I'll go in my studio for a while and paint."

Will and Stacie sat back down, and I walked off to my room. I took off my work clothes and changed into a pair of white sweat pants. As I made my way through the living room area, Stacie's eyes stuck to my body like glue. She placed her hands between her legs and crossed them. I knew Will saw her lustful eyes, but he tried to play it off.

"If you want it, there's a cold beer in the fridge," he said.

"No thanks," I said, trotting into my studio. I picked up a canvas and placed it on the easel in front of my stool then reached for my paint tray and started on a new painting.

When Will came in and handed the cordless phone to me, I'd been working for about an hour. I asked who it was, but he shrugged and told me that he and Stacie were leaving. I cleared my throat and placed the phone on my ear.

"Hello," I moped.

"Hi, handsome. Did you miss me today?"

I wanted to hang up, but sadly, the sound of Evelyn's voice weakened me. "Yeah, I really did. I missed you a lot."

"Then I guess you can't wait to see me."

"I won't see you because I'm not going to work tomorrow."

"Why not? Are you okay?"

"I was, but I just found out that my mother is ill. In the morning, I'm leaving for Alabama to go see her." I lied because I didn't want to tell her how much her man being at her house hurt my feelings. If I confronted her about it, then she would have known that I'd been checking up on her.

"I'm sorry to hear about your mother. Is there anything I can do to help?"

"Nope."

She hesitated. "Would you like some company tonight?

Before you go to Alabama, I'd like to see you. Maybe I can help lift your spirits."

"Didn't you call in to work sick today?"

"Yes, but I'm feeling better."

That was bullshit, and her answer caused me to challenge her response. "I'm sure you are. Your ex must have really put something on you today."

"Listen, is there something on your mind? Your tone is awfully shitty, and I don't like it one bit."

"Then don't call me no fucking more!" I clicked her off and laid the phone on the floor. It rang two more times, and then it stopped.

I hadn't intended for my relationship with Evelyn to go down this road, but I was hurt. I walked over to the tall windows and looked outside. Many pedestrians strolled up and down Washington Avenue, as if the night was still young. The lights from the ground glared off the Gateway Arch, and Highway 70 was packed.

Why me? I thought. Why was all this bad shit happening to me? The thoughts of how serious Jabbar and Cassandra's relationship had been was making me crazy, and so were the thoughts of Evelyn kicking it with her man. All she had to do was tell me she was still involved with him. The truth would've made it easier for me, but I guess that was asking too much of her. The most painful thing about it was that I'd thought Evelyn was a straight-forward woman. She claimed to be, and pretended as if playing games wasn't in her vocabulary. Then again, I'd thought the same thing about Cassandra. How did I ever let this happen to me again? My mind was on overload as I stood by the window, looking outside.

I got back to my picture, and almost an hour later, there was a knock at the door. I laid my paints and brush on the floor and got up to see who it was. I asked who was there, and that's when I heard Evelyn's voice. I opened the door, and she couldn't wait to tear into me.

"I know for a fact that you didn't hang up on me. Your phone better be disconnected, and if it's not, then you've got some explaining to do," she said, walking inside.

I cut my eyes at her and showed major disinterest. "I don't have to explain nothing to you, Evelyn. I'm tired of you calling the shots. If you came here to argue with me, I'm not in the mood."

"I bet if I came here to fuck you, you'd be in the mood for that."

I slammed the door. "Don't flatter yourself, baby. Your sex ain't all that."

"And neither is yours," she said, making her way over to my couch.

"Well, get the hell out then! Go back to your ex-boyfriend and pretend you never met me."

She took a seat on the couch. "I wish it were that easy, but it's not. I . . . I don't know why you keep bringing up my ex, but ain't nothing going on between us anymore."

I walked to the arm of the couch and sat on it. "Then what was he doing at your house today? And don't lie, because I stopped by there after work. I saw his car in your driveway, and there wasn't one light on in your house."

Her eyebrows arched. "Are you checking up on me or something?"

"No. I stopped by to see how you were feeling, but I guess he beat me to it."

"For your information, he was there because I'd blown several fuses and didn't know how to change them. I called you at work, but Jennifer said you'd already left. When he called, he said he was in the neighborhood, and I asked him to stop by.

"While he was there, yes, he tried to do more than change my fuses, but I wasn't having it. I'm not going to lie and tell you we're not friends, because we are. But that's as far as it goes."

"What about earlier today? I've been trying to reach you all day, Evelyn."

She snapped. "I don't have to tell you my every move. But since you're all bent out of shape about this, I called in sick because my son and his wife have been having some marital problems. I spent the day with them to see if I could help them work things out."

I cut my eyes at her again. "Why you got all that snap in your voice? You need to chill out with that shit."

She stood up and headed for the door. "I see that coming here was a waste of time. You don't want to listen to me, so go ahead and clutter your thick head with what you want to believe. It just proves to me how immature—"

I didn't let her utter another word. I grabbed her neck, and in her defense, she dug her nails into my hands. Her anger toward me always turned me on, and she knew how to push the right buttons. She often played hard to get, and it was times like this that I wanted to show her she could be easily got. I lightened up on my grip and gently pecked down her neck. She tried to avoid me, but couldn't.

"Why do you like to play these rough games, Brandon? Grabbing my neck like that is no way to handle me."

"Then tell me how to handle you, Evelyn. Since I'm so immature, why don't you share with me how to handle you?"

"Gently." She spoke softly. "I like to be handled gently."

"Well, sorry. That doesn't work for me all the time."

She reached for the doorknob. "Then I'm out of here."

I picked up Evelyn and tossed her on my shoulder. She resisted as I carried her to my bedroom and laid her back on the bed.

"Brandon, we can't continue to do this—mad at each other one minute and having sex the next. I have never had this much sex with one man in my life!"

I chuckled, and before things got started, I made a suggestion. "I want you to tie me up."

She looked at me as if I'd called her a bitch or something. "What did you say? Tie you up?"

"Yes. I want you to tie me up and ride me. When I get loose, I want to tie you up and work you from your backside. I have some other things in mind, but my toys are in my closet. If you—"

Evelyn stood up and held her ripped dress together. "Look, I gotta go. I don't know what kind of sex you like to have, but I'm not into that kinky stuff."

I grabbed her arm. "Don't leave. If you haven't tried kinky sex, how you gon' say you won't enjoy yourself?"

She snatched her arm away from me and spoke calmly. "Don't grab on me like that anymore. Right now, I don't know what the hell I'm feeling. But I do know that no matter what your request may be, I don't get down like that, all right?"

I lay back on the bed and stared up at the ceiling. No doubt, as I listened to the front door slam, I was pissed. If she wanted this relationship to continue, she'd have to eventually get with the program.

CHAPTER 15

Icalled in sick for two days. I knew I was putting my job in jeopardy, but I couldn't face Evelyn, and I was also kind of upset because Will told me he was moving with Stacie. That, of course, cut into the money he'd been giving me, so I knew I'd either have to find another job or somehow put in more hours. I wasn't prepared to do either one, and my absences from work weren't helping me at all.

Down and out, I sat on the living room couch and flipped through the channels. Will had his belongings placed at the door, and had gone to the bathroom to take a leak. When he came out, he zipped his pants and reached out his hand to grab mine.

"Nah, that's all right, man. No need for the handshake . . . and you didn't wash your hands," I joked.

"Fuck you, man." He laughed and then sat on my legs. "Why the long face? I know you ain't gon' miss me."

"Hell, naw. Now, get your bony ass off my legs. It ain't like they doing no damage, but you need to get the hell up."

We both laughed, until I saw a familiar face on TV and told Will to be quiet. We stared at the TV in disbelief, as it displayed a picture of Ruby. The news reporter said that Ruby had been arrested for the murder of Cassandra White. I couldn't believe it. My mouth hung wide open. Jabbar said she'd be arrested, and I guess he must have gotten the evidence he needed. I felt so bad for Ruby as I turned up the volume to listen to the details.

According to the reporter, the chief of police said he had enough evidence to incarcerate her for a long time. He didn't go into details, but expressed that the prosecutor would be able to win the case unquestionably.

"Damn," Will said, standing up. "That's messed up. You mean to tell me that Ruby murdered her own damn niece?"

I was confused and very hurt that Ruby had been lying to me all along. Cassandra really loved her, and Ruby put all of us in a bad and hurtful situation. "I . . . I guess she did do it. I can't believe she's been lying to me all this time."

"Shit, if you killed somebody, you'd lie too. She had to know that she'd get busted sooner or later."

My phone rang and I looked over at it. "Do you want me to get it?" Will asked.

"Naw, man. It might be Ruby, or possibly Cassandra's mother. I don't want to talk to nobody. As a matter of fact, I'm getting my number changed."

"I don't blame you one bit. How did you manage to get yourself involved with such a whack-ass family? You should've known something was up when Cassandra was closer to her aunt than she was to her own damn mother. I bet it's some drama that follows that story."

"Yeah, and I never really asked why. I knew her for all those years and never got a chance to really get to know her family. I mean, Ruby and me were cool, but I always thought she was a bit weird. And her house . . . you've never been inside, but that motherfucker is scary. I could shoot myself for being so blind. And if this mess is finally over, I'll be glad about that."

* * *

Will hung around for another hour before he jetted. I told him if things didn't work out with him and Stacie, he'd always have a place to come back to.

After Will left, I went to my room and lay back on the bed. I was having a hard time dealing with what Ruby had done. If she was responsible for the murder, then I was pleased she was behind bars.

Throughout the entire day, I didn't answer the phone because I didn't want to talk to anyone. But what if it was Evelyn? I thought. I hadn't heard from her since Monday night, and I missed her already.

Finally, I reached for the phone and answered it the next time it rang. Surprisingly, it was Jabbar.

"Did you see the news today?" he asked.

"Yeah." I swallowed. "I guess your case is finally closed."

"Solid," he said. "We found more evidence, and Ruby is going to spend the rest of her life in jail. Just a word of advice: if she calls you, I wouldn't take her calls. She'll probably try to manipulate you into believing her, and it's best that you get on with your life and leave well enough alone."

"I agree. Besides, tomorrow my number will be changed. I never got a chance to thank you as well, so, on behalf of the woman I once loved, thank you for handling your business."

Jabbar hung up. As much as I wanted to believe that this was all over, I couldn't. There was something missing, but I couldn't quite put my finger on it. My gut still wouldn't let me trust Jabbar, but maybe that was because of his connection with Cassandra. I had to admit that the information he'd provided me with seem factual and was credible. And as much as I didn't want to, I had to give credit to the man for working so hard to find the killer of the woman he loved. He'd definitely earned my respect.

Either way, I decided that day to put full closure to the situation. Cassandra's killer had been arrested, even though, after the way she disrespected me and our relationship, a huge part of me didn't give a damn if the killer was caught.

The next day, I went to work feeling well rested. As soon as I walked in, Jennifer was waiting for me. She asked me to come to her office, and once inside, she closed the door.

"Have a seat, Brandon."

I took a seat and looked across the desk at her.

"You've been taking too many days off. Now, I know your mother is ill, but you haven't called me since Tuesday."

"I'm sorry, Jennifer. My mother was tested for cancer, and the whole family was on pins and needles as we waited for the results. Everything came back okay, but the doctors want to run more test on her because something is definitely wrong."

"I'm sorry to hear that. The only thing I ask is you not forget about your job. All you have to do is call in and tell me what's going on. I'm very flexible, but I have to find someone to cover for you when you're not here."

"I understand. Going forward, if I ever have to take off again, I promise to keep you informed."

"Good," she said. "Now, your early tour will be arriving shortly. You're doing a good job, Brandon, and I hope you'll be around for a long time."

"Me too," I said. I stood up, thanked Jennifer for being so kind, and left.

I didn't see Evelyn until almost noon. She gave me a fake grin and walked right past me. It bothered me, but I wasn't going to cry about it. If my way of lovemaking scared her away, then too bad.

By day's end, it was evident that she wasn't bothered by me ignoring her either. I saw her hurrying to her car, and a man was on the driver's side. As they drove off, she seemed to be all smiles. I shook my head. I could only be mad at myself for getting involved.

* * *

The weekend was nice and rather quiet. I dabbled around in my studio, and then changed clothes so I could go check out an R&B band on Laclede's Landing. The night before, Will told me that he and Stacie would be there, and he asked if I had a date to bring along. I told him I didn't, but foolishly, I called Evelyn and asked her to meet me there. She didn't answer, but I left the message on her voicemail.

When I got to the club, all I could hear on the outside were drums beating, singing that sounded more like yelling, and symbols crashing. I paid the ten-dollar cover charge and walked inside. The place was packed with white folks, and fake smoke covered the dance floor while people danced. The band for damn sure wasn't R&B, sounding like a rock group instead. I counted the mere six black people in the club, and just as I was about to head out, I spotted Will and Stacie. He yelled at me over the loud, disturbing music.

"Where are you going?" he asked.

"Home! I can't take the noise!"

"Just bear with it! They'll be wrapping it up in a bit. Soon, this place will be swarming with black folks."

Not having much else to do, I opted to stay. I went to the bathroom, took a leak, and checked myself in the mirror. My black bootleg jeans with a rugged cut at the bottom hung over my square-toed shoes. The jeans worked well with my black silk shirt, which had a single button and revealed my chest and six-pack. I had a silver dog tag around my neck, and my diamond earring put me in a class of my own. My hair was neatly lined, and I'd shaved my thin beard and goatee. To my satisfaction, I left the bathroom on a serious high.

The music was going wild, and the white chicks were all up on me. I couldn't find Will or Stacie, so when this attractive, tall blonde asked me to dance, I went to the dance floor with her.

As we danced, I couldn't help but laugh to myself. These

people seriously had no rhythm. All they knew how to do was rub against each other and jump up and down on the floor. When Blondie rubbed herself against me, I went with the flow. One of her girlfriends came over and worked me from the back. They made a sandwich out of me and rubbed their hands all over my body.

After a few more songs, I called it quits. My sweat had my shirt sticking to my body, and I had to go cool off. When I exited the floor, I saw Stacie sitting in a chair by herself. I walked over to her, but the white chicks followed behind me.

"Hey," the blonde said, tugging on my shirt. "Would you like something to drink?"

"In a minute," I yelled over the loud music. "I'll be over to the bar in a minute!"

They giggled and danced over to the bar. I made my way to Stacie.

"Where's Will?" I asked.

Stacie looked bored. "I'on know. He said he'd be back in a minute."

I nodded to the fast beat and looked around the noisy club. "I ain't never been to a place this packed. White folks sure in the hell know how to party, don't they?"

"Yeah, I guess. It's pretty cool. Do you feel like dancing?"

"Not right now. Later."

I looked over at the bar and saw the two chicks I danced with sitting on top of the bar, taking shots from the bartender. They were downing drinks like water.

"I'll be back," I yelled. "When Will comes back, tell him to stay right here, okay?"

Stacie rolled her eyes and nodded.

I eased my way through the crowd and felt many hands rubbing on my dick. The place was too packed to see who it was, but as I looked for the culprit, I noticed several more white girls dancing in a circle giggling. I stepped up to the bar, and Blondie and her friend rushed over to me.

"Are you ready for something to drink?" the friend asked.

"Yeah. I'll take an ice cold Pepsi."

They laughed and yelled for the bartender to bring me a Pepsi. He hurried to our end of the bar and fixed me a drink that tasted nothing like Pepsi. I squeezed my eyes and damn near choked. My chest burned like fire.

"What in the hell is this?" I said, looking at the glass.

"Pepsi. One more shot," they chanted.

I laughed, and since I decided to get a bit loose tonight, I asked the bartender to hit me with another shot.

"Damn," I said, taking a big swallow. "How do y'all drink this shit?"

They laughed and pulled me back onto the dance floor. Soon, I didn't know what the hell I was doing. My vision was blurred, my forehead was sweating, and my dick was hard as ever. My dance partners kept touching it, and they whispered all kinds of nasty and freaky things in my ear. After a while, my body got limp and my eyelids were slowly fading. A headache had formed from the loud music, and I was feeling very light on my feet.

I glanced over at the chair where Stacie had been sitting, but she wasn't there. I scanned the club for Will, but I didn't see him either. I did, however, see Evelyn leaned against a pole, watching me. My eyes connected with hers.

I excused myself from the ladies and headed in Evelyn's direction. The closer I walked to her, the farther away she seemed. All I could see was a blurred vision of her angry face.

Appearing to be closer, I reached for the pole and held on to it. I stood face to face with her and smiled.

"Wha . . . what took you so long getting here?" I slurred.

"I've been here for about thirty minutes. Just thought I'd sit back and enjoy the scenery."

I looked Evelyn up and down. She was dressed in brown leather pants and a matching halter with fringes. Her stilettos went well with her fit, and so did her brimmed hat, which set the whole outfit off. She looked better than any woman in the place, and from the stares she was getting, she knew it.

She took my hand and escorted me back to the dance floor. This one chick jumped in front of me, and Evelyn put her hand up in the chick's face.

"If you don't mind, he's with somebody. Please don't be rude."

The chick backed away, and Evelyn turned to face me. The beat was still jumping, and even though everybody around us was dancing wildly, we stood close and left no breathing room between us. I slowly rubbed my hand up and down on her bare back, and she reached her hands up my shirt to touch my chest.

"I'm ashamed of you, Brandon Fletcher. I didn't think I'd ever see you so sloppy drunk."

I was so happy to see her that I decided not to question her about the man she'd gotten in the car with. Now wasn't the time nor the place to kick up a heated conversation. I was just glad to be enjoying myself.

"I . . . I'm not drunk. Tipsy, but not drunk."

"Before you pass out on me, can we get out of here?" she asked.

"And what . . . where would you like to go?"

"I don't care. Your place? Mine? It doesn't matter."

I removed her hat from her head and placed it on mine. I took her hand and we maneuvered our way through the crowd once again. I headed in a direction away from the exit. Evelyn asked where we were going.

"We need to chill for a minute. I don't think I can make it to your place or mine."

I pushed the doors open to the men's restroom, and Evelyn tried to ease her hand away from mine. "I'm not going in there, Brandon."

"Come on, baby. I just need to splash some water on my face or something. I don't want to pass out in there all by myself."

Evelyn pulled me toward the ladies' lounge.

"I'll get you some water in here. Come on and follow me."

I followed Evelyn and we made our way inside. All the ladies looked at me, but most of them just smiled. We stood by the sinks, and Evelyn grabbed a paper cup and filled it with water.

"Here," she said, handing it to me. "Drink this."

I took the cup and splashed the water in my face. I gave the cup back to her.

"Ahhhh, that felt good. More," I said. "Put some more in there."

She filled the cup again and tossed the water. She aimed it at my face, but it splashed on my neck and on my shirt. She covered her mouth.

"I'm so sorry," she said with a laugh. "My aim isn't worth a damn."

"And neither is mine," I said. I reached for another cup, filled it up, and tossed it on her. She got soaked.

"Oh, no you didn't," she said. She grabbed another cup, and we went back and forth, splashing water on each other. The other ladies in the bathroom cleared out, and I slid over to the door and locked it.

"Your ass is in trouble now," I said, sliding on the wet floor. Evelyn tossed more water on me, and I went crashing to the floor on my butt. She thought it was funny and laughed hysterically. I hurried off the floor and grabbed her around her waist. I backed her into the first bathroom stall and closed the door.

Of course, she resisted. "Brandon, hell no. Let me out of this stall right now. I don't get down—"

I covered her mouth with my hand. "Shhh, let's do something wild. We only got minutes, maybe seconds, before somebody bangs on that door. Let me into your pussy for a few minutes, please."

Evelyn didn't respond, so I unzipped my pants and they dropped to my ankles. I unfastened the button on her pants and unzipped them. I pulled them over the hump of her ass, and once she stepped out of them, I lifted her. She wrapped her arms around my neck and straddled my hips.

Instantly, I went inside of her. I slapped her body against mine and we fucked hard against the stall. There were no interruptions, so I pulled down her halter and placed her wet and sweaty breast in my mouth. I laced her nipple with the saliva from my tongue, and continued to slide my dick deep inside of her. Several knocks interrupted us, but we ignored them.

"Brandon, wha . . . what kind of woman are you turning me into? I've never—" she moaned in a soft, pleasing voice. She pulled my head up from her breasts and kissed me like kissing was going out of style. "I can't believe you've got me giving myself to you in such a way. It's like I'm becoming a totally different woman."

"You're only becoming the woman I always knew you could be," I whispered.

I focused hard on making us come together. Soon, the bangs on the door got harder, and we heard shouting.

"Are you ready?" I said, taking deep breaths. "Let's do this together."

She nodded, and I circled my tongue on her nipple again. I flicked and licked around it, and sped up my pace down below. I made sure that each of my entries rubbed against her clitoris, and used my finger to assist. Evelyn was on major fire, and so was I. Our *uhmm*s, *damn*s, and *ahhh*s loudly echoed through the bathroom, and once our juices flowed, we both needed a moment to regroup.

"That was good," I said with my head lying against her chest.

"Yes, it was. But we got to open the door and get out of here."

I snapped out of my trance and quickly raised my pants. I left the stall, but Evelyn stayed behind to straighten her clothes. When I unlocked the door, several women pushed on it and rushed in. They knew what time it was, but only one of them said something to me.

"Next time, get a room. When a girl's gotta tinkle, she don't want to wait."

I smiled and walked out. Shortly after, Evelyn walked out and looked at me standing with my hands in my pockets. She walked up and stood in front of me.

"You look so sexy," she said. "But by the lines on your forehead, I can tell your headache is banging. Next time, hopefully, you'll think twice before drinking so much alcohol."

"Maybe so," I said. I took her by the hand, and she led us out the door. Tonight, I wanted to talk to Evelyn about her ill treatment of me at work, and about her relationship with this other man. It was seriously becoming a problem for me, and as strongly as I felt for her, I knew I couldn't continue on the way things were. She had to make a decision; either it was going to be me or him. There was no way for her to have us both.

CHAPTER 16

I tossed and turned, sweat dripping from my forehead. When I squinted, I was lying naked in my bedroom, with no covers over me. I blinked a few times, and then widened my eyes to check the time. My alarm clock showed 5:15 AM. I sat up quickly and held my stomach, feeling the need to throw up. I didn't know if it was from the alcohol or from the dream I'd had about Cassandra.

In the dream, she was angry at me for allowing Aunt Ruby to take the rap, and she felt as if I knew who was responsible. When I told her there was nothing I could do, she smacked me. That's when I woke up.

I heard the TV on in the living room, so I stumbled to my doorway to see what was up.

Evelyn was a sight for early-morning, tired, and hung-over eyes. I was so drunk last night that I didn't get a chance to speak with her about my concerns. I knew it would possibly lead to an argument, but there were some things that I had to get off my chest.

Evelyn sat on the couch, eating a bowl of ice cream, with

her bare feet pressed against the edge of my table. She wore a black lace bra, which gave her somewhat small breasts a lift, and matching lace high-cut shorts. I couldn't see her butt, but I could only imagine.

"Good morning, sleepyhead," she said while licking the spoon.

"Good morning," I said. Naked, I plopped down next to her and leaned my head on her shoulder. "I'm almost afraid to ask how we got here, but you must tell me."

She pulled her shoulder away, and I lifted my head. "Do you really want to know?"

"Yes, I really want to know."

"Well . . ." She paused and licked the spoon again. "Let's just say that you passed out on me. One of the bouncers from the club helped put you in the car, and when we got here, the building's manager was on hand to assist."

I was shocked. "Are you serious?"

"As a heart attack." She smiled.

"But how did my clothes get off? Last I remember, I had on my clothes."

"And you did, until we got here."

Evelyn stood up, and my eyes immediately jumped to her juicy butt cheeks bulging out of the bottom of her lace shorts. That fast, my dick had swelled, and she watched it grow. She smiled and reached for a pillow on the couch. She dropped it into my lap to cover my hardness.

"You'll have to wait until I get another bowl—"

I removed the pillow and pulled her down sideways on my lap. I wrapped my arms around her and looked into her eyes.

"What did you do to me last night?" I asked.

"What do you think a woman would do to a man who's passed the hell out while lying naked? I had fun with you, that's all. Too bad you don't remember."

I grinned and leaned in for a kiss. Evelyn placed her fingers on my lips. "Wait until I get back. I want another bowl of ice cream."

"The ice cream can wait."

"No, I said wait, okay? I want some ice cream, and I need to discuss some things with you."

I removed my arms from around Evelyn and she stood up. She purposely teased me with the swish in her hips, and turned around to see if I was watching her.

"Yeah, you got my attention," I said, holding my dick in my hand.

Evelyn winked. "I'd better." She walked off.

I couldn't help but think how lucky I was to have her. Maybe I did need to consider being the other man. Eventually, as good as I'd be to her, she'd be forced to tell the other man to go to hell. I just didn't know how serious this thing was between them, and Evelyn had to be truthful with me about her situation.

Evelyn held the bowl of ice cream in her hand and sat sideways on my lap again. I held her as close to me as I could. She put a scoop in her mouth, and then scooped up some ice cream for me.

"Open your mouth," she said.

I shook my head. "I don't eat ice cream this early in the morning. I would like another kiss, though."

"By the way, your manhood is poking me from the back. It's obvious that you'd like more than just a kiss. But . . . did you brush your teeth yet? You talking about all this kissing and—"

I took the bowl of ice cream from Evelyn's hand and placed it on the table. I went in for my kiss, and this time, she didn't complain. I leaned her back on the couch, but she stopped me and sat up.

"What's on your mind?" I asked.

"A lot. For starters, the last two times we've had sex, we

haven't used condoms. That's being irresponsible on both of our parts, considering all of the diseases that are out there."

"Is that all you can think about right now is a condom? Baby, I don't have a damn thing—"

"How do you know, Brandon? How do you know if I don't have nothing?"

I wasn't up for this kind of conversation, so I eased away from Evelyn and stood up. "If you did have something, I hope you'd be woman enough to tell me."

I walked off to the kitchen to get a cup of coffee. When I got back into the living room, Evelyn was lying back on the couch. I sat on the floor in front of her.

"You're right, baby. If we continue to get down like we do, then I promise you we'll use condoms, okay?" I said.

"Fine. And it's nice that you agree. Now, last night, while . . . while you were asleep, I did something that maybe I shouldn't have done."

"And what's that?" I asked.

"I searched around your place. I know it was wrong, but I couldn't help it."

"Okay. All's forgiven, because I have nothing to hide."

"So . . . maybe you don't, but I have to ask you some questions about some things I found."

"What if I don't want to answer your questions?"

Evelyn stood up and rubbed her hands together. She took a seat in the chair across from me.

"Damn," I said. "Since you moved all the way over there, I suspect this might get ugly."

"I hope not. And if you don't want to answer—"

I raised my voice a bit. "Evelyn, get to the point, okay?"

She took a hard swallow. "What kind of sexual fetish do you have? I saw all kinds of things in your closet: whips, extension cords, burnt candles, handcuffs . . . vibrators. What's up with that?"

"Depending on who I'm with, I like to take sex to a whole new level. But when I mentioned you tying me up before, you broke out of here like a bat out of hell. I figured you wouldn't want to explore some of the things that I like to do, so that's why I hadn't shared my toys with you. I hope you don't feel that my toys are abnormal."

"Honestly, yes, I do. There couldn't be anything normal about tying yourself up, using whips, burning yourself with candles . . . and a paddle is taking things too far. The pictures I saw of you and another woman were ridiculous. What woman in her right mind would allow such torture?"

"That's your opinion, Evelyn. There are plenty of women who enjoy exploring sex as I do."

"Well, I'm standing my ground. I can't even begin to understand why someone would let you spank them with a paddle or burn them."

"The paddle doesn't hurt. It's used as a form of arousal, and it's intended to cause exciting pain."

"Exciting pain? Why would I want to cause the person I'm making love to any pain?"

"Because maybe the person you're making love to likes it. Besides, you've caused me pain before."

"How and when did this happen?"

"The day I came to your house and you kept smacking me. The harder you smacked, the more I got turned on. Couldn't you tell how excited I was?"

"Brandon, that's crazy. I don't care what you say, but that kind of stuff can be dangerous."

I snapped. "Dangerous? There's no need to go any further with this conversation because that's your opinion, and I have mine. I will not change who or what I am, and I hope you don't try to make me."

She snapped back. "And I won't. But you need to know that if you ever bring any of your *toys* into the bedroom while we're together, it's not going to work out for me. I'm letting you know now, because I'd hate for you to get disappointed."

I placed my index finger on the side of my face and glared at Evelyn. "Next . . . what's your next question?" I asked, letting her know I was ready to change the subject.

"I wasn't finished talking about your toys."

"Well, I'm finished. You've made it clear that you don't want to mess around like that, so we won't."

"And if we don't, does that mean you'll be having sex with other women?"

I rubbed my chin and thought about lying before I answered her question. "Yes, Evelyn, I will definitely have sex with other women. Now, what's your next question?"

"Thanks for being honest, but maybe we shouldn't waste our time thinking that something special is going to come out of this."

"Or maybe we should just take it one day at a time and see what this leads to. That seems like a better approach, wouldn't you agree?"

Evelyn looked away and rolled her eyes. "Who is Cassandra?"

"My ex."

"Ex-girlfriend, ex-wife, ex-lover . . . what?"

"All of the above. First she was my girlfriend, then my lover, and then she was supposed to be my wife."

"And what happened?"

"She left me. Why are you asking?"

"Because for her to be your ex, her presence is awfully visible around here. She's the woman I saw in the freaky photos with you. Even though I'd seen her pictures on the mantle, in your studio, and in your bedroom before, I thought she was a family member. I didn't think you'd be bold enough to display pictures of a woman you'd been intimate with. That's why I hadn't asked about them, but now that I found the pictures in your closet . . ."

"So, I've had a hard time letting go." I looked behind Evelyn at the picture of Cassandra on the mantle.

"I guess my question is, are you still in love with her? And
if she comes back to you, where does that leave us?"

"She's not coming back." My eyes shifted to Evelyn. I was
not going to tell her about Cassandra being murdered because I knew she'd have more questions for me. That kind of
news would scare her, and she already seemed turned off by
my willingness to see other women. So, I kept with my lie.
"She's never coming back because she's happy with who and
where she is. Now, is there any more interrogation?"

Evelyn smiled. "Just a tiny bit. Where's your family? You
seem to be a loner and never have anyone close to you.
Friends . . . do you have any?"

"My family, I don't care to discuss. Bad blood between us.
And friends, I only have one person that I trust. I've mentioned him before. His name is Will."

"Okay, that's fair. Now, my final question: Since I've opted
not to indulge in your sexual escapades, is there anything
that I can do to prevent you from seeing other women?"

I sat silent for a moment, and then stood up, stretched,
and walked over by Evelyn. I kneeled on the floor in front of
her and eased my hands up the sides of her legs.

"Before I answer that, I have a few questions for you."

"Shoot."

"Who was the man who picked you up from work the
other day?"

"My son."

"Have you still been screwing around with your ex? And
how serious is or was your relationship with him?"

"No, I have not been screwing my ex, and a very long time
ago, our relationship was serious. He messed up, and I've
moved on."

I reached my hand up to the back of her bra and unhooked it. The straps fell to her shoulders. "You're a liar, Evelyn. And a good one, at that."

She pushed me gently and I lay back on the floor. She straddled my hips and touched my chest. I reached for my dick, but she squeezed it in her hand. "You're the one who's a liar, Brandon. You promised me, only minutes ago, that you would not go inside of me without a condom. And since we're planning to have an open relationship, I think we need to make sure we protect ourselves."

"So I lied about the condom. But I'm being straightforward with you when I say that if you don't get with the program and accept my ways of exploring lovemaking, there will be nothing that you can say or do to prevent me from seeing other women."

She reached for a condom in her purse and slid it on me.

"Since I know where things stand, I want you to know where they stand as well. What's good for you is good for me. Don't expect something you're not willing to give in return. What's been said today might very well change tomorrow. So, going forward, I want you to be open and understanding of anything that might come your way."

I knew what Evelyn was getting at. It was her way of implying that she was going to see other men. Which, by the way, was something I felt she was doing anyway. Today, I finally knew where things stood between us: the only thing this relationship had going for it was sex.

CHAPTER 17

For the next several weeks, things were just okay between Evelyn and me. We were spending a lot of time together, but she was the one sexually satisfied, not me.

For my own pleasures, I'd been back to the club I went to the night I got drunk. I found many women who were willing to let me have it my way, and I did so on two occasions. I wasn't trying to disrespect Evelyn, but what I told her was true. What one woman wouldn't do, another one surely would.

She kept insisting that her ex was a man of her past, but I didn't trust her word. For my own peace of mind, I'd scoped out her house last Friday night. Sure enough, the Mercedes pulled up, and the same man I'd seen picking her up from work, her ex, went inside. He stayed for quite some time, and when I placed a call to her, of course, she didn't answer. I drove by early the next morning, but his car was gone. He must have gotten what he wanted.

When I called again, she said the ringer had been off. That was a bunch of bull and she knew it. I never mentioned one word about what I knew, because it was obvious that Evelyn couldn't bring herself to tell me the truth. She'd lie again, and that would cause us to argue about something we'd already discussed before.

Whether or not she was truthful, I'd made a decision to go with the flow, and that's what I'd been doing. It made me feel as if I was reliving my situation with Cassandra all over again. This time, however, I knew that another man was involved. And as much as I wanted to, I tried my best not to get mad.

Late Saturday night, I called Evelyn to see if she wanted some company. Earlier, we'd made plans to go to the movies, but she cancelled on me, saying that she wasn't feeling too well. I pretty much knew what that meant, so instead of being cooped up, I put on some clothes and headed for Stacie's place to chill with her and Will. He'd invited me over several times, but since I was so wrapped up with Evelyn, I always told him I had something to do.

When I arrived, Stacie opened the door with a wide grin on her face.

"Brandon, come on in. Your friend know he's crazy," she said with a laugh.

"What's going on?" I said. I stepped into the kitchen, where they sat, playing cards.

"He over there pouting like a baby cause he losing this game; that's what's going on."

"Shut up," Will said. He slammed the cards on the table and gave up five dollars. Stacie slid the money down inside of her bra and laughed.

"Come on, man," he said. "Let me show you around the place."

I followed Will, but a tour wasn't necessary. The place was tiny, the furniture was old and dirty, and the whole place smelled like week-old garbage. Will really wasn't used to nice things, so he bragged a bit about Stacie's place. All I could say was, "That's nice."

After the two-minute tour, we went back into the kitchen and got another game of poker started. I didn't have any money on me to waste, so I played with change instead of dollars. Will dealt the cards and looked suspiciously at his hand.

"Hey, man," he said. "Have you been keeping up with Aunt Ruby's case?"

"Nope," I replied. "Not at all."

"When her trial starts, you should go to the courthouse and stare her ass in the face. Make her feel guilty about what she done."

"I thought about it, but I don't think I could sit there and listen to them bring up all that happened. I got my number changed, and since then, I've been at peace."

"I guess I don't blame you. I still can't believe Cassandra had all that shit going on behind your back. It ain't funny or nothing, but you should've listened to me when I told you something wasn't right with her. I swear to God that I sensed it from day one."

"Will, please don't go there. Can we not talk about this right now? I got a hand over here that's banging, and I need all of the money I can get."

"Me too," Stacie chimed in with her ghetto fabulous self.

We laid our cards on the table, and the first round belonged to me. I was only up six dollars, but a few more hours of this could be beneficial.

For the next several hours, we had a blast talking, laughing, and cheating at cards. Stacie had been busted twice, and it was clear why she'd been winning at almost every hand.

"I quit," I said. "If y'all ain't gon' play right, then ain't no need for us to keep playing."

"I quit too," Will said. "Before you got here, that's what I was complaining about. She be cheating and taking every dime I got."

"Oh, quit your whining, Will. As much money as you borrow from me, this is payback."

Will couldn't say much else. He reached in his pocket and pulled out his wallet. He emptied it and searched through his mess on the table. When I noticed Jabbar's business card in his pile, I picked it up.

"Man, what are you doing with this in your wallet?" I asked, looking suspiciously at Will.

He took the card from my hand and looked at it. "Oh . . . he came to see me a while ago. He asked some questions about you, but I didn't have nothing to say to him. He told me to call him if I came up with anything."

"Why didn't you tell me? You never mentioned that Jabbar questioned you about me."

"Because I didn't want you tripping, that's why."

"Tripping or not, you should have told me. I can't believe you didn't tell me that he questioned you."

"I know, Brandon, but at the time, you were going through so much shit, and I didn't want to upset you. Jabbar talked to everybody you knew. But all that crap is over now. If you're mad, what you want me to do, tear up his card?"

"You can do whatever you want to do with it. It don't matter right now, but as my best friend, you still should have told me."

"Okay, I fucked up. Maybe I was wrong for not telling you, but I thought I was doing you a favor. He only asked if I thought you had a reason to kill Cassandra, and I said no."

Will avoided the concerned look on my face and looked over at Stacie. "Loan me ten dollars so I can go to the corner store and get some beer."

"See," she said, and then slammed ten dollars in his hand. "Bring me some chips and a strawberry Vess soda."

Will hopped up from his chair. "Are you going with me, or are you going to stay here and trip off some shit in the past?"

"I'm good, Will. Don't sweat it, but if it had been me, I would have told you. I'm staying 'cause I need to call Evelyn. She might be up for some company tonight."

"I'm sure she will be. But give up the keys. I need to use your car."

I gave Will my keys and a few dollars for a soda and chips. He pecked Stacie on her cheek and jetted.

"Do you mind if I use the phone?" I asked.

Stacie pointed to the receiver on the wall. "Help yourself. Just don't dial long distance."

I stood up and walked over to the phone. I dialed Evelyn's number, but of course, got no answer. I dialed again, and still, she didn't pick up.

I tapped the phone against the palm of my hand and stood in deep thought. The next thing I knew, I felt something tugging at my zipper. It was Stacie, and she was stooped in front of me. I backed up, but she held onto my pants.

"Come on, Brandon. Let me taste it. You know I've been wanting to taste it."

A risky and wild man I was, but not with my best friend's woman. "Naw, baby, we ain't going out like this. Do—don't do this to my boy. He don't deserve—"

She ignored me as she worked down my zipper. I could have gotten away from her, but my adrenaline rose, causing me to back into the wall behind me. Her mouth covered me, and my eyelids went limp.

After barely three jabs to the back of her throat, I'll be damned if the door didn't fly open.

Will ran in."I forgo—" He was stunned into silence.

Stacie hopped to her feet, and I stood with my limp dick still hanging out of my pants. This was one moment in my life that I wished like hell I could take back.

Will rushed me. Stacie moved out of the way as he charged

at me fist first. I tried to move, but his fist caught me on the bottom of my chin. It stung like hell.

"Cool out," I said, attempting to back away from his punches. He drew another punch and caught me close to my left eye. I could have taken Will out with one blow, but since I was in the wrong, I tried like hell not to hit him. Stacie yelled for him to stop, but he kept charging at me. He went full force into my body, and rammed me into the door that he'd come into. We landed on the ground, and that's when I had to defend myself.

"I said cool out!" I yelled. I punched his jaw and then his mouth. We went back and forth with punches, until I was able to get myself from underneath him.

I tried to get away, but he tugged on my shirt and ripped it. He tried to kick me in the groin, but I caught his foot and shoved him backward. When he fell, I grabbed my keys from the ground and hurried down the steps.

"Pussy-ass nigga!" he yelled. "I hate your punk ass!"

I heard a door slam. Moments later, there were sounds of breaking glass, yelling, and screaming. At that point, all I could do was find the nearest payphone and call the police. My cell phone had been turned off for two weeks, and it was times like this that I wish I'd paid the damn bill.

No doubt, I felt terrible about what I'd allowed to happen. For as long as I could remember, Will had been my best friend. How did I let a trick-ass bitch fuck up the friendship we'd had for so many years? I'd seen Stacie eyeballing me, but I had no feelings whatsoever for her. Shit just happened so fast, and I seriously thought that it could be our little secret. Damn, had I messed up this time around. I wasn't happy about it, and I surely wasn't happy about calling the police on him either.

While at the payphone, I called Evelyn's house again. Tonight, I needed her. I needed someone to hold and somewhere to lay my burdens. She didn't answer, so I drove over to her place. I was relieved when I didn't see a car in the driveway. I walked up to the door and knocked. The porch light quickly came on.

"Brandon, what are you doing here?" she asked. She looked shocked to see me. "It's almost one o'clock in the morning."

"Can I come in?" I said, licking the inside of my sore and bloody mouth.

She widened the door and closed it behind me. "What happened to your clothes? And why is your lip busted?"

"I had a fight with Will. He got upset with me about something."

"Let me go get you some ice for your lip."

She turned, but I grabbed her hand and pulled her body to mine.

"Just hold me for a moment."

Evelyn seemed distant, but she slowly wrapped her arms around me. When I rubbed the silkiness of her robe, she backed away.

"Let me go get your ice."

Before she made it to the kitchen, the doorbell rang. She turned in her tracks and gave me a disturbing look.

"Wait, ju–just a minute, okay," she stuttered.

I stood by the couch. When she opened the door, in walked her man. She didn't know it, but I'd seen him before. He was the man driving the Mercedes, and the one who had picked her up from work. This man was not her son, and it was time for her to 'fess up. He stood tall and dark, had wavy gray hair, wore an expensive suit, and carried a briefcase by his side. To me, it looked like the brotha was home. A smile covered his face, until he looked over and saw me; then his smile vanished.

Evelyn was nervous. "Darrell, this is Brandon, the young man I work with."

Darrell hesitated to speak, and so did I. His face scrunched as he looked at me. "What is he doing here at one o'clock in the morning?"

His baritone voice caused Evelyn to fidget even more. "He . . . he was—"

"I was just leaving," I said. "I came by to see if I could use the phone."

Evelyn didn't say one word, and neither did Darrell. He set his briefcase beside the couch and unloosened his tie then walked off, leaving Evelyn and me standing there to deal with each other.

"I'm sorry," she whispered.

"So am I," I said, heading for the door. She touched my hand, but I snatched it away. "Bitch, don't touch me." I tightened my fist, wanting to punch her in her fucking face. Instead, I swallowed the lump in my throat; it went straight to the pit of my stomach.

When I got inside my car, I saw Evelyn standing at her door, looking at me. I waited until she closed her door, and then I drove off, mad at myself. I should have seen this coming.

At this point, I hated Evelyn. She was a fake, and I'd had just about enough of her.

The next several days were a living hell. The setback that I experienced with Evelyn felt worse than losing Cassandra, because I could have controlled the situation, but I didn't.

I called Jennifer with another excuse about my mother, and told her I wouldn't be able to make it to work all week. She told me one week was more than enough time off, and if I didn't make it in by next Monday, I could consider myself jobless. I didn't trip too much about her comment because I knew she had to do what she had to do. Anyway, I'd planned on looking for another job, but my hurt feelings wouldn't let me do anything but sit at home, lay in bed, paint, and sleep. That was my routine for the entire week.

On Saturday morning, I was devastated that I hadn't heard from Evelyn or Will. I couldn't wait a moment longer, so I called Stacie's place and asked for Will.

"Is this Brandon?" she asked.

"Yeah, is he there?"

"No, he left. Before the police got here, he heard the sirens and left."

"Do you know where he went?"

"He's back at home with his mother. He called a few days ago and apologized for hitting me. I didn't press charges because I kind of brought it on myself."

My heart ached for Will back at his mother's place. "I guess we both did. I wish you would've never stepped to me like that, Stacie."

"It's too late for me to apologize, but I wanted so much more than just that. Will and me decided not to work things out, but maybe I'll see you around."

It was obvious Stacie had no regrets. I said nothing else to her before I ended the call. Fucked me up, too, because the woman I wanted in my life didn't want to be a part of it, and the ones I didn't want were sweating me.

I got up enough courage to call Will's house. His mother answered, and when I asked for him, she dropped the phone.

"This boy on the phone for you!" she yelled.

Several minutes passed before Will picked up.

"Hello?"

"Hey, what's up?"

"Nigga, don't be calling me. I ain't got nothing—"

"Will, I'm sorry for what happened. Man, you know I would never let a woman come between us. I don't know what's been wrong with me lately."

"Excuses, excuses, excuses. You've been so full of them, Brandon. Just admit that you've wanted a piece of Stacie ever since the day I met her."

"You know that ain't true. You've seen the way Stacie looked at me. With your own eyes, you can't deny that she's been trying to get at me, dog."

"With my own eyes, I saw my woman with your dick in her mouth. I saw no resistance on your part, brotha, none whatsoever."

"And I didn't resist. Hell, I couldn't. I'd like to see a woman giving you head and you telling her no."

"But that was my girl, Brandon. I had a comfortable roof over my head, money in the bank, and was thinking about marrying her."

"Well, maybe you need to thank me for doing you a favor. I don't understand how we can be boys for years, and you not listen to my side of the story. You still talking to her, but you won't talk to me."

"I'm talking to you now, nigga."

"But you ain't listening. You ain't listening to me tell you that she jumped my bones as soon as you jetted. If anything, you should be mad at her ass."

"I am. I'm pissed at yo' ass, but I ain't no fool. I knew Stacie was digging you. Since we've been kids, the girls always went for you first. When they couldn't get to you, they'd try to go through me."

"Stacie was always questioning me about you. I didn't trip because things got real close between us. I know she likes me, but she's a woman. When one man won't do, another one will."

"After twenty-eight years of knowing you, I couldn't agree with you more."

Will laughed, and so did I. I couldn't believe that he didn't hang up on me. By the time I told him about what had happened with Evelyn, we were well into an hour on the phone.

"So, she didn't run after you or get you no ice or nothing?"

"Nope. Busted lip, swollen eye, torn shirt and all; she simply did not care. Had I stayed a moment longer, old boy would've thrown me out and she wouldn't have done shit about it."

"Does he live with her?"

"I don't know. But if that bed is his, all the fucking we been doing on it, it fo' sho' got my sperm all over that motherfucker."

We cracked up.

"Damn, that's messed up," Will said. His mother yelled something in the background, and he told me to hold on. I waited for a few minutes, and then he got back on the phone.

"She be getting on my damn nerves! I can't wait to get out of here already."

My money was running low, and Will's extra income would sure as hell help me right about now. "If you want to, you can always move back in with me."

"Naw, but thanks. I got this place lined up on the South Side. Hopefully, it'll come through for me soon."

"It ain't through shacking up with nobody, is it?"

"Hell naw! It'll be mine and only mine."

"You live and learn, don't you?"

"You got that shit right. I couldn't have said it any better."

CHAPTER 18

I was heartbroken and hated to go in to work to face Evelyn. But since I hadn't gotten my butt out of bed to find another job, I had to cope with it. For the first several hours, I ducked and dodged her. Just as I was leaving the men's restroom, she finally caught up with me.

"So, you can't even speak to me," she said.

"Hello, Evelyn," I said dryly. I saw Jennifer, so I excused myself from Evelyn, called Jennifer's name, and walked away.

My ignoring Evelyn lasted for two more days. As I was heading out on Wednesday, she followed behind me. She called my name, but I kept on walking. I got in my car and sped off. In my rearview mirror, I could see her following behind me. I wanted to make a stop at the grocery store, but I didn't want to argue with her in public. Instead, I headed for home.

When I pulled into a parking spot, she pulled next to me. I got out, placed my hands in my pockets, and started to whistle. I was trying to piss her off, like I didn't care, but honestly, I did. She ran up from behind and grabbed my arm.

"Now, I drove all this way to talk, and you're going to listen to me!" she yelled.

"Get the hell away from me," I said.

I jogged up the many stairs to my loft. Evelyn couldn't keep up because of the high heels she wore. At my door, I reached in my pocket and fumbled for my keys. She came up from behind and snatched the keys from my hand.

"Damn you, Brandon! What in the hell is it that you want from me? So I lied about being with my ex. So what? It's not like you haven't lied to me!"

I held out my hand. "Hand me my keys, please."

She dropped them in my hand and I unlocked the door. I walked in, removed my jacket, and tossed it on the couch. She stepped in after me and closed the door. Pretending as if she wasn't there, my whistling started again as I headed toward the kitchen. I opened the fridge, leaned down to look inside, and she damn near chopped off my head trying to close it. No doubt, my blood was starting to boil.

"Look," I said, "why don't you get the fuck out of here? What we had is over, baby. The other night, you made that perfectly clear."

"I didn't make anything clear. You showed up without calling, so what in the hell did you expect?"

I wanted to fuck her up for putting the blame on me. "Bitch! I did call! I called you all day long, but—"

A hard smack landed on my face. "Who are you calling a bitch?" She smacked me again. "I don't give a shit how angry you are!"

I reached out and grabbed Evelyn's collar, nearly lifting her off her feet as I pulled her to me. "If the definition applies, bitch, then wear it!" I shoved her backward and took a few steps away from her.

"All right then, you whining young punk! You need to grow up and be a real man! A real man would've known that he couldn't compete."

I jumped back and caught myself before hurting her. Instead, I grabbed her collar again and pulled her toward the door. "A real man would throw your ass out of here like I'm getting ready to do!"

Evelyn strongly resisted, using her nails to scratch up my arms. I squeezed my eyes shut when I felt the pain.

"Oh, now I got your attention, don't I?" she said.

I knew what she was trying to do, so I let her continue to push me to the edge. I shoved her again, and her back slammed against the door. I jumped in her face and grabbed her neck, pressing my fingers deeply into her throat. "I know what you're trying to do, Evelyn. You're trying to get me mad so I'll fuck you."

She pulled at my hands and strained to talk. "If you know my motive, bastard, then act on it!"

She smacked me again, and I quickly tripped her to the ground. She fell hard, and I dropped down to one knee in front of her. She rose on her elbows, and a tear fell down her cheek.

We took deep breaths as she tore at my shirt and I tore at hers. I yanked her pants from her, and she yanked mine from me. I didn't waste any time slamming my dick inside of her. She let out grunting sounds as I pounded her hard.

"What kind of woman are you turning me into?" she cried out. "I hate the way you make me feel, Brandon . . . I hate the need that I have for you."

Sweat dripped from my forehead, and it fell right on to Evelyn's bare chest. Her groans got louder and her body started to slide along the hardwood floors. She used her hands to force my hips back, while her legs were high up on my shoulders.

"My back is burning, Brandon. Slow down, and please, get me off the floor."

"Unh-uh. You asked for this, and I'll be damned if you don't get it."

I continued on with my pace. Evelyn seemed to be in great pain. She stopped stroking with me and moved her head from side to side.

"Okay, I'm sorry," she said. "I'm sorry for not being completely honest with you."

"You're sorry?" I dropped her legs then rolled her body on top of mine and rubbed her back burns to cool them. "Let's go in my room."

"I'm afraid to ask why," she said.

"Then don't. You asked me to get you off the floor and I did."

Evelyn rose up. I took her hand and we headed for my room. As she sat on the bed, I opened my closet and pulled out an extension cord. I tossed it on the bed then sat next to her. She didn't say a word, so I lay on my back and put my hands behind my head.

"Take the extension cord and tie me to the bed," I asked.

She reached for the cord and held it in her hands. She took a hard swallow and looked at me. "Brandon, I don't want—"

I pulled her on top of me and stared deeply into her eyes.

"Do you have any idea how much you hurt me?" I asked. "I was really feeling you, and for you to play me like you did was wrong."

"I can't say anything to you other than I'm sorry. I love Darrell, but I'm not ready to let you go. I figured if I told you the truth, you'd end this relationship. I needed you so much, and I wasn't about to lose you."

"Why do you need me and you have him?"

"Because even though I love him, I'm excited about the way you make me feel. At times, I feel like a teenager in love for the first time. You know, that unsure feeling that maybe something will evolve from this, but then again, maybe not. I know so little about you, Brandon, and this feeling is scary."

"I guess knowing that I'll have to play second best in your

life is scary for me too. Thing is, I don't know if I can do it. I've never been in this situation before."

My dick had gone down, and Evelyn lowered herself to give me a rise. As she worked me, I stared at the ceiling, feeling unsure about where things were headed from here. More than anything, I realized that as much as I wanted her, this was too painful for me to continue.

Thursday morning was bright but cold. The temperature had dropped to single digits, and as I got dressed for work, I couldn't help but think about my relationship with Evelyn. After she left, I hadn't gotten a wink of sleep. Now I knew what Jabbar felt like when he secretly saw Cassandra behind my back. He was probably going crazy, loving a woman who wanted to have her cake and eat it too. I wasn't sure what the hell Evelyn had told her man, but I hoped he wasn't a fool like I'd been.

As I looked back on my relationship with Cassandra, the evidence was all there. The long trips out of town, the unanswered calls when I called her condo . . . she always had an excuse. I trusted her, and I didn't think she had a reason to lie to me. I never challenged her explanations; I just accepted them as legit.

With Evelyn, I knew better. I could see right through her, but still let myself fall for her. Yesterday confirmed her lust for me, and all I could do was fuck her well.

I stood in my kitchen in a daze as I put cream in my coffee. The phone rang, and I reached for it. It was Will. When I asked why he was up so early, he said that he couldn't wait to call me.

"Call for what?" I asked. "You sound as if it's urgent."

"I guess you haven't heard the news. Do you ever look at your TV?"

"Yeah, sometimes. Why?"

"Ruby was convicted of murder. She's looking at life, possibly the death penalty. They found the knife that killed Cassandra, and supposedly, Ruby's fingerprints were all over it."

"You lying, right?"

"Nope. I just heard it. I'm surprised you didn't."

"Will, all I can say is I guess they had a strong case, because without it, they wouldn't have been able to convict her. I hate to sound harsh, but all of this has left a real bad taste in my mouth. I washed my hands of Cassandra and her family."

"I don't blame you. Anyway, what you got up for the weekend?"

"So far, nothing. Why?"

" 'Cause I might need your help moving. I got my place and bought some nice furniture."

"Of course I'll help. I'm glad things are looking up. I'm real proud of you."

"Thanks. I'll see you early Saturday morning. The earlier the better, all right?"

"I'll see if I can get Mr. Armanos' raggedy-ass truck so we don't have to make too many trips."

"That's cool, but one trip is all it'll take. Most of my furniture is being delivered."

"Okay, cool. See ya Saturday."

I hung up and rushed to work because I was running late. When I got there, I didn't see Evelyn anywhere in sight. I guess she was running late too, so I went on with my tours for the day.

By day's end, I looked everywhere for Evelyn, but it seemed she was a no-show. I even stepped into Jennifer's office to see if she'd heard from her. She said no, but invited me in to take a seat.

"Is everything okay, Jennifer?"

"I don't know, Brandon. You tell me."

"Yes, everything is fine. Why are you asking?"

"Because you and Evelyn have been calling in a lot. Before you started working here, she'd been here for almost ten years and barely called in. Now, I'm lucky if I even hear from her. I don't like the changes, so it's only fair that I try to find out what's going on."

"There's nothing going on with me. I had a family crisis that required my attention. As for Evelyn, you'll have to talk to her."

"Okay, Brandon. If you say there's nothing for me to worry about, then I won't worry. At times, I can see the tension in your relationship with her, and all I ask is that you guys keep whatever you have going on separate from work."

"We do the best we can, Jennifer. If I hear from Evelyn, I'll let you know. In the meantime, if you hear from her, you do the same."

Jennifer nodded and I walked out. I didn't know Evelyn had been taking a lot of days off. Maybe Jennifer was exaggerating. Evelyn was absent today, but she was probably just exhausted from what I put on her last night. For the first time, she'd let me work her from another hole, and even though I took it easy, she complained about the pain.

After work, I stopped at the bank and cashed my check. I wanted to do something nice for Evelyn, since she'd let me have a bit of my way with her last night. I saw her actions changing each and every time we had sex, and I expected her to give in to my way of sex soon.

I stopped at Target and bought her a fluffy stuffed dog and a card. When I got to her house, I left the card and stuffed dog on the porch. I didn't want her to think I was there to check up on her or that I had stopped by without calling. All I wanted to do was show her that I'd been think- ing about her and I appreciated her trying to make progress in the bedroom. I wrote her a tiny note that said just that.

For the rest of the evening, I did what I knew best and stayed in my studio. I was up until two in the morning, and then I passed out on the floor. When I woke up, it was 7:00 AM. I told Will I'd be there early, so I showered and got ready to leave. Before I left, I called Evelyn's place to see if she'd gotten my surprise. She didn't answer, so I left her a message. The thought of her being with her man crossed my mind, but what more could I do about it? The least she could have done was call and thank me for the gifts.

After I got Mr. Armanos' keys, I headed for Will's mother's apartment. I wasn't too thrilled to see her, and she didn't look too happy to see me either.

"In and out, out and in," she complained as I helped Will carry some of his clothes to the truck. He was already outside, and she put up her arm to block me in the doorway.

"I hope this is the last time you and that nigga come in here. If you're his friend, you'd better tell him that this ain't no hotel where you check in and check out when you want to."

"Yes, ma'am," was all I could say. Her breath was clowning, and I seriously could've gotten high just from smelling it.

She moved out of my way, and I headed to the truck. Will was coming toward me.

"Man, you'd better hurry up," I warned. "She's on a roll."

Will laughed and then quickly ran inside. I put his clothes in the truck then went back inside. This time, his mother stood outside the doorway, puffing on a cigarette. She eyeballed me and grinned. She sucked her decayed, brown-and-yellow teeth.

"Nigga, where yo' mama and them move to?" she asked, as if she didn't already know. I wanted to ignore her so badly, but I knew she'd act a fool if I didn't respond.

"Alabama," I said. I rushed back in as Will rushed out.

"Mama, why don't you stop bugging him so he can help me with my things? You said you wanted me out, and I'm trying to get out."

She raised her voice. "Motherfucker, you need to stay out! The key is staying out and not bringing your pissy ass back here, boy!"

Will gave her a simple look. "Now, I would disrespect you, but I ain't gon' even go there. You just sad," he said, shaking his head. "Truly sad."

That, of course, sparked a nerve. She got even louder. "Your broke ass the one sad! If you really want to know, I'm happay! Happay that yo' black ass getting the hell away from here—again! Remember, you need me, fool; I don't need you!"

Will and I walked away from her.

"Would you please keep quiet until we get finished?" I whispered. "The more you talk to her, the more wound up she gets."

"Man, I'm just messing with my moms. That's how we get along. She mad because I'm leaving, and if I were to go back in there right now and tell her I'm staying, she'd throw her arms around me."

"Yeah, right. I don't believe that bullshit for one minute."

"Okay," he said. "Come on."

I bravely followed behind him. When we got back inside, she was in the bathroom, sitting on the toilet with the door wide open. Will stood in the doorway, as if the stench didn't bother him. I turned my back and stood far away from the door.

"Mama, I changed my mind. I really don't have enough money to move out on my own, so I'm staying, all right?"

Her voice was calm. "Will, take your bony butt somewhere and get out of my face. Bring me two aspirins in here and close my damn door."

I was shocked. Will went to the kitchen, got her two aspirins, and handed them to her. He closed the bathroom door, looked at me, and smiled.

"Told ya," he whispered.

While his mother was in the bathroom, we continued to gather his things. We were on our last trip when she came out of the bathroom and looked around for Will.

"He out by the truck," I said. "He'll be right back."

She looked at me with her beady eyes. "What in the fuck you still doing here?"

"I was waiting for Will."

When Will came in, he saved me. He kissed his mother on the cheek. "I'm gone, Mama. If things don't work out, I'll be back."

"Gone where? I thought you were staying."

"I was just joking with you." He laughed.

That fast, she turned into a demon. She pulled off her shoe and threw it at the back of Will's head. We both ran fast. "Silly-ass, broke-down niggas!" she yelled from behind us. "Don't bring y'all's butts back over here again!"

"I love you, Mamaaaaa!" Will yelled to her as we hopped in the truck.

From a distance, she gave him the finger.

Riding in Mr. Armanos' truck, we laughed our hearts out. If it wasn't about Will's mother, it was about the truck stopping on us three times before we got to Will's new place. Normally, the ride would've taken only thirty minutes to the South Side; instead, it took us two hours.

Will's new place was pretty nice. It was spacious and looked a lot better than the hellhole he'd been living in with Stacie.

"Man, this is nice. How can your broke butt afford something like this?"

"I've been saving my paychecks and tips from the burger joint. I got a raise, and things are looking up."

Once we pulled everything into the house, we sat on the floor. I lay back and looked at the high white ceilings.

"I can't believe how nice this is. It's gon' take you forever to furnish something like this, ain't it?"

"Not really. My bedroom furniture being delivered tomorrow, and hopefully, I'll be able to get my kitchen and living room out by my next payday."

"Damn, if the burger joint paying like that, then you might have to hook me up."

"I thought the art museum pays pretty good. They got to if you ain't late on the rent and you still driving your Acura."

"The pay is all right. I'm still struggling, though. I took the job because I thought I'd meet some people who wanted me to paint something for them, but I only met one person, and his cheap ass gave me fifteen hundred for a painting that was worth at least four thousand."

"That's your fault for undercharging him. You've always done it, and that's why you can't make no profit."

Will and I sat quietly for a moment.

I sat up and yawned. "Where ole girl at?" I asked.

"Who, Stacie?"

"Yeah. Have you talked to her?"

"Nope. After we talked that day, I stopped calling her. I thought about what you said, and after what she did to me, I ain't got no business dealing with her."

"I agree."

"So, how you and Evelyn doing? Since she played you like she did, have you heard from her?"

"Not today," I said. I couldn't bear to tell Will what a fool I'd been for her. "Things are going all right. I'm still trying to recover from how she played me."

I got up to use the bathroom. When I came back, Will was in the kitchen, getting some water.

"You want some water?"

"Yeah, that's cool. I wish you had some ice, though."

"Tomorrow. My fridge will be here tomorrow."

I looked over at his phone on the counter. "Is this thing hooked up yet?"

"Yep. I had it turned on a few days ago."

I picked up the phone and punched through his numbers on the caller ID. Twice, there were calls from the St. Louis Metro Police Dept.

"Why the police on your caller ID?"

Will walked over to me and took the phone. He looked at the numbers and punched through them. "I'on know. That's odd, ain't it? Why would the police be calling my black ass? Maybe they got the wrong number. Do you think I should call the number back?"

"Nah," I said. "But it is odd that they've been calling your new number. You didn't give it to them, did you?"

"Hell naw. Give it to them for what? You know I don't got no love for the police."

I felt that Will was telling the truth, and it was possible that the police were dialing the wrong number, especially since it was new. Still, something told me to watch my back. Will hadn't told me about Jabbar questioning him, and now the number showed up on his caller ID. I had to be real careful with trusting so many people.

To change the subject, I picked up the phone and dialed Evelyn's number. As usual, she didn't answer.

When I got ready to leave Will's house, it was way after six o'clock in the evening. He walked out with me to the truck, teasing me about how it would take hours to get home.

"I hope this damn truck make it," I said. "I ain't got time to be pulled over on the street somewhere. Stay by your phone. I might have to call you for some help."

"Like you said before, I can't come rescue you on no bike. You'd better call Felicity, or hope that Evelyn answers her phone."

"Man, I haven't heard from Felicity in a long time. The next time I see her, she got a good ass kicking coming. As for Evelyn, if I wait on her to come get me, I'll be a waiting fool."

"Just drive slow, real slow. It seems like when you go gunning it, that's when it cuts off."

We laughed, slammed hands together, and said our goodbyes.

I almost made it home without a problem, but three blocks from where I lived, the truck cut out on me. I was already tired from moving Will into his new place, and walking home didn't make it easier for me.

I was nearly one block down, with two more to go, when a police car pulled up beside me. When I looked inside, I saw Jabbar. What in the hell did he want? I hoped that he didn't want to talk to me about Cassandra or Ruby.

He unlocked the door and I opened it.

"Do you need a ride?" he asked.

"Ye . . . yeah, thanks," I said, relieved that he was just trying to offer me a ride. "A friend of mine's truck stopped on me back there. You're right on time, because it's colder than Alaska out here."

Jabbar laughed and nodded. "You need a jump or something?"

"Naw. I'm gon' go home and tell my landlord what happened. He'll probably call somebody to tow it. Honestly, I don't think a jump will do a damn thing for it."

Jabbar grinned, and for a moment, we sat quietly.

"So," he said, "by now I guess you've heard about what happened to Ruby."

"Yeah, I heard about it." I looked out the window.

"How do you feel about it?"

"I'm confused, but I'm pleased about the outcome. If her lawyer couldn't help her, I guess nobody could."

"You got that right," he said.

We pulled in front of my place, and before I got out, Jabbar asked how things were going between Evelyn and me.

"It's been okay. I found out that what you said was true.

Thanks for the tip. You know I didn't want to believe you, but now I'm trying to deal with the situation as best as I can."

"Well, if it helps, take advice from somebody who already knows. A situation like that will cause you many headaches. Back off, and if she wants you, she'll come around. Don't force her like I forced Cassandra. I think it only made matters worse."

I turned to Jabbar. "Do . . . do you think Cassandra loved you?"

He looked straight ahead. "Naw, I don't think she loved me. I think she lusted for me. I do believe she loved you, but I couldn't help myself from falling for her. We both know what kind of woman she was."

"She was wonderful when she wanted to be, but it's obvious there was a dark side to her as well—one I didn't know existed."

"It be like that sometimes, Brandon. You learn and move on. All you can do is hope that whatever happened to you before doesn't happen to you again."

I nodded, slammed hands with Jabbar, and thanked him again. Before going inside, I stopped and told Mr. Armanos about his truck.

That night, I thought about everything Jabbar had said. It would've been stupid of me to repeat the same old mess I'd been in with Cassandra and live it again through Evelyn. At that moment, I decided that going any further with her wasn't in my best interest.

The following week was tough to get through. Even though I said Evelyn was out of my life, I surely expected to hear from her. There was no "thank you" for the stuffed dog or for the card. She hadn't shown up for work all week, and Jennifer was furious. She acted as if I knew where Evelyn was, and on Friday, she called me into her office to confront me.

"I've had enough of this, Brandon. I don't know why

you're trying to protect Evelyn, but at this time, I'm gonna have to let you go."

"What?" I yelled. "Why in the hell are you letting me go? All week, I've been here busting my ass at this job."

"I'm letting the both of you go. One week you're not here, the next week she's not. I need people who are dedicated to working, and not the kind who take turns calling in sick."

"For your information, Jennifer, I haven't spoken to Evelyn. I don't know where the hell she is, and you are wrong for telling me that I do."

"Wrong or not, I've put up with enough." She handed me my check. "Tell Evelyn that I'll put her check in the mail. I'm sorry it didn't work out, Brandon. I was really hoping that it would."

I snatched my check, calling her an ignorant bitch in my mind. How in the hell could she fire me when I hadn't done anything wrong? I needed this job. I didn't have any money to back me up, and I knew it would be a while before I'd find another position.

I didn't know if I was upset with Jennifer for firing me, or with Evelyn for not showing up all week. I drove recklessly to Evelyn's house. When I saw the Mercedes in her driveway, I kept on driving. My intentions were to tell her about her job, but fuck her!

Mr. Armanos was outside wiping the windows when I pulled my car into a parking spot. On my way home, I'd thought about making arrangements with him on my rent, until I could find another job. I knew he'd understand because he'd worked with me many times before. This time, however, he didn't agree to it.

He slapped the back of his hand against the palm of his other hand. "By the end of the week, I need money. No later than the end of the week, or you must go. You still haven't fixed my floors, and I give you much time."

"Two weeks, Mr. Armanos. Give me two weeks, all right?"

He hesitated. "Two weeks, okay. If no rent, I put your things outside."

Damn, I couldn't believe how messed up things had gotten. Where in the hell was I going to get twelve hundred dollars in two weeks? Since I'd taken off for those few days, my check was not enough. I had to pay my car note, and my electric bill was scheduled for disconnection. Even if I let the car payment slide, I still had a nice chunk to come up with.

I jogged upstairs to my loft and went inside. I took a shower to relax me and thumbed through my phone book to see who I could call for help. My mother's number was the first one I saw, but I hadn't talked to her in months and was too ashamed to call her. I couldn't let her know that her grown-ass son had fallen flat on his face, so I overlooked her number and went to the next. Felicity, Will, or Annette didn't look promising, and neither did the several other females I'd dated before I met Cassandra.

Coming up empty, I shut the book and fell back on my bed. Soon after, a thought hit me: Stacie. What if I asked Stacie for the money? I knew I'd be playing with fire by talking to the woman who came between my friendship with Will, but I was desperate. He would be pissed, but he didn't have to know. She'd been dishing out money to Will like crazy, so maybe she'd kick me out some as well.

Instead of calling her, I put on my burgundy sweat suit and splashed on some cologne. I reached for my car keys and jetted.

CHAPTER 19

I got to Stacie's place around eight o'clock that night. As I rang the doorbell, I could hear her on the inside, yakking on the phone. She asked who it was, and when I told her it was me, she unlocked the door. She told the caller she'd call them back then widened the door so I could come in.

"Is, uh, Will here, Stacie?"

"No," she said, putting her burgundy-tinted braids into a ponytail. "What would he be doing here?" She closed the door, and I followed her into the living room.

"I thought y'all made up. I stopped by his mother's house to see him, but she said that she hadn't seen him. I just knew he'd be over here."

"Nope," she said, and then took a seat on the sofa. I sat in a chair. "Brandon, I haven't heard from Will. I called looking for him at his mother's house too, but she said he'd moved out."

"Moved out?" I pretended as if I didn't know. "Did she say where he moved to?"

Stacie laughed. "Now, you know that woman ain't told me

nothing. If she did know, she for damn sure wouldn't tell me."

"You got that right," I said with a laugh. "She is a piece of work, ain't she?"

"You know better than I do. The first time Will took me over there, she called me all kinds of bitches and hoes. Woman didn't even know me, and she was out of line for going off like she did."

"You shouldn't have taken it personal. She's been like that for years."

Stacie laughed again and stood up. "Can I get you something to drink? Nothing hard, but I got some Kool-Aid and some orange juice in the fridge."

"Some Kool-Aid would be nice."

She walked away, and I checked her out in her short, deep purple nightgown. She didn't have much in the way of breasts, but her ass was jiggling loose underneath her gown. I planned to beat around the bush about the money, but I also had a feeling that I'd have to "show some interest" in Stacie in order for her to up the funds. I was in no way turned on by her, but a broke-ass man like me had to do what he had to do.

When she came back, she handed me a glass of red Kool-Aid then sat back on the couch.

I took a sip and almost gagged. "Girl, this Kool-Aid is too, too sweet. Not as sweet as you, but it's sweet enough."

Stacie blushed. "Would you like some orange juice instead?"

I placed the glass of Kool-Aid on the table and changed my whole demeanor. "No, no orange juice. But I . . . I gotta be honest with you about something, Stacie."

"What?"

"I knew Will wasn't here. Actually, he did get a new place, and I know that because I helped him move. He told me you and him called it off, and . . . and I thought maybe—" I paused.

"You thought what?" She spoke anxiously.

"I thought maybe you and me could hook up some time. Not like boyfriend, girlfriend hook-up, but like let's just be there for each other and see where things go."

She unfolded her legs and placed them on the floor. "I'on know, Brandon. Will was really upset about what happened, and if he finds out that something's going on between us, I know he'll be even more upset."

"Stacie, Will ain't tripping off me or you. He's already met somebody, and he's been chilling with her."

She rolled her eyes. "Men. That's so typical of him. I knew there was a reason he stopped pursuing me."

"He stopped pursuing you because he knew how you felt about me. You can't be mad at him for moving on. It's just time you did the same."

"I want to, but I don't want no trouble from Will."

"There won't be any trouble. I mean, we can start off slow. Maybe go on a few dates and take it from there. What do you think about that?"

"I'm for it, Brandon. I liked you from the first time I saw you. I know you noticed how attracted I was to you, and when I was at your place, I started to tell you how I really felt. Will was cool, but he be acting like a little boy sometimes. I think he knew how much I liked you, too."

"He did. He told me so, and I did notice you checking me out. Did you notice me checking you out too?"

"Nope. Will said you were in love with somebody, so I didn't think I had a chance."

"Will lied. I wasn't in love with anybody." I looked her over from head to toe. "But I'm surprised you didn't notice me checking you out."

She didn't say anything, so I picked up my glass of Kool-

Aid and stirred it around. "I'm getting thirsty again. Would you mind switching my Kool-Aid for some orange juice?"

She grinned and went into the kitchen to get my orange juice. Her phone rang while she was in the kitchen, and I heard her laughing and joking with someone over the phone. I sat on the couch feeling terrible about what I was about to do, but what other choice did I have? I knew I could get some money from Stacie, and if she'd given Will all that money, I knew she'd give me more. Until I got what I wanted from Stacie, I had to figure out a way to keep this a secret from Will. The last thing I wanted was for him to be hurt again.

I took another sip from the sweet Kool-Aid then stretched when I stood up. I went into the kitchen and crept up behind her just as she was putting the orange juice container back into the fridge. I wrapped my arm around her waist and pecked my lips down the side of her neck.

"I want to feel you," I whispered. "Let me feel your insides."

Stacie tilted her head and reached up her hand to rub my hair.

"Do as you please," she said. "Take your time and do as you please."

From the back, I flipped up her nightgown and stared at her naked ass. She bent over further, and I reached in my pocket and pulled out a condom. I lowered my sweat pants, placed the condom on my dick, and rammed it inside of her. I had to make it good, so I stroked her well. The rhythm that I chose had her moaning like crazy and caused her knees to buckle. Within a few short minutes, she screamed out loudly and exploded.

"Daaaamn, Brandon," was all she could say.

"That was too quick," I said with my dick still resting inside of her. "Take me to your room, baby. We need to make this last a little while longer."

She smiled, took my hand, and led me to her room. I got down to major business, and surprisingly, so did she.

Once the action was over, Stacie and I lay in bed together. I held my arms around her while she rubbed up and down my chest.

"Did you enjoy yourself?" she asked.

"Do you have to ask? That was some good stuff, girl. I can't believe you were setting it out for my partna like that."

She laughed. "Well, now I'll be setting it out there for you. You gotta promise me something, though."

"What's that?"

"That you won't tell Will about us. I don't feel comfortable letting him know about us."

"Stacie, I don't know if I can make you that promise."

"Why not?"

"For one, in a few weeks, I might be kicked out of my place. My rent increased and I can't afford it. Will told me I could move in with him, and that's where I'm possibly headed. If you and me are still kicking it, how in the hell can I keep our relationship a secret?"

"Simple. Don't move in with Will. Move in with me."

"That would be even worse. I would love to, but it would be so much better if I could keep my own place. That way Will wouldn't know nothing. A friend of mine supposed to loan me the money, but he won't be able to give it to me until the end of the month. I can't wait that long."

"How much do you need? I could loan the money to you, but you gotta give it back."

"Naw, I couldn't ask you to do that. Besides, I don't want to start things off with me owing you money."

"Look, like I said, just make sure I get it back. Now, how much do you need?"

"Fifteen hundred dollars. I really need more than that, but I already got some money in the bank."

"I don't have that kind of money on me. I got about two hundred here, and the rest I'll have to write you a check."

This was easier than I thought it would be. Stacie was either stupid or downright desperate. Either way, she had just saved my ass, and I was grateful. I gave her an appreciative kiss on the forehead. "Thanks, baby. By the end of the month, I'll be sure that you get every dime back."

Stacie nodded, and just because sex between us turned out to be pretty good, I decided to give her another shot.

On Saturday, I caught up with Mr. Armanos and paid him. I signed over the check Stacie had given me, and paid the rest in cash. I even had enough to pay my car payment, and I sent that off as well.

No doubt, I had to find a job and do it fast. I thought about working at the burger joint with Will, so I called his house to see if they were doing any hiring.

"I don't think so. But if you want me to, I can put in a good word for you. Maybe my manager will create something for you," he joked.

"It ain't that much creativity in the world. Either there's an opening or there ain't."

"I don't think so, but next week, I'll check into it. I got the weekend off, so I'm just chilling in my new place and enjoying it. You should stop by and check it out. It's looking tight."

"I'll probably get over that way next weekend. I gotta work hard at finding a job. For me, next week ain't gon' be no joke."

"I'll do what I can and check on things for you. If anything, you need to call a lawyer or somebody about how that bitch manager of yours played you. That was wrong. I ain't never heard of nobody being fired because somebody else didn't show up."

"I thought about checking with the EEOC, but I guess Jennifer did me a favor. Anyway, I was about to quit because I didn't want to see Evelyn on an everyday basis."

"You still haven't heard from her?"

"Nope. It's like she's just vanished. I drove by her house, but her man's car was there. I guess she decided to leave my black ass alone and work shit out with him."

"That's fucked up. Women. And you have the nerve to wonder why I treat them the way I do."

"I feel you, but I guess you got to keep on trying until you get it right."

"That's your motto. Mine is totally different."

"And what's that?"

"Fuck'em, fuck'em, and fuck'em again."

We laughed, and I told Will I'd most likely see him next weekend.

Over the next several days, I got my résumé together and pounded the pavement, trying to find a job. This time around, I didn't have much luck. I started to hear the same old bullshit: "We'll call if we need you," or, "The interviewing process isn't complete. Once we make our decision, we'll be in touch." I left one place after another, pretty much upset. I guess the frustration showed on my face, and that's why I wasn't offered a job.

By Thursday, things started to look more promising. Kline Technologies was looking for customer service representatives, and I'd gotten an on-the-spot interview. When things wrapped up, the supervisor told me she'd call me next week to come back for a second interview. She expressed how pleased she was with me, and she basically promised me the job.

Of course, since the position paid $13.50 an hour, I was on cloud nine. It was a step up from the art museum, and I made a promise to myself to keep my rent current, as well as my car payment.

As I drove toward home, I noticed several people standing around, searching through a bunch of junk and furniture. The furniture caught my attention, as many of the items looked familiar. I hopped out of my car and ran over to the crowd. Sure enough, the items were mine.

"Move!" I yelled. "Get away from my shit!"

Everybody looked at me like I was crazy as they slowly backed away. I couldn't believe Mr. Armanos had set my belongings out on the curb. Almost everything was gone, except for my mattress, a few of my paintings, my sofa, and some clothes. I grabbed as much as I could and packed it inside my car.

When I looked down and saw Cassandra's cracked picture, I wanted to cry. Ever since her murder, my life had gone downhill. If she were still alive, I would probably be catching drama with her and Jabbar, but this eviction would've never happened to me.

I put some more items in my car then stopped this kid and offered to pay him twenty dollars if he stood by and watched the rest of my things. He agreed, and I headed inside to talk to Mr. Armanos about why he evicted me. Before I could even approach him, he was waving his hands in the air.

"You get out of here. You trick me!"

"What? Trick you? How in the hell did I trick you?"

"Your check no good." He picked up a piece of paper and pointed to it. "No, no good."

I snatched the paper from his hand, and sure enough, the check Stacie wrote me had bounced. Twice. I balled up the paper and threw it on the ground.

I pointed my finger at Mr. Armanos. "Mr. Armanos, this was an illegal eviction! You gave me no notice, and by law, I should have had thirty days' notice. You've got to give me a couple more days, and I promise you that I'll have your damn money. I'll even throw in next month's rent too."

"No, no. You are more than thirty days past due. I gave

you notice and time to pay, and you never pay. Just go. Leave before I call the police."

I had thought Mr. Armanos was cool, but when it came to his money, he wasn't playing. All I could do was shamefully turn away. I couldn't wait to get my hands on that bitch Stacie. I wasn't sure if she purposely gave me a bad check, or if she really didn't have that much money to begin with. If not, she should have said so.

When I got back outside, more people had gathered around. The kid who was supposed to be watching my things had jetted. Since I didn't have anywhere to put my sofa and mattress, I sold them. I even sold some of the items I'd put in my car, just to put money in my pocket that I surely didn't have.

By six o'clock that evening, I left with more money in my pocket and not much in my car. I sold my expensive clothes and the watch that was hidden away in one of my socks. I went straight to Stacie's house to see what the hell was up with this bounced check she gave me.

I stood outside and banged hard on her door. She yanked it open, and looked shocked when she saw that it was me.

"Brandon, why you banging on my door like you're the police?"

I stepped inside and pointed my finger at her. "Why did you play me like that? I thought we were cool, Stacie."

"What do you mean, play you? How in the hell did I play you?"

"The fucking check, bitch! It bounced! If you didn't have no damn money, then you should've told me!"

"I did have the money, bastard, and don't be coming up in here calling me no bitch!"

"Well, why didn't *your* check clear the bank? I got put out of my place because the check you gave me was no good. All of my belongings were set out, and people came by and took my shit!"

Stacie rushed to the phone and dialed out. "I'm calling my

bank right now to see what's up. What you're saying don't make sense to me. I know I had some money in there!"

I took a seat on the couch and waited. She paced back and forth nervously in her tight jeans that squeezed her junk in the trunk. She argued with the banking representative; from the sound of her conversation, the dumb bitch miscalculated.

"Okay. Yes. Thank you. You have a good day too," she said with a slight attitude then hung up. She looked at me.

"I forgot about two checks I'd written. That's why your check didn't clear. It wasn't like I was trying to play you, but I made a mistake."

"Well, your mistake left me with no place to stay."

Stacie walked around the couch, sat next to me, and blinked her overly thick false eyelashes. "I'm sorry. Like I said, you can always stay here if you ain't got no place to go. If you want, by the end of the week, I can give you some of your money back."

"That would be nice, since I don't have much of nothing. Until then, how do you plan on making this inconvenience up to me?"

"However you want me to," she said.

I leaned back on the couch and patted my lap. I was horny as hell, and it was rough days like today that made women like Stacie useful. I knew that from this moment forward, she'd do anything I wanted her to do. I believed her about the mix-up with the check, but unfortunately, after I got her to fuck me the way I wanted to, she'd be history. I had no intentions of making my way back to her broke ass ever again.

CHAPTER 20

I spent a few days at Stacie's place, but that was not working out. She was just nasty, and the way she kept her place was too uncomfortable for me. Dishes stayed in the sink for days, musty clothes were piled high on her bedroom floor, and when I had to kill five roaches in the bathroom, that just about did it for me. I hated like hell that the first time we had sex, my condom tore. I had to make it my business to go to a clinic to get checked for STDs. I also planned to make a phone call to Kline Technologies to see if they'd been trying to reach me; then I wanted to get the hell out of Stacie's house and go ask Will if I could stay with him.

I called Kline Technologies, and the supervisor asked me to come in for a second interview. I quickly got dressed and left. I had a short wait, and then, I was called into Mrs. Eldrige's office to interview with her and another gentleman. The interview went well, and I was offered the position. They asked when I could start, and I told them the sooner the better. They suggested next Monday, and I agreed to be there.

As I was leaving, I stopped by the receptionist's desk and

waited for her to end a call. Earlier, while I waited for Mrs. El-drige, the receptionist told me her name was Morgan. We'd talked for a short while and made an instant connection. Be-fore I left, she told me to stop by and say good-bye. She smiled at me and rolled her big, beautiful eyes as she tried to hurry the caller on the other end.

"Sorry about that," she said, hanging up. "It's bound to get busy again, Brandon, so if you write down your number for me, I promise I'll call you later."

She passed me a piece of paper and pen and I wrote down Will's number, since I figured I'd be staying with him.

"My roommate might answer, so don't be alarmed." I handed the paper and pen back to her. "I hope I hear from you."

"Most definitely," she said.

I smiled and walked away.

As I waited for the elevator, I turned and looked at Mor-gan. She was downright gorgeous, with smooth dark choco-late skin, buttered brown lips, and long, shiny black hair. It was neatly combed back into a ponytail to accentuate her make-up free baby-doll face. Since she'd been sitting, I couldn't really get a feel for her body, but I knew it was thick—thick breasts, thick hips, and thick everything that had me licking my lips all the way back to my car.

When I got to the burger joint, I put my hand on the door handle to get out of my car, and that's when I saw something that caught my eye. Jabbar and another officer walked up to Will. The three of them stepped away from the table Will had been servicing, and they seemed to be indulged in a deep conversation. They smiled at each other, and then Jab-bar handed Will a white envelope. Will nodded, and Jabbar gave him a pat on his back.

Now, what in the hell was that all about? I know my boy hadn't been backstabbing me, had he? Something wasn't adding up with him, but as usual, I'd put those incidents to the back of my mind, or swept the shit under the rug. Damn, how was I going to handle this situation?

Jabbar and his partner left the burger joint. I watched as they sat conversing in the police car for a few minutes, and then they drove off.

When I walked in the door, I didn't see Will anywhere. He must've gone in the back. I took a seat at a table and waited for him to come out. I decided not to confront him right away about what I'd just seen. I wanted to see if he'd mention anything to me first. If he didn't say anything, I had to hang tight on opening my mouth about it because the last thing I needed was an argument between us. For the next couple of days, or at least for tonight, I needed a roof over my head, and that was the priority. Another night with Stacie wasn't even possible.

Will spotted me and came over to the table.

"You looking all spiffy and shit," he said. He pulled back the chair, placed a pencil along the side of his ear, and worked a piece of gum.

"I got a new job. It starts next Monday. Until then, I really need a place to stay."

"What's up with your place?"

"Mr. Armanos put me out. I was late on my rent and he set my things out."

"That's foul, man. But you know you can stay with me." Will reached in his back pocket. "Here. Take my keys and go put your stuff in my pad. I don't get off until eleven o'clock tonight, but when I leave here, I'm coming home."

"Thanks, man. I appreciate it. Things been going downhill for a brotha, but after I start this job, hopefully my luck will change."

"I'm sure it will. When I was down and out, you helped me, didn't you? That's what friends do. I got your back."

Will went back to work without mentioning anything about his meeting with Jabbar. I smelled a rat, but I had to be smart about how I moved forward. I needed money in my pocket, and the only way I could get that was by working. My first paycheck wasn't coming anytime soon, so I had to hang tight; then, I'd deal with Will and make sure he paid for stabbing me in my back. I didn't know what he was up to with Jabbar, but whatever connection they had, I knew it meant bad news for me.

I took the few items that I had to Will's place and placed them in his empty bedroom. He wasn't getting off until eleven, so I got busy looking around for anything out of the ordinary. First, I started with his bedroom, which was awfully fancy for a person who worked at a burger joint. It wasn't that much fast food working in the world that he could have afforded the flat screen TVs in his bedroom and in the living room, the leather sofa and loveseat, nor the stainless steel appliances. If that wasn't enough, the king-sized bed was a dead giveaway that somebody was giving big money to Will. I knew it was Jabbar, but why? Had they been plotting against me since Cassandra's death? Did Will have anything to do with her murder? Damn, I wanted some answers, and it was going to be hard as hell to keep my mouth shut.

At almost midnight, Will came through the door. He had an iPod clipped to his jeans, and the headphones were in his ears. I had made myself comfortable, sitting on his couch and watching a movie. Will removed the iPod and plopped down on the loveseat across from me.

"What you watching?" he asked, stretching his arms.

"*Diary of a Mad Black Woman.* I ain't really been watching it, 'cause my mind can't stop thinking about all the crazy shit that happened this week."

Will yawned. "It be like that sometimes, man. All I can say is take as much time as you need here. You ain't under no time constraints. If anything, I know what it feels like to be homeless."

I felt the bullshit coming down. Suddenly, I thought of a

reason he might have decided to talk to Jabbar. "Hey, you ain't still upset with me about Stacie, are you?"

"Man, I ain't tripping off Stacie. She's old news. I thought about what you said when you told me to put myself in your shoes, and had it been me, I probably would've let her get her suck on." Will laughed and stood up. "I'm gon' call it a night. This negro here awfully tired. I got the morning shift, so by the time you wake up, I'll probably be up and out."

I nodded, pleased that I'd contained myself from jumping up to beat his ass. He closed the door to his bedroom, and I assumed he was out like a light. I couldn't get a lick of sleep. I tossed and turned on the couch as I plotted my next move.

CHAPTER 21

Will was at work, and I sat in front of the TV drinking wine. I was calm after having spoken to my mother earlier about loaning me some money. I hated to call her, but I really had no other choice. I couldn't stand the sight of Will, and I was so ready to bust this thing wide open. My mother told me she'd think about loaning me the money, and said she'd give me a call tomorrow. I figured one more day of keeping quiet wasn't going to hurt, so that's what I planned to do.

As usual, Will came in upbeat one minute and tired the next. I told him to go in the kitchen to get a glass, and after he did, he joined me in the living room.

"If you're drinking wine, that must mean you got good news," he said.

"Yes, I did. I probably won't be a thorn in your side too much longer. I called my mother for some money, and she's supposed to loan it to me. "

Will didn't say much. He twirled the wine around in the glass and looked at it. Before we could even toast, he'd already taken a sip.

"Damn, man," I said. "Couldn't you wait?" He stood up and paced the room. "Will, what's on your mind? You seem—"

"It's Stacie," he said. "Last week, she called my mom's house and said she was pregnant. My moms called, going off and shit, and when I called Stacie, she confirmed it. She started crying and told me how sorry she was for everything. And even though I'm angry for what she did, I gotta be a part of my li'l shorty's life. You know I ain't never been one to forget about my kids."

My mouth hung open. "Did she say how far along she was?"

"According to her, only weeks. She missed her period, took a pregnancy test, and she said it showed positive. I don't think she's been to the doctor yet, but I told her I'd go with her."

"Man, I'm confused. I thought you'd stopped fucking with her. You told me you hadn't seen her."

"I lied because I didn't want you to know what a sucker I was. I'd been dipping into that, even though she played me."

I was at a loss for words because even though I put on a condom the first time we got together, we fucked so wildly that it tore. There was a possibility that this baby was mine. I felt that Will had to know.

"Man, if Stacie was so eager to get down with me, how do you know the baby is yours?"

He grinned and headed back toward the sofa. "Aw, we gon' get a blood test done. You can be damn sure of that." He sat back down.

"Please get one, especially since . . . you know what happened between her and me."

"Since when does a woman get pregnant from sucking dick, fool?"

I gave Will a serious look. "Since that wasn't the only time she sucked my dick. Not only have you still been having sex with her, but I've been having sex with her too. I thought—"

Will hopped up, jabbed his finger at me, and yelled, "I can't believe your ass, man! What the fuck is wrong with you?"

I held up my hand to avoid the spit that came out of his mouth as he yelled. "You told me that it was over," I said defensively.

"Over or not, your punk ass—"

No more words left his mouth, as he swung his fist around and punched me. While he continued to pound away at me, I covered part of my face. He eventually backed off and grabbed his jacket.

"By the time I get back, your ass better be gone!"

I knew he was headed to Stacie's house, and I hoped he gave her exactly what she deserved—a good ass-kicking.

Tasting blood in my mouth, I got up and went to the bathroom. This motherfucker had put a scratch underneath my eye, and my lip was busted again. I dabbed my lip with a towel. Will was just as stupid as that bitch Stacie, and he deserved whatever he got.

An hour had gone by, and I continued to look out the window for Will. Finally, I saw him walking down the street with his hands in his pockets. I knew things would get ugly between us, but I still had to remain cool.

Will came inside, his eyes burning with fire. He looked at me standing by the window and charged at me. We fell backward, and the lamp next to us crashed to the floor right along with us. I purposely let Will get the best of me, and when one of his neighbors shouted that she was calling the police, I was glad about that.

When the police sirens sounded, Will kept at it. He was in a rage, and simply couldn't be stopped.

"I—hate—your—punk ass—Brandon!" He let out a blow to my face with each word he spoke. "You and that bitch can go to hell! I know you warned her that I was on the way over, because I saw my number on her fucking caller ID, pussy!"

I held my hands over my face. "I didn't—"

Just then, the police rushed in and grabbed Will off me. He tussled with the officers, and I sat up and watched as they roughed him up and placed handcuffs on him.

"I got plans for your ass, Brandon!" he yelled. "You better believe that I won't forget about this shit!"

Two of the officers dragged him outside, and one stayed behind to question me about what happened.

"Officer, Will and me been boys for years. He just found out that I had sex with his girlfriend, and he went crazy. I don't blame him, though. I tried to explain myself, but he wouldn't listen. I think he might have gone to her house to hurt her."

"Do you want to press charges against him?"

"No. He's still my friend, and we gon' work through this, like we always do."

"Well, he's gonna spend the night in jail. Hopefully things will cool down and we'll release him tomorrow. In the meantime, it might be a good idea if you go elsewhere."

"I agree. I'll gather my things and cool out at my mother's house for the night."

The officer left and I locked the door behind him.

Tonight, I was staying right here. By the time they released Will tomorrow, or even *if* they released him, I'd have my money from my mother and could get a room at a motel. Once I got settled in, I'd catch up with him, so we could have our discussion about his connection with Jabbar. So far, things were going according to my plan.

The following day, I called the police station. They said that Will wouldn't be released until he saw the judge on Monday. Apparently, he'd gotten into a major scuffle with the of-

ficers, and they decided to hold him a while longer. He was
making matters worse, but that was very beneficial to me.

My mother had wired the money to me, and on Sunday, I
decided to make my way to a motel for the next couple of
weeks. That would give me time to get a paycheck from my
new job and possibly put a security deposit on another apartment. The motel was cheap, but it simply had to do until I
could do better. I didn't have much but clothes, so I packed
them into the tiny room and lay down on the bed.

Feeling down, I gazed at the ceiling, and my eyelids
started to fade. I'd spoken to Morgan several times while at
Will's place, and I saw a vision of her pretty face. I wanted to
see her, so I opened my eyes and reached for the phone. I dialed her number and smiled when she answered the phone.

"You have one of the sexiest voices I've ever heard," I said,
without acknowledging who I was.

"This must be Brandon. You seem to always know the
right things to say."

"That would be me." I smiled. "Listen, I was wondering if I
could take you to see a play, *Two Wrongs Don't Make a Right.*
It's at the Fox Theatre, and from what I heard, it's supposed
to be off the chain."

"This is kind of a short notice, don't you think? . . . But if
we could make it to the seven o'clock show, then maybe
that'll be cool."

"I'll pick you up around six. Give me directions to your
place."

After all that had been going on, hopefully Morgan would
be able to take most of the bullshit off my mind and keep me
from going insane.

I searched through my wrinkled clothes to find an outfit. I
wanted to look nice, so I chose my black suede pants that

hugged the nice-sized print in my pants and a flimsy V-neck burgundy sweater that draped on my muscles. I decided to sport my thin beard and goatee together, so I trimmed my facial hair to perfection. As for my hair, I lined it well and added some sheen to give it a shine.

As it neared five o'clock, I got dressed and jetted. My car was kind of messy, so I stopped by a car wash and vacuumed it. I sprayed a dash of cinnamon oil inside and headed for Morgan's house to pick her up.

She didn't live too far from the Fox Theatre, so when I got to her house, we still had plenty of time. She opened the door looking workable. I was left breathless, and didn't even hear her when she asked me to come in.

"Brandon, I said come in. I was finishing up in the bathroom, so come in and have a seat."

"Thanks," I said. "I didn't mean to trip like that, but you look amazing."

She smiled, and I took a seat in a chair by the window. I watched as she switched back to the bathroom in her strapless fuchsia jumpsuit. She accessorized it with silver and wore her hair pulled back into a long ponytail that rested on her shoulder.

Within moments, she came back into the room. She grabbed her silver purse off the table and opened the closet door to get her coat. I stood up and helped her put it on.

"You're so polite," she said.

Morgan and I got to the Fox Theatre early. I went inside to purchase our tickets while she stayed in the car. When I got back, I suggested going somewhere for a quick meal.

"Let's just chill here for a moment," she said. "We have less than an hour, don't we?"

I looked at my watch. "Just about. Fifty-four minutes to be exact."

"Then we'll stay in here and keep each other company. How about that?"

"That's fine with me."

"I know we've been talking on the phone a lot, but tell me more about yourself, Brandon. You're a very attractive man, and I find it hard to believe there's no woman occupying your time."

"Like I told you, I just ended a relationship. She wanted to be with somebody else, and I couldn't do nothing about it. Things ended badly, and I had my heart broken. I'm not in the market for another relationship; just looking for somebody I can have fun with."

"Fun? Like what kind of fun?"

"Fun like 'make me laugh' fun. 'Let's go hang out somewhere' fun, or even, 'let's have sex' fun. I don't mean to be blunt, but you asked."

"I like a man who's real. The ones I can't stand are those fake ones who try to be something that they're not."

"Well, I'm as real as it gets. I don't put on no front for nobody." There was silence. I looked over at Morgan. "If you don't mind me asking, how old are you?"

"Thirty-four," she said. "Why? Am I too young or too old for you?"

"I asked because I usually date older women. Thirty-four is right up my alley because I'm only thirty-two."

"If you don't mind me saying, you're one of the finest thirty-whatever-year-old men I've seen. You're groomed well, drive a nice ride, smell good, and you have the prettiest eyes. And your dimples . . . they are definitely a plus in my book."

We stayed in the car yakking until the play got started. It lasted for a little more than two hours, and on our way out, she saw several of her girlfriends, and they stopped to talk. I slipped my arm around her waist, and she stopped talking to introduce me.

"Ladies, this is Brandon. And Brandon, these are my friends, Ally, Gail, and Beatrice."

"What's up, ladies?" I said, keeping a tight grip around Morgan.

Ally fanned herself. "Moe, you didn't tell us Brandon was this handsome. You wouldn't happen to have a brother or cousin, would you?"

I smiled. "Naw, it's just me. Sorry."

She shook her head and looked at Morgan. "That's a shame. Tonight, you make sure you have plenty of fun for all of us. If not, you need to let him go home with me."

The ladies laughed, and I slid my hand down to Morgan's hand and held it.

"Brandon, you have to excuse Ally. At times, she seems a little desperate and out of control."

"I'm sure it's all in good fun," I said.

They all agreed, and we walked out together. Of course, they followed us to my car to see what I drove. Morgan seemed impressed as I opened the door for her to get inside.

"I'll call you tomorrow, Gail," Morgan said. "As for the two of you, Bee and Ally, don't stay out too late. Curfew is at two o'clock in the morning."

"Same to you," Ally said as they walked off and waved. "Bye, Brandon!"

"Goodnight." I smiled and got in the car.

"Where to now?" Morgan asked.

"It's late, and if you haven't forgotten, I have a new job to start in the morning. You wouldn't want for me to be late, would you?"

"No, but I was hoping that you'd take me to your place so I'll know where you live."

"My place is being renovated. We can't go there because it's not ready yet. Right now, I'm staying at a motel, until my place is ready."

"Then I guess I'll have to show you around my place."

"I guess so," I said. I stuck the key in the ignition and drove off.

When we got to Morgan's house, she reached for the doorknob, but I stayed in the car.

"Aren't you coming in?"

I wanted to, but I knew that if I went inside, we'd have sex. I had too many other things on my mind. "Let me take a rain check. I gotta get up early, and I'd like to be prepared for my first day of work."

"Are you sure? I promise not to keep you all night."

"Woman, ain't no need in me lying to you. If I go inside, there's no doubt we'd be up all night."

"So, I see you're a bragger."

"No. Normally I never talk about it, I just be about it. But you'll soon see."

"What if I want to see tonight?"

"Bad timing. Being prepared on my first day of work is important to me. We'll have our time; trust me."

Disappointed, Morgan leaned over and placed her hand on the side of my face. Her eyes dropped to my lips, and we both leaned in for a kiss. It was a long, wet, and juicy one that almost had me changing my mind about going inside.

"Umm, now, that was nice," I said. "I love a woman who's a good kisser."

"It says a lot, doesn't it?"

"A whole lot." I laughed.

She laughed with me then pushed the door open to get out.

"I'll see you tomorrow, Brandon. Until then, you be good."

"You too," I said.

Morgan closed the door, and I watched as she went inside. She closed the door, and I drove off. I thought about how easy it was to get almost any woman I wanted. These days, the possibilities of finding, dating, and screwing the woman of my choice seemed simple. As far as I was concerned, the total package wasn't even necessary. All I had to do was look okay, drive a nice car, and be able to lay my pipe well. As long as I did that, nobody knew or even cared about my horrific past and currently messed up situation.

CHAPTER 22

I was dressed to impress and ready for work. I couldn't wait to see Morgan, but more importantly, I couldn't wait to start making some money again. This time around, I had big plans. I couldn't wait to get out of this hellhole motel room.

I tossed my suit jacket in the back of my car, got inside, and pulled off. As soon as I was halfway down the road, a police car pulled me over. I wasn't sure what for, and when I saw Jabbar get out of the car, he completely caught me off guard.

I lowered the window, and he bent down to talk.

"I waved and tried to get your attention, but you didn't see me," he said.

"I was on my way to work. I'm starting a new job, and I don't want to be late."

"Well, you might have to be. Your friend Will is in big trouble. Yesterday, we found his girlfriend's body, and—"

"Stacie?"

"Yes. Stacie Delaney. A recent police report stated that you and Will had a fight over her. You claimed he left that night and came back a few hours later, right?"

I was at a loss for words. I couldn't believe this shit was happening all over again. First Cassandra, now Stacie? What in the hell was going on? It was time for Jabbar to tell me what his connection was with Will. If Will was responsible for any of this shit, I was not going to cover for his ass.

"Yeah, he left right after our argument. But I need to talk to you about something else."

"We can talk at the station. I need you to follow me. It shouldn't take long, but some detectives want to question you. If you need any type of clearance with your new job, I'll be happy to provide it for you."

"All right."

I followed Jabbar to the police station, where he led me to an interrogation room.

"While you wait, do you want something to drink?" he asked.

"Right now, a shot of anything would be cool, but a Pepsi will do."

Jabbar patted me on the back, and shortly after, came back with a Pepsi. I was more than nervous because I couldn't believe that Will was upset enough to kill Stacie. Something just wasn't right about the whole thing, but all I could do was sit back and wait.

After some small talk with Jabbar, his pager went off. He said he'd be right back. I sat in the room by myself and sipped on my Pepsi.

Thirty minutes must have gone by before I heard the door squeak open. My face was resting in my hand, as I'd gotten rather bored. When I looked up, I was shocked to see my mother enter the room. Her face looked confused, and her eyes were puffy and red. I could tell she'd been crying, so I stood up quickly.

"Mama, what are you doing here?"

She hurried over and wrapped her arms around me. Her

body trembled. "Baby, I'm so glad to see you. Why haven't you called me, Brandon? Why?"

I moved her back. "I did call you—about the loan. Why are you here, though?"

She rubbed the side of my face, and tears continued to pour from her eyes. "Baby, tell me you didn't do what these people say you did. Please tell me you didn't."

I snapped. "What are you talking about? Who told you I did what? What is it that I supposedly did?"

Her voice got loud. "Did you kill Cassandra?"

"Hell no, I didn't kill Cassandra! Ruby killed Cassandra! She . . . she was sent to prison for life for kill—" I paused and grabbed my mother by her arms. "Did the police tell you I killed Cassandra?"

Her eyes fluttered and she nodded. I let go of her and tightened my fists. "I can't believe this shit is happening all over again! Damn! Why can't this bullshit just go away?"

The loud cries of my mother echoed in my ears. I covered my eyes and started to cry as well. "Mama, you gotta believe me. I loved her. You know how much I loved her, didn't you?"

She nodded and closed her eyes tightly. Her hands trembled as she held them together and placed them on her quivering lips.

"Why, Brandon?" she yelled. "How did you get yourself into trouble like this?"

I grabbed her arms and shook her hard. "Are you listening to me?" I sobbed. "Why are you here? The police . . . Jabbar asked me to come here to talk about Will's girlfriend! I think he killed her! I'm not here about Cassandra, and you need to listen to me!"

She smacked the shit out of me. "Don't you yell at me like that! They got evidence, Brandon. Evidence that you killed Cassandra and Evelyn! Who in the hell is Evelyn?"

I snapped again and held my sore cheek. "Evelyn?" My voice calmed. "What happened to Evelyn?"

My mother gritted her teeth. "You tell me. Brandon Fletcher, you tell me right now! What the hell did you do to that lady?"

I dropped in the chair behind me and glared at the mirror. I was sure that the detectives and Jabbar were watching me on the other side. I rubbed my shaky fingers across my forehead and sat for several seconds in deep thought. "I . . . I didn't do nothing to Evelyn, Mama. The last time we were together, she—"

My mother pounded her fist on the table so hard that my whole body jumped.

"I am your mother, Brandon, and you will not lie to me! Tell me, what in the hell did you do?"

I looked up at the bright light hanging from the ceiling, and then turned to look at my mother, who knew me so well. I spoke calmly to her.

"I love you, Mama."

She gave me a partial smile and placed her hand over mine. "I know you do, baby. And no matter what, your mama is always gon' be here for you. So, tell the police the truth, okay? Even if it's dirty, you've got to tell it."

I nodded slowly, and she leaned forward and gave me a kiss. When Jabbar came back in, he pulled her away from me.

"I love you," she cried before leaving. She looked at Jabbar and swallowed the lump in her throat. "I . . . I hope you get your confession. But please take it easy on my child. He's ill, and without taking his medication, I knew something like this would happen." She turned to me in tears. "That's why I wanted you to move with me, Brandon. I knew you wasn't capable of taking care of yourself. Look at what you've done," she sobbed.

I placed my fingers on my lips, kissed them, and held my hand out to her, "I'm sorry, Mama. I . . . I didn't mean for any of this to happen."

Detective Banks came in and rushed my mother out. Jabbar closed the door and sat at the table with me. He held several folders in his hand. He laid them calmly on the table and opened the first folder. There was a picture of Cassandra clipped to the edge of the folder. I stared down at it, and tears fell from my eyes.

"We both know who this is, don't we?" he said.

I nodded.

"Tell me what happened to her."

It was time to lay it on the line. My mother was deeply hurt, and I had to reveal the dirty truth. I placed my index finger on the side of my temple and gave Jabbar a serious look. "I had to do it. Cassandra left me no other choice. She told me we'd get married, and then, weeks later, she told me she wanted to be with someone else. I was devastated."

"That had to be quite painful." Jabbar sounded sincere.

"It was. I planned the whole thing out. I even drugged myself to make sure I blacked out. I knew you all would find the pills in Ruby's house because she'd been on medication for quite some time."

"Ruby was an easy target, wasn't she?"

I snickered. "Hell yeah, she was. She was already losing her mind, so I made sure you all went after her. When I was at her house, I planted the knife that I used to kill Cassandra in her basement. I knew you'd find that too. Thing is, though, when I was there, Cassandra tried to stop me. She spooked me the hell out, man." I laughed. "You should've seen her. Then she kept fucking with me in my dreams. The bitch just wouldn't go away. Damn!"

"I bet she wouldn't." Jabbar lowered his eyelids and gave me a devious look. He closed Cassandra's file and opened another one. This one had a picture of Felicity in the corner. I lowered my head and rubbed my temples.

"What about Felicity?" Jabbar asked.

"What about her? You tell me. You knew her better than I did, didn't you?"

"Yeah, I knew her."

I dropped my head back and swallowed. "She was a shitty lover, wasn't she? I was really disappointed with her sexually, but I needed her just in case my plans for Ruby didn't work out."

Jabbar cleared his throat and folded his arms in front of him.

"They did work out, so what happened to Felicity?"

I smiled with pleasure. "I fucked her up, that's what happened. She was becoming a pain in the ass. Right after she tried to play me with Evelyn, I caught her ass tripping, and . . ." I used my index finger to slash across my throat.

Jabbar took a hard swallow. "What did you do with her body? There's been a missing persons report filed, and it would help if we knew where her body was."

I shrugged my shoulders. "I really don't remember. Let me think about it for a minute, all right?"

Jabbar slid her folder back and opened yet another. I looked down and saw the most beautiful woman I'd ever met. Evelyn. I rubbed my fingertips on her picture as if I could really feel her. My eyes welled with tears.

"Do you need a moment?" Jabbar asked. I shook my head. "Then tell me what happened to Evelyn."

"I fell in love. She . . . she showed me how to love all over again. I was starting to feel happiness again, until—" I paused.

"Until what, Brandon? Take your time."

I swallowed. "Until she hurt me. I loved her, and she hurt me just like Cassandra did. I thought she was different and she cared, but she didn't."

"When's the last time you saw her?"

I cracked a quivering smile. "We made love at my place that day. She'd finally let me have my way with her, but then she got mad because I wanted to tie her up. She tied me up, but when her turn came around, she didn't want to play fair. Right then and there, I knew I had to end it. We took a long drive that night, and that's the last time I saw her. No matter how hard I tried to make her like Cassandra, she just wouldn't cooperate."

"Let me guess," Jabbar said. He slashed his index finger across his throat, and I nodded.

"Yep. That's pretty much how it happened," I said.

"I'm afraid to ask what you did with her body."

I tapped my fingers on the table. I seriously didn't know where Evelyn's body was. "You know, I blacked out and can't remember. Let me think about it."

"Think hard," he said. "If you come up with something, let me know."

"Will do." I winked then placed my hand on my chest. "I did, however, find it in my heart to buy her a stuffed dog and card the day after I killed her." I paused and shook my head. "The bitch didn't even have the decency to call and thank me."

Jabbar cleared his throat again. He opened one last file. Not surprisingly, it contained a picture of Stacie.

"This is where you messed up," he said. "Even after Ruby's trial, I still had concerns about you. My gut told me that we had the wrong person, so I stayed on you. The first time I went to your boy, Will, he wouldn't help me; then, right after your fight with him, he started looking at things differently, and he couldn't deny the money I offered him.

"You decided that the blow job Stacie gave you wasn't enough and went back for more. I told Will about it, and trust me, he wasn't happy at all. I paid him more to help me out, and he put on quite a performance that day. We knew Stacie was dead, but we couldn't find her body.

"So now, Will's in a safe place and Ruby is a free woman. You, on the other hand, got some serious problems. Do you see how the power of pussy can get you all fucked up? If you hadn't been so desperate, you could still be a free man."

I slammed my fist on the table. "I didn't kill Stacie! Will was angry. He was the one—"

"Forget it, man. Will need to be starring in movies because he's the best damn actor I've seen in a long time. You tried to set him up, Brandon, but it didn't work. You killed Stacie, and you knew if you told Will that you had sex with Stacie, he'd get angry. You allowed him to beat you up so you'd look like the victim. When he got back from Stacie's place, which, by the way, he never went to, you were hoping someone called the police.

"We figured Stacie was already dead because Mr. Armanos showed us a copy of a bounced check she'd given you. I'm sure that made you mad."

I giggled. "Boy, I could have killed that bitch."

"You did."

I looked puzzled. "Did I?" I snapped my fingers. "That's right, I did. She came between me and my boy." I pounded my chest. "Will was my boy. Don't nobody come between us."

"Nobody," Jabbar replied. "Now, what did you do to Stacie?"

I quickly turned my head and stared at the wall. "Damn, Will played me? I can't believe he played me." My eyes shifted back to Jabbar. "Anyway, what did you say?"

"I asked about Stacie."

"Stacie was one of the most trifling-ass people I ever met. Pussy was guuuud, but"—I took a deep breath—"she was nasty. In a good and bad way, of course. And she sho' knew how to suck a dick. She had me sh-sh-sh-shaking like a leaf. You ever had a woman that made you shake like that?"

"Can't say that I have. But I guess I don't have to ask you where her body is."

"Shit, I don't know. But I do know that had she not given me that bounced check, things might have been different."

Jabbar closed her file.

"Is there anything else you'd like to share with me, Brandon?"

"Naw, not really. That about sums it up."

Jabbar eased the chair back, stood up, and leaned down face to face with me.

"I told you I'd get you, didn't I?" He smirked.

I whispered, "Question is, what took you so long, motherfucker?"

He backed away and headed for the door. I whistled for a few seconds.

"Say, Jabbar," I said.

"What?"

"Do you think I can get a clearance to get out of here?" I looked at my watch. "I'm almost two hours late for work. I can't make no bad impression on my first day, can I?"

"Brandon, I plan to bring your clearance to you real soon. As for work, you'll be working for a very long time."

"As long as I get paid." I chuckled.

Jabbar cut his eyes at me and walked out.

CHAPTER 23

I sat in the interrogation room for a few more minutes; then two detectives came in and handcuffed me. One read me my rights and escorted me to a holding cell. After they removed the cuffs and shoved me inside, I took a seat on the bottom bunk and looked at my hands, which were still cuffed together. For the first time, I didn't like being cuffed.

I fell backward on the bed, realizing that maybe my time was finally up. Whether I'd have the chance to plead insane or not was yet to be seen. I could damn sure do it, because there was a part of me that wanted to be a good man. I wanted to be true, loving, and faithful to any woman who would have me, but they were the ones who turned out to be the real demons.

I chuckled about my relationships, and turning to my side in a fetal position, I cracked a wide smile.

Maybe it wasn't their fault; maybe I had my own demons to deal with. I had been the perpetrator, hadn't I? And a damn good one at that. I had good looks, was a smooth talker, wore fancy clothes, drove a decent car, and I dished out dynamic sex. Those things rewarded me, and the women

I'd been with all fell for it. They had no clue what type of man I truly was.

Most of all, they didn't know that I had past mental issues, but my obsessive behavior should have been a clue that something was wrong. I had been prescribed medication for years, and instead of searching through my closet for my toys, the medicine cabinet might have been an appropriate place to check.

My charm got me anything I wanted, and I hooked plenty, didn't I? But, you couldn't be mad at me. I wasn't your average Joe; my game was tight. So tight that just maybe I'd manage to manipulate myself out of this mess. And if I did, I was sure that there would be plenty of women who would judge a book by its cover. My cover was one that couldn't be denied.

If released, I'd make my way back to sweet and innocent Morgan first—the one who was mesmerized by my looks and so willing to drop her panties on our first date. I was positive that things wouldn't have worked out with her either. During our date at the Fox Theatre, I noticed her flirting with other men. And when I conversed with her in the car, her cell phone rang, but she didn't answer. Being very observant, I saw Montell James' name appear as the caller. If anything, I figured she'd call him to fuck her that night, since I declined her offer.

I sat in my car for less than an hour before I saw another brotha show up at her house. She was a game player, and I wasn't the type of man she could play her games with. I came with a guarantee that if you fucked me over, you'd for damn sure pay with your life!

So, yeah, if I somehow got out of this mess, I'd have to make my way back to her and finish my business. After dealing with her, who knows what kind of woman would invite me into her home next?

I smiled as I thought about how I could work my magic to get out of this mess. After all, anything was possible.